Five Golden Wings

ALSO BY DONNA ANDREWS

For Duck's Sake

Rockin' Around the Chickadee

Between a Flock and a Hard Place

Let It Crow! Let It Crow! Let It Crow!

Birder, She Wrote

Dashing Through the Snowbirds

Round Up the Usual Peacocks

The Twelve Jays of Christmas

Murder Most Fowl

The Gift of the Magpie

The Falcon Always Wings Twice

Terns of Endearment

Owl Be Home for Christmas

Lark! The Herald Angels Sing

Toucan Keep a Secret

How the Finch Stole Christmas!

Gone Gull

Die Like an Eagle

Lord of the Wings

The Nightingale Before Christmas

The Good, the Bad, and the Emus

Duck the Halls

The Hen of the Baskervilles

Some Like It Hawk

The Real Macaw

Stork Raving Mad

Swan for the Money

Six Geese A-Slaying

Cockatiels at Seven

The Penguin Who Knew Too Much

No Nest for the Wicket

Owls Well That Ends Well

We'll Always Have Parrots

Crouching Buzzard, Leaping Loon

Revenge of the Wrought-Iron Flamingos

Murder with Puffins

Murder, with Peacocks

Five Golden Wings

A Meg Langslow Mystery

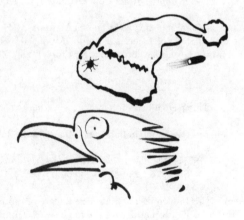

Donna Andrews

MINOTAUR BOOKS
NEW YORK

This is a work of fiction. All of the characters, organizations, and events portrayed in this novel are either products of the author's imagination or are used fictitiously.

First published in the United States by Minotaur Books, an imprint of St. Martin's Publishing Group

EU Representative: Macmillan Publishers Ireland Ltd, 1st Floor, The Liffey Trust Centre, 117–126 Sheriff Street Upper, Dublin 1, DO1 YC43

FIVE GOLDEN WINGS. Copyright © 2025 by Donna Andrews. All rights reserved. Printed in the United States of America. For information, address St. Martin's Publishing Group, 120 Broadway, New York, NY 10271.

www.minotaurbooks.com

Title page illustration by Gabriel Guma

The Library of Congress Cataloging-in-Publication Data is available upon request.

ISBN 978-1-250-40730-6 (hardcover)
ISBN 978-1-250-40731-3 (ebook)

The publisher of this book does not authorize the use or reproduction of any part of this book in any manner for the purpose of training artificial intelligence technologies or systems. The publisher of this book expressly reserves this book from the Text and Data Mining exception in accordance with Article 4(3) of the European Union Digital Single Market Directive 2019/790.

Our books may be purchased in bulk for specialty retail/wholesale, literacy, corporate/premium, educational, and subscription box use. Please contact MacmillanSpecialMarkets@macmillan.com.

First Edition: 2025

10 9 8 7 6 5 4 3 2 1

Five Golden Wings

WEDNESDAY, DECEMBER 17

Chapter 1

The breeze rustled gently through the palm fronds overhead. I took a sip of my margarita, then parked it in the sand by my side and settled back on my beach towel. Somewhere behind me, someone was playing "Over the Rainbow" on a ukulele.

"Mom?"

I cracked one eyelid. Michael and the boys were still clowning around in the surf. So who was calling me?

"Mom?"

Then I woke up and opened my eyes for real. Hawaii or Bermuda or wherever I'd been dreaming about vanished. Ocean breezes gave way to chill air and the faint sound of Christmas carols in the distance. At least the gale-force winds that had kept me awake part of the night seemed to have died down. My son Jamie was peering down at me with an anxious expression on his face.

"What's wrong?" I asked. I braced myself to hear another complaint about his brother, Josh. The twins, normally the best of friends, were codirecting Trinity Episcopal's annual children's Christmas pageant and were suddenly having creative differences. Noisy creative differences that sometimes ended in scuffles.

"Cousin Lexy and Cousin Emily are fighting again."

I stifled my first reaction, which would have contained words I tried never to utter in front of my twin sons.

"Actually fighting?" I asked. "I mean, have they come to blows? Or are they just arguing?"

"They're yelling a lot," he said.

I was opening my mouth to say that they did that all the time and to come back and wake me when their disagreement came to blows, when he added something.

"And they both yelled at Rose Noire and told her to shut up."

"That tears it." I threw back the covers and hopped out of bed. Bad enough that they were being beastly to Mother. Mistreating my gentle New Age cousin? "I won't stand for them being rude to her. Go back downstairs and keep an eye on them. I'll be down in a couple of minutes."

He nodded and turned to leave, looking less anxious.

"Is your grandmother there?" I asked.

"No," he said. "And I don't think we should call her. They were awfully nasty to her yesterday."

"They were indeed." I knew that Mother had gone home early, with a stress-induced migraine. I was pleased that Jamie had noticed. "I don't want her to have to deal with them. So if she shows up, see if you can distract her until I get downstairs. Take her outside to see what that wedding photographer is up to out in the yard."

He nodded and raced out, partially closing the bedroom door behind him. I began grabbing clothes and getting dressed. I'd hurried into my underwear and a t-shirt when I heard the door open again.

"Merry Christmas, Meg. Who are those two . . . harpies downstairs in the kitchen?"

I turned to see my friend Caroline Willner standing in the doorway.

"Merry Christmas, and welcome." I was at the closet, grabbing a clean pair of jeans. "And a virtual hug. The harpies would be Alexis Turner and Emily Winningham. Cousins. First cousins to each other. Only second cousins once removed to me, actually. Not that I particularly want to claim even that much shared DNA right now. Harpies fits. Harridans and termagants would work, too."

"A good vocabulary's so useful." She settled into the comfy chair, as I sat on the bed to pull on my jeans. "I was going to say witches, but I didn't want to insult Rose Noire and all her New Age and Wiccan buddies. So who are they?"

"Witches with a *b*," I said. "Emily and Lexy are the brides."

"Your mother mentioned something about a wedding," she said. "Brides, plural? They're having a double wedding?"

"Alas, no." I began pulling on my socks—a little distractedly, since I had one ear cocked for signs of trouble downstairs. "They're having competing weddings. Apparently Mother has been doing too good a job of selling her relatives on what a wonderful place Caerphilly is for a destination wedding. And how beautiful Caerphilly is at Christmas. Both Lexy and Emily are having their weddings here on the twentieth, since that's the closest Saturday to Christmas."

"Here? At your house?"

"Ceremonies at Trinity Episcopal," I said. "Receptions at the Caerphilly Inn. All the wedding party members and quite a few visiting relatives are staying with us or at Rob and Delaney's next door or over at Mother and Dad's farm, plus we're hosting all kinds of ancillary events, like the final fitting parties and the hen parties and who knows what else. And before you ask, yes, it would be a lot easier and cheaper if they joined forces and had a double wedding, but that was never an option. Their mothers, Aunt Betty and Aunt Letty—"

"Twins, I assume?"

"Only sisters, actually," I explained. "They were best friends growing up, but Lexy and Emily, their daughters, have hated each other since they were both in diapers. If you ask me, they're spending less time organizing their own events than trying to ruin each other's festivities, and their mothers aren't helping much."

"Your poor mother," Caroline said. "Because I know she's probably been doing everything she could to keep the peace."

"She has." I looked around for my sneakers, and settled for my gardening Crocs. "They only arrived yesterday, and Mother went home last night with a raging migraine, and now I'm told they've been mean to poor Rose Noire. So even though I've been telling everyone for months that I wasn't going to get involved, it looks as if I need to rethink that. I'm going downstairs to deal with them."

I drew myself up to my full five foot ten and practiced my menacing gaze on the dresser. It appeared uncowed by the threat of my wrath. I wasn't all that optimistic about the effect I'd have on Lexy and Emily, either.

"I'll help." Caroline also drew herself up to her full height, and even though she was at least half a foot shorter than me, she made a pretty imposing figure. "Is your grandmother here? I bet she'd be a help."

"No." I headed for the door. "She's on Dad's side of the family, remember. These brides are from Mother's. We invited her, but she decided to pass. She's coming down for her holiday visit once the weddings are done with. She's met Emily and Lexy before."

"A wise woman. Let's go confront them!"

I picked up my notebook-that-tells-me-when-to-breathe, as I called my giant calendar and to-do list, and hoped, just for a moment, that the brides wouldn't be adding more pages of tasks to it. Then I squared my shoulders and marched out of the room.

"So what are you doing in town?" I asked as we headed for the stairs. "Not that you aren't absolutely welcome, either to join the festivities or to scorn them at close range. But you don't usually manage to get here quite this early for the holidays."

"I've got a possible big donor for the refuge." Caroline had retired from her career as a nurse to run the Willner Wildlife Refuge, where she rehabilitated wounded animals and provided a peaceful sanctuary for former racing greyhounds and over-the-hill horses. "I'm doing what corporate types call a dog-and-pony show for him. Actually more like a possum-and-eagle show in this case. I was wondering why the Inn was so full. Ekaterina managed to find a room for my donor guy, but she looked so stressed when I asked if she could find another for me that I told her not to worry—you'd find me a bed."

"We absolutely can," I said. "Even if I have to kick Lexy to the curb."

"Only Lexy?" she asked. "You have a favorite bride, then?"

"Only Lexy because she's the one staying with us. We decided it was wise to separate the two hostile factions. Lexy and her bridesmaids are here with us, and Emily and her tribe are wearing out their welcome next door with Rob and Delaney."

"Sensible," she said. "And don't worry. Rose Noire's letting me bunk with her."

"I'm starting to think it was a mistake, having both bridal parties so close to each other," I said. "Maybe we should have sent one of them out to Mother and Dad's farm, so they'd have to travel farther to annoy each other."

"You could switch things around," Caroline suggested. "I'm sure we could come up with a plausible-sounding reason."

"We've got the brides' parents staying with Mother and Dad," I said. "And both grooms. Strangely enough, the guys seem able to coexist quite peacefully. And I think they're both happier, staying out of the worst of the chaos. Plus, after yesterday, I think the only thing that will keep Mother sane is knowing she can go home at the end of the day to a bride-free house."

We had arrived at the kitchen door. I took a deep breath. All the little speakers Mother had tucked away behind the wreaths and bows and garlands decorating the hallway were pouring out a beautiful dulcimer version of "What Child Is This?" I tried to focus on the music for a few seconds, but it wasn't having much of a calming effect. So I put what I hoped was a stern but neutral expression on my face, and pulled the door open.

Chapter 2

Both brides turned to stare at me when I walked in. Growing up, if Mother ever saw me with an expression like the ones they were wearing, she'd have warned me that if I wasn't careful my face would get stuck that way.

"Caroline, this is Emily Winningham and Alexis Turner—Lexy for short," I said. "Caroline Willner, an old family friend."

Caroline beamed sweetly at them, but showed no inclination to approach for a handshake. The brides responded with rather perfunctory nods and murmured greetings.

"Isn't it time we took off for the Inn?" Lexy asked.

Emily frowned, as if her cousin had stolen words that were rightfully hers to utter.

"You need to light a fire under that photographer," she said instead. She was looking straight at me.

I needed to light a fire? In the interest of preserving family harmony, I choked back what I thought about this demand.

Emily and Lexy were both attractive young women—at least when they weren't sulking and frowning. Both blond—though Lexy was slightly blonder, her hair a thick mane of gleaming gold. Mother had hinted that Emily planned to have some highlights done before the ceremony, which probably meant she'd emerge from the Caerphilly Beauty Salon with her hair the same shade as Lexy's. Lexy liked to describe herself as tall, though from my lofty height of five foot ten, she wasn't. She was around five foot seven, which made her only slightly taller than Emily's five foot five. Also slightly thinner, though no one could call Emily fat. I'd have said more fully recovered from the anorexia of their teen years.

I'd heard that Emily was the smarter of the two—she'd actually graduated from a four-year college, although not one whose name stuck in my mind. Lexy had barely managed to finish a two-year degree from a Richmond-area community college. But I had the impression that it wasn't so much a lack of brainpower on Lexy's part as a lack of interest. She was now, like her two older brothers, working at some kind of job at her father's insurance agency—a job we all predicted she'd quit as soon as possible after the marriage. Since Emily lacked a father who could provide gainful employment—hers had died way too young, while she was still in high school—she had probably been more highly motivated to do well in school. She'd taken a degree in hospitality management and met her husband, an aspiring chef, while doing an internship in the restaurant of a posh hotel in the historic Fan District of Richmond, Virginia. I wasn't sure where Lexy had met her groom, but I suspected sports were involved. Or at least tailgating parties.

They'd grown up a few miles from each other in the Richmond suburbs. Both were in their early twenties—twenty-two and twenty-three, if memory served. Enough younger than me that we hadn't hung out with the same crowd at family gatherings.

Although even if we'd been closer in age, I'm not sure I'd have spent that much time with them. I think Mother had felt much the same about their mothers, Aunt Betty and Aunt Letty. I'd rarely heard Mother say anything negative about them, but she did have a habit of remarking, "but of course they're *very* sweet"—as if afraid she'd accidentally said something aloud that she needed to contradict.

I'd been helping decorate the Christmas tree at the Caerphilly Women's Shelter most of yesterday, and hadn't witnessed much of what went on when the bridal parties had arrived. But I'd gotten an earful from my cousin Rose Noire and my sister-in-law, Delaney. It would be interesting to see if Mother would still maintain her diplomatic stance toward the brides or if she'd let her hair down and tell me what she really thought. Speaking of her . . .

"Has Mother arrived yet?" I asked.

"She's meeting us over at the Inn," Emily said.

"If you can ever get that miserable photographer to stop taking pictures in your backyard," Lexy said, with a sniff.

"He's taking pictures of your llamas," Emily said. "He's a wedding photographer. Why is he taking pictures of llamas?"

I decided not to suggest that he found them more interesting than brides. I hoped someone had warned him that llamas were touch averse, and prone to spitting at people who offended them.

Then again, a lot of the brides he dealt with probably came with the same warning. At least these two should.

"If you like, I can see about sending the photographer over to the Inn," I said. "Are you meeting with him together or—"

"Hell, no," Lexy said.

"I need to meet with him first," Emily said. "After all, my wedding's first."

"By all of two hours," Lexy said. "And I need to get my meeting with him over first. I have other things to do."

"And you think I don't?" Emily snapped back. "We have to meet the minister at the church at noon and—"

"Ladies!" Caroline called out. "No need to fall out over this."

I glanced at the clock. Only nine thirty.

"One of you can meet the photographer at ten, and the other at eleven." I plucked a blueberry from the bowl of fruit salad on the table and held it up. "And whoever picks the blueberry gets her choice of appointments."

I put my hands behind my back, moved my arms to emphasize that I was shifting the berry from one hand to the other, then brought them back into view. They both frowned and glanced suspiciously at each other. Finally Lexy reached out and tapped my left hand. I opened it to reveal the berry.

"You get to choose." I popped the fateful berry into my mouth and reached for a few more. "Ten or eleven."

"I'll take the second appointment." Lexy's tone dripped with fake sweetness. "Since Emily's wedding is first."

Which meant she had probably thought of some way she could use going second to her advantage. Like finding out what her cousin wanted and convincing the photographer to change it.

Not my problem.

"Why don't you two head out, then?" I said. "And I'll send the photographer over to the Inn."

They both sailed out of the kitchen without another word. I breathed a sigh of relief when I heard the front door slam behind them.

And found myself actually smiling when I heard their cars starting, followed by racing engines as they both drove off. Going too fast, as usual, by the sound of it. They were probably both trying to be the first to arrive, although I had no idea why they would care. Was it unkind of me to hope that they'd encounter one of the chief's deputies on the way into town?

I could even warn one of the deputies to keep an eye open for them. My cousin Horace, or my good friend Aida. Or would that be a Grinch-like thing to do? I'd think about it.

Caroline was frowning at the doorway through which Emily and Lexy had disappeared.

"If I were you, I'd steer clear of those two," she said.

"I did yesterday," I said. "But I think Mother needs help."

"Heavens, yes," she said. "You're a good daughter. Now I'm dreading going over to the Inn myself."

"They'll be gone by noon," I said. "Why not take your donor guy on a tour of the town's holiday decorations until then?"

"Good idea," she said. "But I do have to go now to see about relocating my eagles—the ones I brought up to charm him. Apparently one of the brides needs the room where we were going to keep them, and I want to make sure they're settled properly in whatever new spot Ekaterina has found for them. I should go. I'll see you down there."

"I hope not," I said, but she was already halfway to the front door.

The basement door opened.

"They gone?" My nephew Kevin peered out.

"The brides? For the moment."

"Hallelujah." He emerged and headed for the refrigerator.

I frowned. Kevin, an expert at all things cyber, lived in a computer-filled lair in our basement. In addition to being a department head at Mutant Wizards, the company my brother, Rob, had founded, and a well-respected computer forensics examiner for law enforcement, he teamed with a buddy to run a successful true-crime podcast, and in his spare time kept all the family electronics humming along. We jokingly called him our human firewall. I worried, occasionally, about his relative lack of a social life, and had been encouraged when he'd shown some interest in the arrival of the wedding parties. "It'll be interesting to see if any of the bridesmaids are hotties," he'd said. But since the arrival of the bridesmaids he'd barely poked his nose out of the basement. He wasn't normally quite that antisocial.

"Have Emily and Lexy done anything in particular to alienate you?" I asked. "Or are you simply a good judge of character?"

"I've seen them in action, remember." And he probably had, through the dozen or so security cameras he'd set up in our yard. "Get a DNA sample from those two if you get a chance."

"Why?" Surely he wasn't suggesting that either bride could be a suspect in any of the true-crime cases he followed with such enthusiasm.

"Maybe it'll turn out that we're not related to them after all." He was filling two plates with food.

"Yeah," I said. "Hard to believe we come from the same gene pool."

"I'd say they're from the shallow end. Is there such a thing as too much exercise?"

"Probably," I said. "But don't worry—I don't think you're anywhere near the danger point yet."

"No, but I think that groom might be."

"Which groom?"

"The one who's been working out in our gym since around dawn," he said. "The beefy blond one."

"That would be Blaine," I said. "Lexy's groom. Did he wake you?"

"I was still up," he said. "And he apologized when I asked him to turn down his music just now so I could go to sleep. Seemed sincere. Nice guy. Dim, but nice."

With that, he took his plates and disappeared back into the basement. While the door was open, I heard the familiar metallic clank of weights being deposited back on their rack.

I should have guessed that Blaine was an exercise buff. He was tall, blond, and visibly fit. He was pleasant enough, and friendly, and arguably handsome, though in a beefy, preppy way that didn't much appeal to me. But he didn't seem to have any interests beyond beer, sports, and his budding career at Lexy's father's insurance agency. Sitting beside him at a recent family dinner had been boredom personified.

But if it happened again, at least now I'd have better luck finding a topic that would interest him. He'd probably love bragging about how many pounds he could lift. Doubtless he had informed opinions about the relative merits of Gatorade and Powerade. We could discourse about the importance of a proper warm-up before jogging.

And I decided I was relieved that none of the bridesmaids had piqued Kevin's interest. Maybe I'd gotten off to a rocky start with them, but they seemed to have no interests beyond clothes and makeup, and it was obvious that they thought by coming to Caerphilly, they had left civilization far behind.

"Yes," Mother had said, when I mentioned this to her. "They're all much of a muchness, aren't they?"

Then I shoved the brides and bridesmaids out of my mind. I had things to do. I grabbed the coat I kept by the kitchen door and went out into the backyard to motivate the photographer.

"Bracing," I muttered, as the cold air hit me. Actually, at twenty-eight degrees, I thought "too freaking cold" was a more accurate description, but I was working on maintaining a positive attitude. Especially since the sky was taking on that luminous silver-gray color that suggested we might be getting snow sooner or later. The boys would love having a white Christmas, and now that they were old enough to do most of the snow shoveling, I was philosophical about the possibility.

And actually, the sooner the snow came the better. I gathered that Betty and Letty had been driving Mother crazy with their panic over the possibility that the snow would interfere with the weddings. Once the snow started, they'd be able to see that Caerphilly could cope with it fairly well. Mother had charmed Beau and Osgood Shiffley, who drove the county's two snowplows, into promising to prioritize the route from our house to the church and the Inn. She'd also gotten a commitment from Grandfather and several other locals to make their snowmobiles available for the wedding parties and guests if need be. And she'd taken both mothers to inspect the state-of-the-art generator system that would keep the Caerphilly Inn running normally if a power outage occurred during the receptions. Apparently none of this had done much to calm either Letty or Betty. A good thing Mother was dealing with their angst. I wasn't sure I could refrain from saying, "If you're that freaked out by the possibility of snow, maybe you shouldn't have planned a winter wedding."

Rose Noire, muffled from head to toe in fluffy pink-and-lavender wraps, was filling our many bird feeders and making sure the heaters were still working in both of the birdbaths. Our copper-and-black Welsummer chickens were scratching diligently in the yard for the feed she had scattered for them. Across the fence, in her herb garden, the all-black Sumatras were doing the same thing.

The photographer was standing by the llama pen but he seemed to be aiming his camera at the Sumatras. Not surprising—they were quite photogenic, with their glossy plumage and dramatic tail feathers. The llamas, always fascinated by human antics, were lined up just inside the fence, craning their necks as if they, too, wanted to see what he was photographing.

His assistant stood nearby, shivering slightly. Why was she wearing only a light coat and no hat or gloves? As I watched, the photographer swore, then shoved his camera in her direction.

"Battery!" he snapped.

As the assistant fumbled to open the camera's battery compartment with fingers that were obviously partially numbed by the cold, the photographer stuck his gloved hands into the pockets of his heavy down jacket and scowled at her.

I strode over toward them.

"Good morning." I held out my hand. "I'm Meg Langslow."

"Austin Luckett." He reluctantly pulled his hand out of his pocket and took mine. He was one of those super competitive jerks who seemed to enjoy causing pain with what he probably called a firm, manly handshake. I make it a point never to lose that game—not even to my fellow blacksmiths. He couldn't quite suppress the wince.

"More of the family, I assume." He shoved his hand back into his pocket.

"Your hostess, actually," I said. "Since I seem to recall you're staying here at our house. Meg Langslow," I said, turning to extend my hand to his assistant.

She jumped as if not used to being spoken to.

"I'm Maddie," she half whispered. "Madeline Brown." Her soft, breathy voice seemed perfectly matched to her pale, round face and the ash-blond hair that was falling out of a badly tied ribbon at the back of her head.

"And you look as if you're freezing," I said. "We keep extra coats on a rack just inside the back door—go put a heavier one on."

"I need her to—" Austin began.

"And there's a basket with gloves, scarfs, and hats," I added. "You'll be no good to your boss if you get frostbite."

I accompanied that with a stern look at the inconsiderate boss. Maddie shut the door of the camera's battery compartment, handed it to him, and half ran toward the back door.

"I sent the brides down to the Inn," I said. "And since I assume you'd rather deal with them one at a time, I got them to agree that Emily will meet you there at ten, and Lexy will steer clear until eleven."

"Yeah," he said. "Hard enough to deal with them one-on-one."

Evidently "thanks" wasn't part of his vocabulary.

"You should probably take off in five or ten minutes." I was turning to go when—

"Any chance you can give me a ride there?" he asked.

Was there some reason he couldn't drive himself? His van was right there, occupying one of the three prime gravel-covered parking spaces we usually tried to save for less able guests.

"I've got a bunch of stuff I need Maddie to do for me this morning," he added, seeing my glance. "Including unpacking a lot of stuff and running some errands."

Well, it was better than getting stuck with chauffeuring either of the brides.

"Sure," I said. "As long as you can be ready to leave pretty soon."

"Just give me a minute."

"I'll bring my car around."

I strolled down to the overflow parking by the barn, where I kept my old blue Toyota. I drove it out to the road and pulled in beside his van. He was still giving poor Maddie instructions—and none of them sounded all that relevant to photography. Dropping off his dry cleaning, picking up his preferred brands of cigarettes and bottled water. Evidently she was not so much a photographic assistant as a personal one. Or maybe a nanny.

He was still giving her detailed instructions—now, at least, about finding a part for one of his lights—when a huge RV hove into sight. It was white with pink flowers painted all over the sides. I cut the motor and hopped out of my car.

"What the hell is that thing?" Evidently Austin had finished giving Maddie her marching orders. He ambled over to my car.

"Your guess is as good as mine," I said. "Unless— Yes! It's the dressmakers!"

Chapter 3

As the giant flowered RV drew closer, I'd spotted the word "Bestitched" painted elegantly in purple metallic calligraphy on its side. Bestitched was the dressmaking shop formerly co-owned by Dahlia Waterston, my mother-in-law. When she had decided she wanted to retire and spend more time traveling, Mrs. Tran, her business partner, had bought her out—and from what I'd heard, Bestitched was still going like gangbusters under the revised management.

The RV pulled into the remaining available parking space—the one closest to our front walk. I took a few quick pictures of it and texted the best to Mother, saying, "Look what Mrs. Tran sent!" Then I saw the driver hop out—a young Asian woman with spiky purple hair, dressed all in black, with a velvet-and-tulle skirt and a leather jacket pocked with silver spikes.

"Nikki!" I called

"Hey, Meg!" She ran over and gave me a quick, fierce hug.

"Great to see you," I said. "But what the heck is that thing?"

"It's our new mobile dressmaking shop," she said. "Comes in handy for fancy events, when they want us on-site to do last-minute fitting and pressing and repairs. Used to take hours to set up a makeshift workspace when we arrived. But now, we pull up and plug in the power and we're good to go."

Behind her I could see two diminutive Asian women stepping down from the RV. I recognized them as Mrs. Giap and Mrs. Nguyen, two of Bestitched's most skilled seamstresses. And Nikki Tran had already earned her slot as her grandmother's second-in-command. Mrs. Tran had definitely sent the A-team for the weddings. I waved and called a welcome to the two ladies.

"Also saves us a lot of money on hotel rooms," Nikki said. "You want a tour?"

"I would love one," I said. "Rain check? I have to take the photographer over to the Caerphilly Inn so he can start scoping out the scene. We're meeting the brides there."

"I don't envy you," Nikki said. "Either one of them's a piece of work, and together? Ai yi yi."

"Sorry about that," I said. "I know Mother recommended Bestitched to them. If she'd had any idea how horrible they'd turn out to be—"

"You don't have to apologize," Nikki said. "Your mother's already done plenty of that. And remember, we're in the wedding business. We're used to dealing with bridezillas."

"As bad as these two?"

"We've seen worse," Nikki said. "Not that often, to tell the truth. And these two are already in the running for our hall of fame. But we'll cope."

"And we appreciate it," I said.

"A pity neither of their mothers is the least bit useful," Nikki said. "For dealing with all the wedding stuff, I mean. I wasn't trying— I mean, they're both very sweet—"

"I know," I said. "Very sweet, but neither of them has an organized bone in her body, and they both let their daughters walk all over them."

"Yeah," Nikki said. "Usually works out better if they don't come to the fittings."

"I'll suggest that to Mother. Meanwhile, let's get you and the ladies settled in." I could see both Austin and Maddie snapping pictures of the RV. But I'd already noticed that the photographer had a short attention span, not to mention how impatient the brides would be if we kept them waiting.

"Don't worry." Rose Noire had joined us. "I'll take care of them. You go deal with the brides."

"Are you okay?" I asked her.

"I will be, now that the brides are gone," Rose Noire said. "And I'm hoping to have a very nice day—most of the members of my pagan group are coming over in an hour or so, so we can make plans for our Winter Solstice celebration."

"Ooh . . . can I help?" Nikki asked. "I'd be doing some Solstice rituals myself if I didn't have to be here for the weddings."

"We'd love to have you," Rose Noire said.

"Yay!" Nikki exclaimed. Then she frowned. "Um . . . will the brides be involved? I mean, is that why they both chose the day before the Solstice?"

"Goodness, no." Rose Noire shuddered.

"They didn't choose it because of the Winter Solstice," I said. "They only want it because it's the closest Saturday to Christmas."

"That's all right then," Nikki said.

"All right for them," Rose Noire said. "They're making it very hard for us to have a proper celebration."

"Let me know if there's anything I can do to help," I said to Rose Noire.

"I will." Then she turned to Nikki and the two older ladies. "Let's get you settled in."

I left them to it. Austin and I hopped into my Toyota and I

began backing out. He immediately pulled out his phone and began tapping on it, paying me no more attention than if I was his chauffeur.

I decided I preferred it that way.

I waved to Seth Early, our across-the-street neighbor, who was out in his front pasture, putting his Christmas decorations back in order. As usual, he'd deployed his collection of department store dummies dressed in homespun shepherd's costumes. They'd taken on personalities over the years—they included the napping shepherd, the nosy shepherd with his hand cupped over his ear to hear what the others were saying, the show-off shepherd, who was pointing dramatically toward the star in the east— although the Washingtons, who owned the farm next door to Seth, didn't usually turn on their giant tree-mounted electric star until dusk. I was relieved to see that last night's high winds hadn't done any damage to the star, even though they'd knocked most of the dummy shepherds sprawling.

As usual, Seth had spread some hay and grain near the dummies, to ensure that at least a few of his shaggy Lincoln sheep would show up to play the part of the flocks abiding in his field. This year the display was particularly sheep-heavy, thanks to the two half-grown Great Pyrenees dogs he'd recently adopted to serve as livestock guardians. The Pyrs, he'd decided, were almost as smart as Lad, his Border collie—high praise indeed. They'd already figured out that this time of year he liked to have the sheep hanging out where the tourists could see them, and most days they could be seen in their favorite perch, lolling atop a pair of hay bales, with dozens of sheep—very nearly the whole of Seth's flock—grazing contentedly around them.

"Slow down a sec," Austin said, and when I did so, he rolled down the window and leaned out to snap a few dozen shots of Seth and his sheep. A good thing we were in the digital camera era, or I'd be keeping a close eye on Austin to make sure he wasn't charging the brides for the film he used for photographing llamas and sheep. Since, according to Mother, neither bride had ever been willing to settle for a moderately priced vendor, I expected his charges would be astronomical enough without that.

Eventually he tired of the sheep and grunted that we could go on. But less than a mile down the road I braked and stopped to find out why Isaiah Washington was out in his front pasture taking a chain saw to one of the camels in his life-sized display of the three magi.

"What did that camel ever do to you?" I asked.

"The darned things won't stay upright, even in a slight breeze." He straightened up and put a hand to his back to ease it, casting a curious eye at Austin, who had hopped out of the car and was documenting the alterations to the camels. "And the legs never really looked realistic anyway. So after last night's winds, I decided that's it. We'll have resting camels."

He pointed to one of the other camels, whose legs had already been removed. The camel's saddle was fitted with an ornate tasseled and embroidered saddle blanket long enough to hide the fact that the beast was now legless, especially since the lower few inches of its body were camouflaged by the stubble of whatever crop had been harvested from the field.

"Looks more natural this way anyway," I said.

"That's what I was hoping." Isaiah glanced again at Austin, who was now lying on the ground so he could get an artsy shot of the camel's head against the gray sky.

"Wedding photographer," I explained. "We're on our way to the Inn for a meeting with the brides."

Isaiah nodded and fired up his chain saw again. We waited long enough for Austin to take some pictures of Isaiah sawing the legs off the third camel, and then I managed to coax him back into the car.

Halfway into town I heard a rather unpleasant noise—a loud

and prolonged fart. I braced myself for the odor I expected to accompany it, and began debating whether it would be rude to crack my window for a little fresh, if freezing, air. But then I realized that Austin had pulled out his phone and answered it. Evidently the fart was his ringtone. I hoped my brother, Rob, never heard it. And I made a mental note to warn Mother of the importance of getting everyone to turn off their phones during the ceremonies and receptions.

"Like I told you," he was saying, "that wasn't included in the basic contract. You want all those extra shots, you need to pay for them."

Out of the corner of my eye, I saw him pull the phone away from his ear and chuckle. And an angry male voice was coming from the phone. Evidently his caller wasn't happy with what he'd just heard.

Austin let him rant for a minute or so. I caught the occasional phrase, as the caller variously threatened to sue him, punch his nose, and wring his neck. Austin seemed to be enjoying himself. Then he put the phone back to his ear and spoke.

"Yeah, like I told you. You want all those extra shots, that's what it costs. Now stop calling me unless you're ready to cough up the dough."

He hung up. His phone farted again, and he glanced at it, with a faint smile on his face, until the caller gave up. Or maybe he'd set his phone to go to voicemail after four farts.

He seemed in a particularly cheerful mood the rest of the way to the Inn. I made a mental note to tell Mother about this. Suggest she find out more about it. As an independent craftsperson in my career as a blacksmith, I'd had more than one negative experience with someone who placed a commission and then balked when it came to payment, finding fault with my work or claiming I hadn't delivered what I'd promised. If that was what was happening—an entitled couple demanding something over and above what they'd paid him for—I might feel a certain sympathy for him. But even though I'd only just met Austin, if I had to bet on what was happening, I'd put my money on him getting them to sign a sneaky contract—one that let him charge them a premium price if they wanted more than a bare minimum number of photos. Maybe Mother should suggest that someone take a look at the contracts he'd signed with Lexy and Emily.

Although Austin seemed intent on maintaining an expression of blasé indifference to the increasingly elaborate holiday decorations we were passing, I could see that even he was impressed when we turned into the Inn's mile-long drive. The white-painted fences were bedecked with evergreen garlands, red ribbons, and twinkling fairy lights, with an occasional brightly lit tree in places where Mother had arranged to have suitably sized white firs and Colorado blue spruces planted.

They'd even put tasteful evergreen garlands on the two small tractors that were parked near the entrance with their snowplow blades already attached. Although no amount of decorating would make either of them look like anything other than a very utilitarian piece of equipment. I suspected they were there to reassure the guests. Or maybe just Betty and Letty. "See? We have snowplows!"

I ignored Austin's pleas to stop and let him take some pictures, since we were already running behind schedule. We arrived at the Inn's front entrance a good seven minutes late, with him half hanging out his window. I was surprised not to find Emily standing on the front sidewalk, tapping her foot with impatience. She'd probably ambush him when he went inside. If he ever made it inside. After I dropped him off in front of the entrance, he seemed to be enthralled by the front door, with its wreaths and garlands, and Jaime, the doorman, in his red, green, and gold Christmas uniform.

I decided to take my time parking the car.

Chapter 4

When I strolled up to the Inn's festively decorated entrance, Jaime gave me a sweeping bow.

"Feliz Navidad," I said.

"And a merry Christmas to you, Meg," he said. "And welcome to the Caerphilly Inn."

Jaime wasn't normally that formal, but I suspected he might still be vexed from his encounter with Austin—who had probably treated him like a piece of furniture.

"Have all the brides safely arrived?" I asked.

"They have," he said. "Ms. Ekaterina can fill you in on that."

"Thanks." I tried not to wince at the thought that there was anything I needed to be filled in about.

But I was relieved that by the time I made it into the lobby, Austin was out of sight. And Emily. Lexy was pacing up and down in front of the huge multistory wall of glass that formed one wall of the lobby. And alternating between peering up at the sky and staring at her phone. Maybe she was doing the same thing that Mother had reported Betty and Letty, the two mothers, were doing—refreshing her weather app every few minutes, in the vain hope that the snow prediction would go away.

My friend Ekaterina Vorobyaninova, the Inn's general manager, was standing near the entrance with a stern look on her face. She seemed to be keeping an eye on Lexy. She turned when she heard the door, and I was relieved to see a smile cross her face. She strode over and greeted me, as always, with a quick peck on each cheek.

"How did those wretched brides manage to find a photographer who is just as rude as they are?" she asked, keeping her voice too soft for Lexy to hear.

I winced at her words.

"Sorry," I said. "If we'd known how they would be—"

"No need to apologize," she said. "Your mother has already done so, at least a hundred times. And I gather she had no idea how . . . difficult those two young ladies would be. If they weren't your family, I think I would be trying to find a way to kick them out by now."

"Don't hold back on our account," I said. "If they deserve kicking out, have at it. If they give Mother another migraine, I might start a movement to drum them out of the family."

"That one thinks we should redecorate the entire hotel to match her wedding colors." Ekaterina indicated Lexy with a jerk of her head. "They were shown precisely what the hotel's holiday color scheme would be. Months ago. If it was so important for the decor and their wedding colors to match, they should have chosen different colors."

I liked her attitude.

"What about the other one?" I asked. "She's not demanding that you redecorate?"

"As it happens, her wedding colors match our decorations,"

Ekaterina said. "Or at least they do not clash. I have no idea if that was deliberate or merely good luck, but she is quite smug about it."

"And I'm sure that's making Lexy even more insistent that you redecorate."

"She can insist until she is blue in the face," Ekaterina said. "The decorations are nonnegotiable. And I haven't seen the grooms yet—what are they like?"

"I don't really know," I said. "Neither of them seems to be that involved in all the preparations."

"It's usually like that," she said. "Often the grooms are— Oh, dear. Is your grandfather involved in the planning of these weddings?"

She pointed behind me. I turned to find Grandfather entering the lobby, accompanied by my brother, Rob.

"Not that I know of," I said. "The brides are from Mother's side of the family. No relation to him. And even if they were, I doubt if anyone would invite him to a wedding after all the problems he caused at Rob and Delaney's."

"Problems?" She tilted her head like a bird. "I was unaware that there were problems."

"I didn't hear about it until afterward myself," I said. "Apparently, after a few glasses of champagne at the reception, he held forth at great length about the similarities and differences between human wedding customs and the mating practices of various animal species. Gave several elderly aunts the vapors. If he's not careful he'll get banned from any future family weddings."

"Probably wise," she said. "Then— Ah! I assume he is here to inspect Caroline's animals."

Just then Rob and Grandfather joined us.

"*Rozhdestvom Khristovym,*" Grandfather said, nodding to Ekaterina. I had no idea what he'd said, but it must have been an appropriate holiday greeting of some kind, since she smiled warmly and repeated it back to him.

"And what are you doing here?" he asked, turning to me. "Don't tell me they've roped you into these damn fool festivities."

"I'm only doing what I can to help Mother," I said.

"I knew you were too sensible." He nodded with approval. "You and Michael."

I hurried to cut him off before he went on another rant about how wasteful the typical American wedding was, and how damaging to the environment. I didn't disagree with him—after all, Michael and I had eloped to avoid the kind of show we knew our mothers would try to organize. But I didn't want to run the risk that he'd set off Lexy.

"I gather you're here to see Caroline's animals." I turned to Ekaterina. "Where are they, anyway?"

"At the moment, the possum is sleeping in one of the closets," she said. "Caroline was worried that he was overstressed at being out in the open at a time when he would normally be safe in his burrow."

"Yes," Grandfather said. "Opossums are nocturnal. And very shy."

"And the eagles are over by the Christmas tree," Ekaterina added.

"By the Christmas tree?" Grandfather frowned. "I thought you had a special room for them."

"Unfortunately, we had to repurpose that room," Ekaterina said. "We thought it would be acceptable to have both gift tables in the same room, but the brides were very vocal about each having a separate room for her table."

"Gift tables?" Grandfather gave a puzzled frown.

"At some weddings, they set up a table so the bride and groom can show off the presents they've received," I explained. "And people who bring their presents with them instead of sending them beforehand can drop off the packages there."

"Delaney and I didn't do that at our wedding." Rob looked worried. "Should we have?"

"You didn't smash cake into each other's faces, either," I pointed out. "Some things are optional."

"This gift table thing sounds like a charmingly primitive custom," Grandfather said. "Like something magpies would do." Then he frowned and glanced around. "Of course, maybe that's something I shouldn't say in front of your mother."

"Don't worry," I said. "She'd be fine with you saying it. She's not a big fan of the gift table idea herself. I'm not sure what the origin of the custom is—if it's a regional thing or traditional in some cultures and not in others or what. Could be just a question of differing family traditions—like whether you have a big dinner on Christmas Eve or Christmas Day. But in any case, according to Mother, it's not something the Hollingsworths regularly do."

"That's a relief," Rob said. "So why are Lexy and Emily doing it?"

"No doubt they have seen the custom on social media," Ekaterina said.

"On Pinterest and Instagram," I said. "And Martha Stewart's website."

"And on other brides' websites," Ekaterina said.

"Fascinating," Grandfather said. I'd figured out that "fascinating" was what he said when he thought something was almost too silly for words and wanted to change the subject. "So, let's take a look at our eagles."

Our eagles? I wondered how Caroline would feel about that.

"They are over here." Ekaterina began to lead the way to a small alcove that was somewhat separated from the main body of the lobby.

"Completely unsuitable place for them," Grandfather muttered as he strode toward where she was pointing.

"Until we can find a room to put them in, we wanted them where the staff can keep an eye on them," Ekaterina called after him.

"Cool." Rob was scurrying after Grandfather. "You can tell everyone they're part of the holiday decorations."

"I do not think your mother would appreciate that," Ekaterina murmured, as we followed them to the eagles' temporary lair.

I nodded and followed her, braced for Grandfather's reaction.

Chapter 5

To my relief, Grandfather didn't explode over the eagles' location.

"Ah!" he exclaimed with satisfaction. "The golden eagle! *Aquila chrysaetos*! The world's most widely distributed species of eagle."

"Not an endangered species, then," Rob said.

"Well, its numbers are much reduced." Grandfather craned his neck to get a better look at the birds. "They used to be much more widely distributed throughout the northern hemisphere, but they've pretty much disappeared from a lot of populous areas. We must remain vigilant."

Rob nodded and tried to assume a vigilant expression. Or was he imitating the fierce attitude of the eagles?

There were three of them, seated on tall, sturdy perches. And tethered to the perches, I was relieved to see. They didn't look particularly golden to me, but maybe it was the indoor lighting. The one in the center looked so sleek and healthy that I wondered why he was in Caroline's sanctuary. Maybe he was almost recovered from an injury, and would soon be released into the wild. The one on the left was rather scrawny and bedraggled, with a misshapen beak. Clearly in need of much rehabilitation. I could see him as the before to the center eagle's after. And the one on the right—

"That one's only got one wing," Rob exclaimed, pointing to the eagle on the right. "What happened to him?"

"I think he's the one who tangled with a car." Grandfather stepped closer to inspect the eagle, who stood up slightly straighter and flapped his remaining wing in what he probably thought was a menacing manner. It might have been more intimidating if he'd uttered some kind of loud, challenging, raucous call, but instead he emitted a sort of high-pitched squeak, rather like the whimpering of a scared puppy.

"And I gather it also injured the poor thing's voice box," Ekaterina commented.

"No, that's what a golden eagle's call sounds like," Grandfather said.

"Seriously?" Rob said. "He sounds like a seagull with laryngitis."

"They don't sound like that in the movies," Ekaterina said.

"In the movies, they normally dub in the call of some other bird of prey—one they think sounds more menacing," Grandfather said. "The call of a red-tailed hawk, for example—which sounds something like this."

Grandfather then uttered several loud, raucous shrieks that definitely got the eagles' attention. They all three flapped their wings and squeaked fiercely.

"Pretty pathetic, if you ask me," Rob said, through chuckles.

"Trust me," Grandfather said. "If you were a mouse or a rabbit, the sound those eagles are making would fill your heart with dread."

"Hey, look," Rob said. "When you put them together, you know what you've got?"

"Eagles are solitary birds," Grandfather said. "So there isn't a well-established collective noun for them."

"Okay," Rob said. "But since they're together at the moment, we have *five golden wings*!"

He sang the last three words quite loudly, which set off the eagles again.

We all stared at him for a moment. Then Grandfather turned to me.

"By the way, Meg," he said, "you're welcome to join tonight's festivities at the zoo. Should be a lot more fun than anything those crazy brides have planned."

"And just what are tonight's festivities at the zoo?" I asked.

"I call it Sleep with the Wombats!" he exclaimed. "We'll be having a sleepover in the Small Mammal House."

"In the wombats' habitat?" I asked.

"No, in an empty habitat down the hall from them," he said. "I'm supplying the sleeping bags. Michael and the boys are coming, and a few of the boys' friends, and any children who have come to town with their parents for the wedding are invited."

"I'll think about it," I said. "It sounds like fun, but if today keeps on the way it's started, I expect I'll be so exhausted I'll want my own bed, not a sleeping bag."

And that didn't take into consideration the likelihood that the need to run interference between the brides and the rest of the sane world might continue well past my usual bedtime.

"Your choice," Grandfather said. "Plenty of room if you change your mind."

With that, he focused his attention back on the eagles.

Meanwhile Rob had wandered away and was talking to Jaime. Then he lifted his voice once more in song, and the sound drifted across the lobby.

"Fiiiive gol-den wiiiiings!"

"This is only the first day those poor birds have been here, and already I can see that I will be tiring of that song," Ekaterina said.

"Just ignore him," I said. "He'll be going back to the zoo with Grandfather before you know it."

She sighed heavily. Then her face brightened.

"And here is your dear mother."

We left Grandfather to commune with the eagles and crossed the lobby to greet Mother.

"Good morning," she said, while giving each of us a light kiss on the cheek. "Have both of the brides arrived? I only see Lexy."

"Ms. Emily and the photographer are inspecting the Hamilton Room," Ekaterina replied. "That's where her reception will be held. I told them I would join them when you arrived. Oh—are their mothers coming today?" She sounded wary.

"Betty and Letty are back at our house," Mother said. "Resting. I think they found yesterday quite tiring, so I encouraged them to stay home and regain their strength."

"A very good idea." The news seemed to cheer up Ekaterina. "Shall we go find the first of the brides?"

"If you're sure you're up to dealing with this," I said to Mother.

"Of course, dear," she said. "Let's get it over with."

"I'll stay here and keep an eye on things," I said, nodding my head toward Lexy.

"Good thinking," Mother murmured.

The two of them headed for the door to the conference room area.

"Just let me know if you need me," I called after them.

And then I almost fell into one of the lobby's comfortable chairs. I mentally apologized to Mother—not for the first time—for anything snarky I'd ever said about her decorating. By the time she'd redone the Inn's lobby, she had mastered the seemingly impossible art of picking furniture that was both chic and comfortable.

It was only a little past ten in the morning. Why did I feel as beat as if I'd done a full day's work? If that was the effect the two brides had on me, this was going to be a pretty miserable few days. And yet it was obvious that I'd need to help Mother, to keep her from feeling the full toxic effects of riding herd on the bridezillas.

"Fiiive gol-den wiiiings!"

I was about to go over and suggest that Rob go someplace else when I glanced at Lexy. She was pacing up and down, talking animatedly on her cell phone, and scowling balefully at Rob.

Suddenly Rob's singing became much less annoying. Almost endearing.

Although whatever Lexy was hearing on her phone didn't seem to be making her happy, either. Even when Rob wasn't warbling his new favorite carol her face was scrunched up in anger and she kept shaking her free hand, which was balled up tightly into a fist.

"Your friend seems to be upset about something."

I glanced up to see a pleasant if nondescript couple hovering over me. They were—well, not quite elderly, but well along into middle age. He was balding and slightly potbellied. She was plump, with pretty, pleasant features and carefully permed hair that had started out light brown and was now more than half silver.

"Cousin, actually," I said. "And yes, she's probably upset about something. Her wedding's only a few days away, and she's . . . well, a little too easily stressed."

"Oh, she's one of the brides I've been hearing about!" the woman gushed. "How lovely! She's going to make a beautiful bride."

The man didn't say anything, but he put his arm around her waist and beamed as if to echo her sentiments.

As we watched, Emily and Austin appeared in the lobby. Lexy dashed over as if rescuing the photographer, grabbed him by the arm, and dragged him back in the direction of the meeting rooms. Emily stood scowling after them. And then she followed them back through the door that led to the meeting rooms and the ballroom. A good thing Mother and Ekaterina were there to run interference.

"Two beautiful brides," the woman exclaimed. "And what a lovely time and place for a double wedding."

"Actually, it's not a double wedding," I said. "Two competing weddings. Two of my cousins decided to get married in the same place, on the same day, and for a while I thought they were going to come to blows over who got what time slot."

"Oh, dear." The woman's face fell. "I'm sorry to hear that. How terrible for your family."

"Sad." The man shook his head. "But of course not everyone can be as happy as we are."

The two exchanged the kind of look that I had yet to see from any of the family brides and grooms—full of warmth and affection, yet with a subtle but unmistakable hint of physical heat.

"Terri Meredith," the woman said, holding out her hand to shake mine. "And this is my fiancé, Frank Graves. We came here because we heard such wonderful things about Caerphilly as a wedding destination."

"Meg Langslow," I said as I took her hand.

She sat on the sofa catty-cornered to my chair and sighed as if she shared my appreciation of Mother's taste in seating.

"Not to mention all the Christmas stuff you do around here." Frank also shook my hand, and then took a seat right beside Terri. "We go overboard on Christmas ourselves."

"I lost my husband ten years ago," Terri said. "And Frank lost his Lucy not long after that. We've been keeping company for seven years now. And last month, when Frank popped the question, I started saying yes before he quite finished his sentence."

The two laughed gaily at that, and I found myself joining in.

"About the only argument we've ever had was about whose idea it was to come here for a Christmas wedding," Frank said. "I was pretty sure it was Terri's brilliant inspiration."

"And I remember you being the one to suggest it," Terri said. "We've agreed to disagree on that."

"Do you have a place for the wedding?" I asked.

"We just thought we'd go down to the courthouse, get the license, and tie the knot there," Terri said. "Frank called to make sure they'd be open this week."

"And then we'll have dinner in our suite," Frank said. "A nice *romantic* dinner."

Terri actually blushed at that.

"That will be nice," I said. "Although if you change your mind about the courthouse, I know most of the local officiants—I could find you a priest, minister, rabbi, judge, justice of the peace, or unaffiliated officiant. We've even got a Druid who does a lovely outdoor ceremony, though now's not the best time of year for it."

"Now that's a sweet offer," Terri said. She and Frank exchanged a thoughtful look. "Would you let us think about it and get back to you if we're interested?"

"Of course," I said. "Let me give you my cell phone number, just in case. Or Ekaterina, the hotel manager, can usually track me down." I pulled a sheet out of my notebook and scribbled down the number. "I hope you've had a chance to check out all the Christmas decorations in town."

"Not yet," Frank said. "We were pretty busy getting settled in last night. But we thought we'd do that today."

"Do you recommend going during daylight?" Terri asked. "Or at night, to see the lights?"

"I'd recommend both, if you have time," I said.

After a few minutes of conversation about the sights, I ended up pulling out a second sheet of paper and drawing them a rough map of where some of the most spectacular decorations were, along with a listing of some of the more notable upcoming events, like Michael's one-man show of Dickens' *A Christmas Carol*, the New Life Baptist Choir's public performance, and the nightly concerts in the town square. Terri and Frank thanked me profusely, and she folded my map neatly and tucked it into her purse.

"Meg, dear." I glanced up to see Mother standing nearby. And looking unwell. She actually swayed slightly.

Chapter 6

"Sit down." I leaped up and steered Mother into the chair next to mine. She looked pale. "What have those two spoiled jerks been doing?"

"Nothing in particular," she said, closing her eyes. "It's not one thing—just more of the same." Then she opened her eyes again and noticed the couple across from us. "I'm so sorry," she said. "I didn't mean to interrupt you."

I could see that in spite of her malaise, she was also curious about who they were, so I introduced her to Frank and Terri.

"Are you the one organizing both of the weddings?" Terri asked. "That's quite a job."

"I'm not supposed to be." Mother's voice had an edge to it. "They ought to have wedding planners."

"I thought they did," I said.

"They don't anymore," Mother said. "Emily went through two wedding planners and Lexy alienated three."

"Oh, dear," Terri murmured.

"So now their mothers—my two cousins—are supposed to be doing all the organizing. Unfortunately, they're not very good at . . . moderating their daughters' enthusiasms."

"They've both spoiled their daughters rotten all their lives," I said. "If you ask me, they're reaping what they've sowed."

I half expected Mother to chide me for saying unkind things about my cousins, or perhaps for airing family dirty laundry in public. Instead, she simply leaned back and sighed heavily.

"Now they seem to think the Inn should provide armed security for the gift tables," Mother said. "And even if we knew how to find a pair of armed guards on short notice, paying for it is not something we can expect the Inn to do. If they're that worried about all their silverware and china, they can take it all back to your house and Rob's and hide it under their beds."

"Oh, my," Terri said.

"Those . . . young ladies would try the patience of a saint," Mother murmured.

"Talk to Randall Shiffley," I said. "Our mayor," I added, for the couple's benefit. "I bet he could round up a couple of inexpensive armed guards for you. Some of his cousins would probably do it for the fun of it if you threw in a few meals."

"I don't really think . . ." Mother began.

"Of course, they wouldn't be the kind of neatly uniformed guards the brides are thinking of," I said. "Odds are they'd be scruffy and bearded, dressed in paint- or manure-stained overalls, and waving vintage shotguns. You might even have to install spittoons."

Terri and Frank looked puzzled, but Mother chuckled softly.

"A lovely idea," she said. "If the brides keep harping on guards for the gifts, I'll talk to Randall. Meanwhile, they'll be ready to go over to the church pretty soon. Meg, dear, I don't suppose you could go with them? Robyn would be there to help you deal with them."

Yes, the Reverend Robyn Smith, rector of Trinity Episcopal, was fully capable of dealing with any number of bridezillas. She'd won Mother's heart in record time after her arrival at the church, partly because they shared both progressive social views and a love of the more traditional style of Episcopalian ritual—smells and bells, as some scoffers called it. But it was Robyn's enthusiastic approval of Mother's decorating style that had completely cemented their friendship. Robyn had all but appointed her lifetime chair of Trinity's decorating committee. And I'd already figured out that Mother was feeling intensely guilty about inflicting Lexy and Emily on her beloved rector.

"And you can't enlist their mothers to help out?" Terri asked.

"I don't think either Betty or Letty would be much use right now." Clearly Mother's headache was eroding her usual tact. "They're neither of them very forceful."

She was right. Both Betty and Letty were complete pushovers for their only daughters—actually only child in the case of Emily, and even though Lexy had two perfectly nice older brothers, she'd always been the spoiled golden child. Maybe Mother knew that if she took the mothers along, each would take her daughter's side in any disagreements and make things worse.

"I'd really like to find some Excedrin and rest for just a little while," she murmured.

"Two Excedrin coming up." I made sure I always had Mother's—and my—go-to headache remedy in my tote. I fished out the pill case, along with my trusty water bottle, and handed them over. "I bet Ekaterina could find you a room."

"She's fully booked," Mother murmured as she swallowed the caplets. "And I don't want to be a bother."

But Ekaterina had already seen us and hurried over.

"Are you all right?" she asked.

"Mother's getting a migraine," I said. "Any chance you could find her a place to lie down? Just for a little while."

"Of course," she said. "And I don't wonder—those *zhadnaja sterva* really are intolerable!"

Later, when we didn't have an audience, I'd ask what *zhadnaja sterva* meant, and maybe get her to teach me how to say it. For now, her tone of voice gave me the gist.

"I don't want to be a bother," Mother whispered.

"Come with me," Ekaterina said, offering Mother a helping hand. "Meg can take care of those miserable *cochons*!"

Not for the first time, I envied Ekaterina her ability to swear and sling insults in at least five languages. She led Mother off toward her office—where I knew she had what she called her nap room, a walk-in closet in which she'd installed a twin-sized Murphy bed for when she or one of her friends was facing exactly the same predicament Mother was in. I followed along to make sure Mother had all the help she needed.

"Your poor mother," Terri said, when I returned. "This must be quite a trial for her."

"You have no idea." I was a little distracted. If both Mother and Ekaterina were here, had they left Austin to bear the full force of the brides' demands? Not that I cared much if they gave him a migraine, but there was always the risk that he'd agree to something completely unreasonable. Or balk at something simple and set them off.

I was relieved when both brides appeared a minute later. And glad Mother didn't have to watch them sweep through the lobby toward the exit door, each staring at her phone to avoid having to talk to the other. Not to mention that she'd be glad they hadn't seen her in a weak moment. I'd worry later about what had happened to Austin.

"Will your mother be all right?" Terri asked.

"She will if we can keep her away from the brides for a while," I said. Austin emerged from the door to the conference area, and appeared unharmed.

"I'm still astonished that the brides are dumping all this on your mother," Frank said. "You'd think they were both orphans."

"Neither Aunt Letty or Aunt Betty is very good at organizing things," I said.

"Letty and Betty," Terri exclaimed. "Twins, I gather."

"No," I said. "Although everybody always assumes they are—they were born less than a year apart and look very much alike. Mother says they used to dress alike, so I think they grew up wishing they were twins."

"Still, sad that they don't seem to be getting along all that well," Frank said.

I winced. Had the normally mild-mannered mothers of the brides taken to arguing?

"Oh, yes," Terri said. "We spotted them in the restaurant last night, sitting a few tables apart and both pretending not to see the other."

"What made it kind of funny was that they had ordered identical meals," Frank added. "It's very kind of your mother to do all this for her sisters."

"Cousins, actually," I said. "I only call them 'aunt' out of family custom. Relatives in your parents' generation are honorary aunts and uncles; the ones in the generation below you are nieces and nephews, and all the rest are cousins. Don't ask me how many cousins I have by that definition—even Mother doesn't know for sure."

I noticed Austin lurking nearby, staring at us. In a just world, he'd be feeling at least a little remorse over his contribution to bringing on Mother's migraine, but I suspected he was merely impatient for me to chauffeur him over to Trinity.

He appeared to be studying Frank and Terri. And frowning. Perhaps he had intuited that they were getting married and was scoffing at them because they weren't going to make a particularly photogenic couple. Or perhaps he'd pegged them as people who were unlikely to cough up hundreds or even thousands of dollars for wedding photography. They'd probably just hand their phones to a passerby who could take a few candids of them when the ceremony was over.

Terri and Frank seemed oblivious to his disapproval.

"I should go," I said. "We're going over to the church so the photographer can start planning his shots."

"Which church?" Terri asked. "The big one on the town square?"

"No, that's the Methodist church," I said. "Trinity Episcopal. It's—"

"That lovely gray stone church with the bright red door." Terri clapped her hands in delight. "That's definitely the nicest one."

I smiled at that. I thought the same, though in the interest of ecumenical feeling and general goodwill I would never have said so publicly.

"I'll probably see you here later," I said. "We're having the rehearsal dinners over here, and the receptions, and I forget what else."

"You're not worried that the snow will interfere with the festivities?" Terri asked. "It does look rather threatening."

"Last time I checked, it was supposed to start sometime tomorrow and be over with sometime Friday," I said. "And Caerphilly's pretty good at snow removal. Even if things get a little messy for the rehearsal dinners, they should be fine for the weddings. But please don't mention the snow to the brides," I added. "Or their mothers. They're worried enough already."

"Of course not," Frank said.

"No need to borrow trouble," Terri said.

I was in a better mood as I strolled over to join Austin. Terri and Frank were just the antidote I needed right now. Nice, normal people who were planning to get married without all the expensive fuss and bother my cousins seemed to think necessary.

"Who are they?" he asked, jerking his head toward the couple. "Wedding guests?"

"Just a couple of visitors who have nothing to do with either of my cousins' weddings," I said. "So nice to talk to some sane people for a change."

He chuckled at that.

"Why?" I asked. "Do they look familiar?"

"Just curious." He shrugged. "They have interesting faces. Could make for some good candid shots."

I gave him a sharp look. Was he making fun of Terri and Frank? I felt slightly protective of them. And while they had perfectly pleasant faces, I wouldn't have called either of them interesting. But I couldn't see any signs of mockery in his expression. So I just nodded and headed for the parking lot, with him trailing behind me, eyes glued to his phone.

Under ordinary circumstances I might have been annoyed at the way Austin spent the whole trip from the Inn to Trinity fiddling with his phone. But since the only thing I knew of that we had in common was our connection to the weddings, I was just as happy to duck conversing with him. His phone farted a few more times during the drive, but he just glanced at it, chuckled, and didn't answer it. More calls from the disgruntled client?

When I pulled up in front of Trinity, I found Lexy and Emily in a rare moment of unanimity—or at least shared pique. They were standing on the front steps of the church, banging on the bright red door. They turned when they heard the gravel crunching under my tires, and stood with impatient expressions on their faces. Emily was actually tapping her foot.

"Do you have the key?" Lexy called out, while I was still climbing out of my car.

"Yes," I said. "But we can't go in that door."

I climbed the steps to join them and pointed out the large cardboard sign taped to the middle of the door: CONSTRUCTION

AREA, it read, PLEASE USE SIDE ENTRANCE. A second sign, almost as large, featured a bright red arrow pointing to the left.

"There are workmen in there repairing the floor," I said.

"Why is the church a construction site this close to my wedding?" Emily snapped.

"Are they going to be finished by Saturday?" Lexy asked. "I want to come out through this door."

"They should be finished by tonight," I said. "Assuming they can get a little uninterrupted working time, without people banging on the door and traipsing through their work area. This way."

I led the way to the left side of the church and through a brick archway to where a path of very old bricks ran between the church and the low wall that surrounded the graveyard. The side door was halfway down the side of the building, and directly opposite the wrought iron graveyard gate.

"Nooooo!" Emily shrieked.

Chapter 7

I whirled around to see what was wrong. Emily had retreated back to the archway and was hovering there, looking wild-eyed.

"I don't want to go that way," she wailed. "Isn't there another door?"

"Yes," I said. "But it's all the way at the other side of the building and not nearly as convenient to what we need to do when we get inside. What's the problem?"

"She's a superstitious idiot," Lexy said. "Scared of the graveyard."

Just great.

"I'll close the gate," I said to Emily. "And then I'll open the church door, and you can just scoot in. You'll hardly know it's there." I walked over and swung the gate shut, wincing at how badly it squeaked. I made a mental note to come back and oil it, when I didn't have the brides underfoot.

Emily didn't look reassured.

"It's a very peaceful graveyard," I said. "We've never had any reports of ghosts. And it's been very recently blessed. A few weeks ago, they had some vandalism—people desecrating the graves with spray paint and Silly String—so the rector performed the rite for the Restoration of Things Profaned. If you get a little closer, you can probably still smell the incense."

Emily looked only slightly reassured.

"You can hang around out here if you like," Lexy said. "I'm going inside to take care of what I need to get done."

I unlocked the door and she sailed inside.

"Cool place." Austin had grabbed the camera that was hanging around his neck and let himself into the graveyard. I winced again at how the gate squeaked, both when he opened it and when I swung it closed again. Austin began taking pictures of the graveyard. I stood in front of the gate, blocking Emily's view of it, and smiled encouragingly at her.

The side door we were using to enter the church had a window in it. Inside, I could see Robyn and Lexy talking. Robyn didn't quite look her usual calm, upbeat self. Of course, as Mother and I had agreed, either of the brides could try the patience of a saint, so perhaps it was not a surprise that one of them was getting on the nerves of a mere rector.

"Sometime this year, Emily," I murmured under my breath.

Emily took a deep breath and began inching down the brick walk, keeping close to the right-hand edge—the side away from the graveyard. She was hovering so close to the edge that she occasionally stepped into the flower beds. Not a problem this time of year, since the Grounds Committee had already pulled up the last of the fall mums and dressed the beds for the winter with a thick layer of leaf mold and organic cow manure. With luck, she wouldn't notice the faint residual manure smell her shoes were probably acquiring.

I held the door open and she skittered inside. Austin reluctantly tore himself away from the graveyard and followed us in.

I stopped for a minute to peer through the iron gate at the graveyard. From what I could see, the volunteer work party Jamie and Josh had organized had done a great job of cleaning up the damage the vandals had done. But if Chief Burke didn't manage to catch the vandals—and last I heard, the case was still unsolved—would they strike again?

Maybe I should try again to convince Robyn to let Kevin install a few security cameras to monitor the graveyard. Her objections weren't so much aesthetic—I was sure Kevin could find a way to camouflage them—as ethical. She felt that security cameras would violate the church's mission as a sanctuary.

Maybe it would take another vandalism episode to change her mind. When I went inside I found her talking with Emily and Lexy.

"About time," Lexy said, turning rather abruptly away from Robyn. "Come on, Austin. I'll show you the way to the sanctuary."

She strode off, with Austin and Emily trailing behind her.

Robyn closed her eyes briefly. Was she saying a prayer, or just counting to ten?

"Bless us," she said, when she opened her eyes again. "If they weren't family of yours, I might be reconsidering letting those two have their weddings here."

"Don't let that stop you if you really need to kick them out," I said. "Mother would understand."

"From what I've seen, I bet your mother would cheer," she said. "I'd almost rather have the vandals back."

"Have they made any progress figuring out who they are?" I asked.

"Oh, the chief is pretty sure he knows who did it, thanks to the rumors he heard from Josh and Jamie and a few of their friends. A trio of eighth graders."

"The boys said they were actually bragging about having done it," I said. "Can't the chief use that to nail them?"

"He tried." Robyn set her jaw. "But when confronted with what they said, they claimed they'd just been talking big, taking credit for the vandalism. And then the mother of one of the boys swore up and down that they were at a sleepover at her house that night, playing video games till the wee small hours. And that's what's really upsetting me. We can repair the damage to the graveyard. But we can't repair what she's doing to those children's characters. Oh, and they've hit several other churches, too. Father O'Donnell at St. Byblig's almost caught them, but he slipped on a patch of black ice and ended up in the ER, and now he's limping around with a cast on one foot."

"Poor man," I said. "And at one of the busiest times of a clergyperson's year."

"Well, at least he's still with us," she said. "He could just as easily have busted his head instead of his ankle. Are we all here?"

"Photographer, both brides— Were we expecting anyone else?"

"The mothers? Your mother brought them by yesterday to show them what the sanctuary looked like, and one of them had a million questions about the wording of the ceremony. I kept telling her neither bride had asked for anything customized, so I'd simply be using the standard form."

"Which makes for a lovely, dignified ceremony, if you ask me," I said.

"A lovely, dignified ceremony that she seems completely unfamiliar with," Robyn said. "I finally lent her a copy of the *Book of Common Prayer* so she could read up on it."

"And I bet you'd like the copy back before she leaves," I said. "Which one was it?"

"Hetty, I think."

"We don't have a Hetty," I said. "A Betty and a Letty, but no Hetty."

"Then I have no idea," she said. "I can't tell them apart anyway. And don't worry about the book—she's welcome to keep it if she finds it of any use or comfort. But I have to admit, I'm relieved that we won't have another round of questioning about whether I'm sure I won't be asking anyone's daughter to love, honor, and obey. Does she think we're back in the Victorian era? Let's go see what the brides are up to."

I nodded and made a mental note to ask Mother to retrieve any borrowed books Letty or Betty might have made off with. And another to ask Father O'Donnell if he'd be open to having Kevin install some cameras at St. Byblig's—just until we caught the vandals. Even if he shared Robyn's reservations about surveillance, perhaps the broken foot would erode his scruples.

Or maybe I could talk either Robyn or Father O'Donnell into letting Kevin set up some cameras nearby—cameras that wouldn't violate the privacy of anyone who was actually on church grounds, but would let the chief know who might have arrived at the church at a suspicious hour the next time the vandals struck.

Of course, that was assuming Kevin didn't carry out his threat to evacuate until the weddings were over.

"I've met Lexy and Emily, remember?" he'd said a few weeks ago. "No way I'm going to either of those shindigs. I'm just sticking around to see if any of the bridesmaids are presentable. But since they're friends of the brides, I'm not optimistic."

I'd worry about that later.

In the sanctuary, Austin was poking about the space, presumably scouting out camera angles and light levels and whatever else photographers needed to worry about. And occasionally taking a flurry of pictures, though usually of some small detail of the church, or from a rather odd angle, which suggested that the shots were for his own purposes rather than any kind of preparation for the weddings.

Lexy was sitting in the front row of pews, watching him with an expression of bored impatience on her face.

Emily was standing on a nearby pew, stretching up on tiptoe, looking up at the ceiling and reaching out for something.

"Be careful!" Robyn hurried over to Emily's side. I wasn't sure if she was positioning herself to break Emily's fall if she lost her balance or planning to shoo her off the pew and check the seat for scuff marks.

"They're fabulous!" Emily exclaimed. "Too perfect! Wherever did you get them?"

"Get what?" Robyn asked. "Please come down. That pew seat is very highly polished and I'm worried that you'll slip and hurt yourself."

"The angels!" Emily exclaimed. "They're perfect! Absolutely divine! Where did you get them?"

"One of the Sunday school classes made them," Robyn said. "Are you all right, Meg?"

I gave Robyn a thumbs-up and dialed back the coughing fit I'd been faking to keep them from realizing that I had burst out laughing.

The angels Emily found so divine had, indeed, been made by one of the Sunday school classes. A group of ten- to twelve-year-old girls had found a dozen secondhand Barbie and Ken dolls at the local thrift store and turned them into angels, complete with gauzy white choir robes and tinsel halos. They'd then proudly presented them to Trinity's Christmas decorating committee. Mother, as head of the committee, had only just managed to hide her dismay. The girls had done their best, but no one could call the angels elegant. The ten Barbies and two Kens were all of the era when most of the dolls Mattel produced—at least the less expensive ones designed for actual children to play with—wore perky, vapid smiles. Their choir robes failed to hide that some of their arms and legs had been chewed on or were missing entirely. And whoever had been in charge of decorating the white robes evidently was, in Mother's opinion, "a little heavy-handed with the glitter." She was being tactful. Some of the robes were so heavily encrusted that the underlying white fabric was barely detectable. They looked, in short, exactly like the sort of angels a children's Sunday school class would make, and Mother was daunted by the challenge of incorporating them into her elegant, carefully designed decorations.

But it was my suggestion that had saved the day.

"They don't look half bad if you sort of stand back twenty or thirty feet and squint," Rob had said, in between fits of laughter—although at least he'd waited until the angel-makers were not around.

I tried it, and he was right—so I suggested that Mother could position them up near the soaring ceiling of the Trinity sanctuary. That proved to be the perfect solution. The angels were all in what no one could deny was a highly visible place of honor—half of them were hovering high up over the altar, and the rest deployed along the side walls, three on one side and three on the other, tooting tiny gold trumpets in the direction of their colleagues. And Mother and her decorating crew had surrounded each angel with an exuberant amount of gold tinsel, red velvet ribbon, and evergreen boughs, making them seem like the glittering centers of some sort of exotic winter blooms. Mother was actually pleased with the resulting effect, but I doubted if her migraine would be improved by Emily's next words.

"I want to have them at my reception. Let's take some of them down and bring them over to the Inn."

She looked around, at first eager and then a little petulant when no one jumped to fetch a ladder and carry out her suggestion.

"Not possible," Robyn said when she'd recovered her composure. "They're part of our holiday decorations, and I'm sure the Inn has its own very lovely decorations. You can enjoy them here."

"But you've got so many of them." Emily pouted dramatically.

"Fine by me if you want to send the wretched things over to the Inn," Lexy said. "As long as you keep them all inside your own ballroom. I don't want them anywhere near *my* reception."

"I wouldn't share them with you if you *did* want them," Emily said. "It was my idea. They're mine."

"They're not going anywhere," Robyn said. "Members of our congregation made them, and they expect to see them here at Trinity."

"If you like them so much, why not take a picture and show them to your bridesmaids," I suggested. "They're coming for tonight's hen party, aren't they? You could have them make some angels between now and Saturday. It only took the Sunday school girls a few hours to make all of them—I'm sure a group of grown-ups could do it just as quickly."

"But I want *these* angels," Emily whined. "None of my bridesmaids are the least bit artistic. I have no idea if they can do something like this."

"If they can't, then we'll ask around for someone who can," I said.

"Why not speak to your wedding planner?" Robyn said.

"Her *mother* is planning her wedding." Lexy's tone dripped with scorn. I wasn't sure where the attitude came from, since her mother was also planning her wedding. "She hasn't a creative bone in her body."

"What a mean thing to say," Emily said. "You take that back."

"No one's suggesting that she make the angels herself," I said. "She could find someone to make them."

"Or hire someone," Lexy said. "Not that I'd waste money on such a tacky idea, but whatever floats your boat. Or maybe Meg's mother could find someone. She's actually good at organizing stuff."

Her tone suggested that she considered organizing a rather unimportant skill—perhaps even a slightly disreputable one. Which would have raised my hackles, even if she hadn't been suggesting that Emily dump yet another thankless chore on Mother. I'd make the damned angels myself before letting that happen. Although, if it came down to it, I could probably find a few willing volunteers. I began making a mental list of candidates while Austin and the brides finished their inspection of the church. Well, Austin was inspecting. Emily spent her time climbing up onto the pews to take pictures of the angels with her cell phone, while Lexy followed Austin's progress from her seat in the pew while vigorously plying an emery board on her long, clawlike pink nails.

While all this was happening, I'd begun to notice that one of the side doors occasionally opened a crack and then closed again. I kept watch on the door, and the next time it opened, I saw Josh peer out. Then he frowned and closed the door again.

I pulled out my notebook, checked the calendar, and repressed words that I probably shouldn't be saying inside a church.

"I think the Christmas pageant rehearsal was supposed to have started five minutes ago," I said.

Chapter 8

"Oh, dear!" Robyn glanced at her watch and grimaced. "Mr. Luckett, could you finish up now? We have several dozen small children waiting to get in here for a rehearsal."

Much eye-rolling from the brides.

"Time for us to get moving anyway," I said. "After all, Austin needs to scope out how he's going to shoot them coming out of the church. That's an important moment. And while Trinity's front steps are a beautiful place for a photo, some people find the angles a little tricky."

That worked. Both brides brightened at the thought of rehearsing the poses they'd be striking on their way out of the church. Austin sighed and followed us.

It was a good thing the three workers from the Shiffley Construction Company were still in the vestibule finishing up the floors, because without their help I'm not sure Robyn and I could have kept Emily and Lexy from exiting into the vestibule, marching across it to the front door, and ruining the floor's gleaming new surface.

As we left the sanctuary, the pageant cast began pouring in. Evidently, this was a dress rehearsal, since most of the children were already wearing shepherds' robes, angels' halos, or the fuzzy pajama-like costumes of the various animals who played a part in the Nativity story.

Several adult volunteers were there to ride herd on the children, which was a good thing, because I found Josh and Jamie, the codirectors of the pageant, out in the hall, having what appeared to be a tense discussion.

"Hi, guys," I said. "What's up?"

"Your older son is a real stick-in-the-mud," Josh said.

"Your younger son has some really weird ideas about what a Christmas pageant should be like," Jamie replied.

"Jerk!"

"Creep!"

They both turned on their heels and began striding away from each other. I collared Jamie, who happened to be closest, and turned him around.

"What's going on?" I asked.

"He wants to ruin the whole pageant!" Jamie said. "He wants to add some stuff he thinks would be funny, but it's not really, except maybe to kids even younger than us, and it will just be awful."

He looked on the verge of tears.

"Okay, what is it he wants to add?"

"Ask him." Jamie's face set in a stubborn expression. "It's just stupid."

My twin sons didn't often argue, but when they did, they could be impossible. And not just about trying to strike a compromise with each other. They were also annoyingly reluctant to break the bonds of twinship by divulging to anyone else what they were arguing about.

"I tell you what," I said. "Go sit on one of the comfy sofas in the parish hall and do those calming breath exercises Rose Noire taught us. Can you do that?"

"And you'll take care of it?" He looked up eagerly.

"I'll go talk to him."

He nodded and hurried off.

One of the adult volunteers stuck her head out of the sanctuary and looked at me inquiringly. Just then my phone rang. Rose Noire. I let it go to voicemail.

"Our directors appear to be having creative differences," I said to the volunteer. "Can you keep the kids busy for a little while? Inspect their costumes. Maybe rehearse a few of the carols?"

"Can do," she said, and disappeared back into the sanctuary.

Just then Mother called. I let her go to voicemail, too. But I needed to get back to her and Rose Noire before too long.

I went in the direction I'd seen Josh going. I found him outside, in the graveyard, kicking at piles of fallen leaves. He looked up when he heard me coming, thanks to the squeaking of the iron gate between the brick walk and the graveyard.

"He's so bossy!" he exclaimed, hurrying over to greet me. "And he has no sense of humor. He wants us to have the same old boring, tedious things we always do. I want to liven it up a little, and he's just being a stick-in-the-mud."

"I hear you," I said. "Can you do something for me?"

He nodded.

"Go inside and find an oil can," I said. "There should be one in the janitor's closet. And oil the squeaky hinges of this gate, because it's driving me crazy. And then I'd like you to find a quiet space out here in the churchyard and do that yoga breathing Rose Noire is always recommending."

"When I'm calm I'm still going to think he's a stick-in-the-mud," Josh said.

"Probably," I agreed. "But maybe by the time you're calm I'll come up with a way to solve your disagreement with Jamie."

"Okay." He didn't rush to follow my instructions, but he began trudging glumly toward the church door.

My phone rang again. Ekaterina.

I let her, too, go to voicemail. Then I called Michael.

"Where are you?" I asked.

"If I told you that, I'd have to think of another thing to surprise you with on Christmas morning," he said.

"Good point," I said. "Let me rephrase my question. Are you near enough to Trinity that you can rush over here to help resolve some creative differences between Josh and Jamie over the Christmas pageant?"

"Already on my way for the boys' rehearsal," he said. "What's wrong? Does Josh still think a few fart jokes would enliven the pageant?"

"Good heavens," I said. "I hope not. If that's it, maybe I'll sic Robyn on him. Let her veto it. So when you get here, go to the parish hall and talk to Jamie."

"Can do."

We said goodbye and hung up. I strolled around to the front of the church.

I spotted Lexy walking briskly across the gravel parking lot toward her car. Emily was still on the front steps, striking poses. Perhaps she hadn't noticed that Austin was no longer paying attention to her.

"I think Mr. Luckett has all the test shots he needs," Robyn said.

"What?" Austin looked up. "Oh, yeah. Done here."

"About time," Emily said, as if it was his fault that she was still there. "I'm running late."

With that, she took off toward the parking lot.

I wondered, briefly, what she was late for. I hoped it wasn't anything involving Mother. I texted Ekaterina a heads-up and asked her to fend the brides off if they showed up.

"Call me," she texted back.

"When is this rehearsal thing going to be over?" Austin asked.

Robyn pulled out her calendar.

"They've got it from one to three," she said. "And then—"

"Longer than I want to hang around here," he said. "It's way past time to find some lunch, and then I have some things to do. Can I come back later?"

We compared calendars and discovered that tonight at eleven was the earliest possible time that both he and the church were available and either Robyn or I was free to let him in.

"Let's look at tomorrow, then," Robyn said, turning the page of her appointment book.

"No, eleven's fine with me," he said. "I'm a night owl."

"Fine." I added the appointment to my calendar.

"And now I plan to murder a Big Mac," he said. "Maybe two."

With that he strode off toward the center of town.

"A Big Mac?" Robyn echoed. "Doesn't he realize we don't have a McDonald's in town?"

"Evidently not," I said.

"Should we warn him?"

"I'm sure some kind soul will steer him to the diner when he asks for directions to the nearest Mickey D's," I said. "Although I expect I'll hear him whining about it the next time I see him. Which I hope isn't until I have to let him in here tonight."

"Convenient that you're a key holder," Robyn said. "Just don't let him do anything to the decorations your mother and her committee have worked so hard on. And keep him out of the vestibule. The floor needs to dry overnight."

"Will do." I was watching Austin, who was at the far side of the parking lot, bending over backward, taking some pictures of the iron-gray sky through the bare branches of the towering oaks that surrounded the church grounds. I hoped he realized that if he backed up any farther, he'd be stepping out into a road that carried a lot of tourist traffic.

"And I should be able to join you tonight." Robyn was writing in her appointment book. "We're having the monthly ecumenical meeting over at the New Life Baptist Church, but unless it runs a lot longer than usual, I should be able to get over here by eleven."

"Does that mean you don't trust me to protect the angels and the floor?" I asked.

"I trust you," she said. "I don't trust him. And not just with the angels and the floor. Looks to me as if he has a bit of a roving eye."

"If it's roving in my direction, he's doomed to disappointment," I said.

"Well, I know that, but he might not." Robyn chuckled. "And if I'm here, it should keep him from doing anything he'll feel embarrassed about later."

"No objection from me," I said. "See you at eleven. Meanwhile, could you go talk to Josh? He's in the graveyard calming down. He and Jamie have had some kind of disagreement over the Christmas pageant, and I'm hoping you, as rector, and Michael, as their directorial mentor, can help them work out a compromise. I'd stay around and try to restore harmony myself, but I think some wedding-related things might be blowing up, and—"

"Go take care of them." Robyn gave me a slight shove. "Leave the Christmas pageant to Michael and me. If it's about the whoopee cushion Josh brought to the last rehearsal, I'll confiscate it."

As I headed for my car, I saw Josh wielding the oilcan on the offending gate. I waved to him. He nodded back at me. Then Robyn arrived at his side.

And I was relieved to see Michael's car turning into the parking lot. He hopped out, waved to me in passing, and hurried into the church.

I pulled out my phone and called Mother.

Chapter 9

"What's up?" I asked, when Mother answered her phone.

"Rose Noire could use some help," she answered. "Some of the bridesmaids are arriving, and also some of the more . . . difficult relatives, and that young lady who works for the photographer is having a meltdown in your kitchen, and I need to be here to help Ekaterina with—"

"You need to be lying down until your head is better," I said. "I'll take care of Rose Noire and whatever Ekaterina needs help with. Now hang up and go back to resting."

"Thank you, dear." Her voice was faint. Almost meek.

A good thing the brides had taken off, or I'd have been tempted to kick them.

I texted Rose Noire to say I was on my way home and she texted back. "Thanks. Hurry."

I called Ekaterina.

"What do you need me to do?" I asked.

"Help me keep those horrible brides from bothering your mother," Ekaterina said. "If they come back, I am going to lie and say she went home."

"Don't do that," I said. "They know the way to Mother and Dad's farm. We don't want them lying in wait for her when she goes home. It's bad enough that she has to deal with Aunt Betty and Aunt Letty. If the brides start trying to find Mother, tell them Dad is admitting her to Caerphilly Hospital for observation."

"Oooh, that's much better," she said. "And I will warn your father so he can back me up."

"Perfect!" I exclaimed. "Keep it up. And if there's anything you or she want done—"

"I know where to find you," she said. "At the moment, I am preparing my estimate on the cost of providing armed security guards for the gift rooms. I might call on you for assistance when the time comes to present it to the twins."

"The twins?" I wasn't sure what Josh and Jamie had to do with hotel security.

"The twin mothers of the brides," Ekaterina explained. "Is there a trick to telling them apart?"

"If you mean Betty and Letty, they're not twins—just sisters," I said. "And if you figure out the trick to telling them apart, please share it with me."

"They showed up just now wearing identical forest-green pantsuits," Ekaterina said. "And seemed horrified when they spotted each other. So now I am waiting while they have both gone back to their rooms to change."

"Tactical mistake," I said. "You should have kept one with you. They seem to have exactly the same taste in clothes. What if they change into more identical outfits?"

"Then I will follow your useful suggestion and detain one." Ekaterina's patience was wearing thin, by the sound of it. "It is also possible that I will eventually need your assistance in explaining to Ms. Letty and Ms. Betty that the cost of armed security guards is not covered in their contract with the hotel."

"If it comes to that, I'll be there," I said.

We hung up and I headed for home.

As I drew near the house, I could see that more guests had arrived. The line of cars parked along the side of the road started half a mile away—worse than usual, I suspected, since road construction just beyond our house forced not just our visitors but also those staying at Rob and Delaney's to park here.

"They'd better not have taken my parking spot," I muttered.

Luckily for my mood, they hadn't. I parked in my usual place, by the barn, and strolled back to where the Bestitched mobile sewing shop was parked. Several young women—presumably bridesmaids—were flitting in and out of it. Several more were across the street in Seth Early's pasture, taking selfies with the sheep.

I saw Nikki Tran standing a few feet away, with her eyes closed, taking deep breaths. I strolled over to join her.

"Should I worry that you're already using Rose Noire's calming techniques?" I asked.

"It's mostly preventive." She opened her eyes. "Although this isn't going to be a picnic. I've already begun to notice a certain tension between some of the bridesmaids."

"Not surprising," I said. "I'd be astonished if the hostility between Lexy and Emily didn't spread to their wedding parties."

"Yeah." She chuckled. "Could be a loyalty test. Hate who I hate, or you're out on your ear, and stuck with a beautifully made dress that's so monumentally ugly you probably won't ever want to wear it in public. Don't worry. I've done this before."

I left her to it and went inside the house. Several young women were clustered in the living room, whispering to each other. They looked up when I came in, but seemed unalarmed by my arrival, and went back to their whispering.

The several young women occupying the dining room did much the same thing.

I wondered, briefly, if it would be helpful if I could convince them to wear some sort of identification, so we sane people could tell from afar which faction they belonged to. Like the white and red blooms worn by the York and Lancaster sides during the War of the Roses. Or perhaps more like gang colors in a skirmish between the Sharks and the Jets. Maybe Nikki and the seamstresses could run up some rosettes in the brides' chosen wedding colors—lavender and black for Lexy, green and silver for Emily.

I'd ponder that idea later. Meanwhile, when I got to the kitchen, I found Rose Noire sitting next to Maddie, rubbing her back and gently pushing a cup of tea into her hands.

"That won't work," Maddie was wailing.

"What's wrong?" I asked.

"We need to help Maddie find a new job," Rose Noire said.

"Right now?" I blinked in surprise. "Has Austin fired her?"

"He didn't fire me." Maddie had tears running slowly down her face. "He won't let me quit. I tried that last year, and it was a disaster."

"What happened?"

"Maddie is a perfectly wonderful photographer in her own right," Rose Noire said. "But Austin poisoned the Richmond-area wedding vendor community against her. Made it look as if she was the one responsible for several things he'd done wrong. And after that, no one would hire her or even work with her, and she had to go crawling back to him and ask for her job back."

Maddie nodded, and sniffled.

"He is not a nice man," she said.

"I could tell that from his aura," Rose Noire said. "He has a very nasty, slimy aura."

I never argued with Rose Noire when she diagnosed someone's

aura. I didn't entirely believe in auras, but I absolutely believed in Rose Noire's ability to judge character.

"You might want to warn the bridesmaids," Maddie said. "He's . . . he's a predator."

"He hasn't done anything to you, has he?" Rose Noire exclaimed.

"Oh, no." Maddie's laugh had a bitter tone. "He's told me lots of times that I don't have to worry about him hitting on a chubster like me."

"Chubster!" Rose Noire was starting to look like a broody hen defending her nest. "How dare he? You're a perfectly normal, healthy weight."

"Consider the source," I said. "The man has no taste. He probably likes anorexic bimbos like Lexy and Emily."

Rose Noire nodded vigorously, which showed how very upset she was on Maddie's behalf. Normally she'd have taken me to task for calling our cousins bimbos.

"Warn them," Maddie said. "They don't want to leave anyone alone with him—especially if there's going to be drinking, as there usually is."

Rose Noire and I exchanged a glance. We knew that tonight, when all the bridesmaids had arrived, both brides were holding hen parties. Of course, both of them had already had expensive destination hen parties—Emily in Vegas and Lexy in Acapulco—so I wasn't sure why they needed yet another boozy blowout. Their decision, though. So Lexy's bridesmaids and friends would be carousing in our library while Emily and her posse took over Rob and Delaney's basement game room.

"And they should make sure they have a signed contract spelling out exactly what he's doing for them," Maddie said. "If they don't, he'll try to gouge them for things they would have every reason to assume were included. He does it all the time. I've had to block one of his clients who kept calling today to ask me if I couldn't make him give them all their photos. I feel sorry for the poor man, I really do, but he's the one who signed a contract that let Austin charge extra to give them more than fifty photos, and it's not as if Austin would listen to me."

That explained the call I overheard while I was chauffeuring Austin around. And I wondered what Lexy's and Emily's contracts said. Fifty photos might work if the photographer was only shooting a few posed shots right after the ceremony, but they'd hired Austin for three days' coverage of all official events, plus candid shots. Were they limited to fifty photos? Neither Mother nor I would ever have signed such a ridiculous contract. If we couldn't negotiate better terms, there were plenty of other photographers in the world. But I wasn't sure either the brides or their mothers were that practical-minded.

"Not my circus, not my monkeys," I reminded myself.

Just then we heard screaming outside. Rose Noire and I exchanged a startled look and then raced to the front door.

Chapter 10

We arrived at the front door in time to open it for a small posse of hysterical bridesmaids who stampeded past me and up the stairs, presumably heading for the bedrooms they occupied. Which identified them as Lexy's bridesmaids. Emily's were staying next door with Rob and Delaney.

"What in the world is wrong?" I called after them.

"Alyssa stepped in something horrible!" one of the bridesmaids said, before fleeing upstairs in the others' wake.

Rose Noire was examining the floor in the front hall.

"Probably sheep poop." She turned and headed for the kitchen. "Some kind of poop, anyway. I'll go get the mop."

Out by the mobile Bestitched shop, another group of young women—presumably Emily's wedding party—were laughing hysterically at Alyssa's plight.

Sheep poop. And instead of sensibly leaving her soiled shoes on the front porch, the wretched Alyssa had tracked it inside, all over the floors and rugs that we'd had cleaned so the house would look fabulous for the holiday season and the weddings. Correction: the rugs and floors Mother had arranged to have cleaned.

Rose Noire emerged from the kitchen with a bucket full of cleaning implements.

"You want me to help with that?" I said.

"I'm better at cleaning," she said, in a weary voice. Then she put her hands to her mouth. "Oh! I'm so sorry! I didn't mean—"

"You're right," I said. "You're better at cleaning. I'll read the riot act to Alyssa when she recovers from her ordeal. And meanwhile, I'll bring you as many buckets of fresh water as it takes to clean this up."

Between the two of us, we got the hall back into some approximation of the perfection Mother's holiday cleaning had produced. And Maddie, bless her heart, pitched in to help, along with one of Emily's bridesmaids. I didn't remember the helpful bridesmaid's name and I was too embarrassed to ask, but I figured Rose Noire either knew or could find out. I'd ask her when the bridesmaid was no longer in earshot.

"That's Jenna," Rose Noire said, when the bridesmaid in question had gone back out to the Bestitched RV and the rest of us returned to the kitchen to celebrate our success with Christmas cookies and hot mulled cider.

"The polite one," Maddie said. "This would be such a nice photography assignment if I were here by myself. The brides and most of the bridesmaids are pretty typical, but the rest of you are really nice. Not that I'm trying to undercut Austin or anything like that," she added, hastily. "I didn't—"

"Relax," I said. "We understand. Do you at least get a little time off tonight?"

"Probably not," she said. "Apparently both brides are having girls-only parties tonight, and since they wouldn't want Austin at those, I'm supposed to document them for the wedding albums. So I guess I'll be trudging back and forth between here and the house next door—are they friends of yours, the people next door?"

"My brother and his wife," I said.

"I should have guessed," she said. "I can't imagine anyone who's not a relative letting that bunch party at their house. Are you guys going to be there?"

She looked so hopeful that I felt guilty when both Rose Noire and I shook our heads.

"Alas, no," I said. "Since I expect both events will be dedicated to the consumption of impressive quantities of alcohol, I decided to pass. I'm past the phase of life where that sounds like fun."

"Did they even invite you?" Rose Noire asked.

"Yes," I said. "But I expect they were only being polite. They both looked relieved when I declined. I'll be attending one of the other social events taking place this evening."

"Other social events?" Maddie looked discouraged.

"Nothing anyone expects you to document," I said.

"Neither of the brides invited me," Rose Noire said. "Which is fine with me. I'm having a little get-together out at my herb shed with some of my pagan and Wiccan friends. We'll be finalizing the plans for our Winter Solstice celebration. You're both welcome to join us."

"Maybe once I'm able to leave the hen parties," Maddie said.

"I'll keep it in mind," I said. "Michael has invited me to join the crowd going with him to tonight's basketball games at Caerphilly College. He's invited both grooms, Lexy's dad, Josh and Jamie, a bunch of their friends, plus any visiting family members not eligible for the hen parties, so most of the men and kids. Then after the games, a lot of them will be going out to Grandfather's zoo for his Sleep with the Wombats event."

"Games?" Maddie echoed. "Plural? I didn't know basketball teams ever did doubleheaders."

"The women's team, followed by the men's," I explained. "Which is kind of stupid, since the women's team is actually pretty good and the men nearly always end up last in their league. Most of the spectators will leave when the first game is over."

"Still sounds like fun," Maddie said. "More fun than trudging back and forth between two drunken parties."

"May I add an amendment to whatever instructions you've received from the brides or their mothers or Austin?" I said. "As soon as the parties get to the point where any pictures you might take would be more suited for blackmail fodder than fond memories, you are hereby ordered to cease and desist. And if anyone gives you any guff about it, send them to me."

"It's a deal," she said. "Does that mean you're going to be around?"

"Not in the early part of the evening," I said. "Mother will be hosting an elegant ladies-only dinner down at the Inn for the mothers of the brides and a few other visiting relatives from their generation. I plan on attending that, and then getting home reasonably early, so I'm here to play party pooper if either event is getting out of hand. Oh—and I'm supposed to meet your boss at the church at eleven—he wanted to spend some more time scoping it out. He'll probably ask you to drive him there—and even if he doesn't, that will give you a good excuse to abandon the parties if you haven't already. So if you need to get away, just say that I ordered you to show up at the church at eleven."

"Thanks." She started, then pulled her phone out and looked at it.

"I have to go and pick him up," she said, as she tapped something into the phone. "And he's in a wretched mood. Does Caerphilly really not have a McDonald's?"

"No, but if he'd bothered to ask, we could have steered him to a couple of good places to get a burger," I said. "And if you need directions or if anyone gives you any trouble, call me. I can find someone to take care of it." I made sure she had my cell phone number. I didn't say "don't hassle poor Rose Noire or Mother," but I think she got the point. She nodded and hurried out.

"Are you really going there to meet the photographer?" Rose Noire asked. "Or is that a cover story for staking out the church to see if you can catch the vandals red-handed?"

"I'm really meeting Austin," I said. "But that's not a bad idea, staking out the church. Although I'm not sure anyone's going to want to do it until after Christmas."

"Do we really want to wait that long?"

"That long?" I echoed. "It's only a week. And we can start planning now, so come Boxing Day we're ready for the stakeout. Meanwhile, have we warned Delaney what these parties are apt to be like?"

"She knows." Rose Noire looked slightly anxious. "She recruited eight or ten people from her office to get their basement game room ready for the one that's happening at her house. I think they're putting half of the contents into storage."

"Good," I said. "She'll be prepared."

"But their game room is pretty well adapted to entertaining," Rose Noire said. "Here, they'll be in the library."

"Thanks for reminding me," I said. "I'm going to go and batten it down so we're ready for the invading hens. See you later."

As I headed for the library, I found myself wishing, not for the first time, that there was some valid reason for refusing to let Lexy hold her party there. Or for suggesting some other venue I could exile them to.

Our library was a later addition to the house, built in the 1880s as a ballroom by a previous owner who wanted to make a splash on the local social scene. It had been a ruin when we'd first bought the house, but Michael and I, avid readers both, had immediately had the shared vision of turning it into the library of our dreams. Alas! The estimates we'd received on repairing it and turning it into a functioning library had been so exorbitant that we'd almost given up on the idea. The only thing that had saved it, back then, was that it would cost almost as much to tear it down, fill in the basement, and make the house and yard presentable without it. So we gave it a lick and a promise and hoped that some future financial miracle would make restoring it feasible. Which was exactly what eventually happened. The Caerphilly library was temporarily evicted from its quarters due to a financial crisis, and Randall Shiffley, as mayor, had promised to carry out our library construction plans for a fraction of the real cost, provided we hosted all the town's books until the town was able to reclaim the library building. Which took several years, but now we had exactly the library we'd fantasized about, all white plaster and gleaming Mission oak, and of course bookshelves lining the walls not only on the main floor but also on the mezzanine that ran along three walls of the double-height room.

Sometimes, if I was in a less-than-cheerful frame of mind, I could snap out of it just by curling up on one of the deep turquoise velvet couches and reading a few pages of a favorite book. *The Three Musketeers. To Kill a Mockingbird. Freddy the Detective.*

And maybe I should do just that right now, I thought, as I walked down the long hallway that led to the library. Even ten or fifteen minutes in the library would have a restorative effect.

But when I opened the door, I found that the room wasn't empty. Emily's groom was sitting at one of the sturdy oak tables, reading a book. He looked up with a start when I came in.

And then I reminded myself to stop calling him Emily's groom. He had a name. Although it took a few seconds to recall it. Harry. Which should be easy to remember, now that I'd had a good look at him, since he reminded me of Harry Potter, as played in the movies by Daniel Radcliffe. He was about my height and slender, with a slightly unruly mop of dark hair. He was even wearing round wire-rimmed glasses. And his last name, Koenig, would also be easy to remember, since several relatives had already asked if he was related to Walter Koenig, who'd played Chekov on *Star Trek*.

"Sorry," I said. "I didn't mean to disturb you."

Chapter 11

"That's okay," Harry said. "I'm not intruding, am I? I mean, if you'd rather not have me here I could—"

"Relax," I said. "You're very welcome here. Nothing makes Michael and me happier than having someone appreciate the library. I'll be out of your hair in a few minutes. I just want to make sure everything is battened down before tonight's hen party."

He nodded. There was something different about him. Not that I'd seen all that much of him before, but still—

Aha! I had it. The glasses. Round wire rims, slightly crooked on his face. Every other time I'd seen him, he'd been wearing contact lenses. And either he was still getting used to contacts or he was one of those people who shouldn't even try to wear them— he'd been constantly squinting and batting his eyes and dabbing at them when they watered, which was most of the time. When I'd met him, I'd found him a slightly odd match for Emily, and wondered what was wrong with his eyes. But now it was obvious. The only reason I hadn't seen the difference immediately was that he looked utterly natural in glasses. Put him in the right setting and he was a reasonably attractive young man—well, if you could get him to shed the uncomfortable contacts. And the library was obviously the right setting.

He'd taken off his glasses and was holding them in one hand.

"Oh, for heaven's sake," I said. "Put your specs back on. I won't tell Emily you're cheating on your contacts."

He blushed but followed my instructions. His face looked so much more natural with the glasses.

"Thanks," he said. "I'm sure I'll get used to them eventually."

"So you haven't been wearing contacts long?"

"About six months." He sighed. "Seems as if I should have gotten at least a little used to them by now."

"You look perfectly fine in glasses," I said.

"Emily doesn't think so."

His tone worried me. It wasn't "Emily, the love of my life, prefers me in contacts, so I will keep wearing them no matter what—this is the hill I will die on!" More like "Emily will have a conniption fit if I spoil her picture-perfect wedding by wearing glasses."

"Stay here as long as you like," I said. "The party doesn't start until this evening. Eight or nine."

He nodded. He looked down at the book he was reading. But as I quietly got the library ready for the party, I could see him glancing up occasionally.

Given its size, the library was obviously a great place for parties, but Michael and I had always been a little worried about the danger to the books if one got out of hand. So this summer we'd arranged to have the Shiffley Construction Company install glass doors on all the bookshelves on the lower level. Lockable glass doors. So while our books weren't necessarily protected from a determined vandal, who could break the glass or pry open the doors, they were reasonably safe from getting ruined if party-goers got careless with food or drink. We didn't normally keep the bookcases locked, but it was now part of the prep for any party held here.

I glanced up at one point to see Harry studying me. No, not me. The glassed-in bookcases.

"I see you're locking the bookcases up." He held up the book he'd been reading: *David Copperfield*. "Want me to put this back now?"

"No, you're fine," I said. "I'll leave the bookcase it belongs in open for the time being. Or I could lock that up, too, and you could take the book with you when you leave."

"That would be great," he said. "If you trust me with it. Do those glass doors do a good job of keeping the dust in?"

"I think it's more a case of keeping the dust out," I said. "You have no idea how nice it is not to worry about dusting all of these."

He nodded and continued running his eyes around the library.

"Emily's allergic to book dust," he said. "Having more than a few books around makes her sneeze. And she doesn't like the way they look. She says they make a room look cluttered. I had to put most of my books in storage."

He focused back down at his book, which was probably just as well. He missed the expression of shock on my face. Shock, followed by anger. What the hell was wrong with Emily? And what could they possibly have in common, if he loved reading and she was determined to banish books from their life together? Okay, he could still use e-books. But Harry struck me as the kind of reader who loved the look and feel of a paper book. The smell of ink and paper. The comforting feel of a room filled both with books he'd read—old friends—and a large, enticing to-be-read pile.

Were we knocking ourselves out for a wedding that would be followed, all too soon, by an acrimonious divorce? Or worse, a wedding that would be followed by a life of quiet misery for this shy, bookish man?

And then I reminded myself that it was none of my business. Harry was a grown-up. He didn't really look old enough to drive, but he was twenty-five. I remembered seeing that in the engagement announcement.

And I suddenly felt a stab of anxiety for him. If he'd had to put his books into storage . . . how long would that last? Once they were married, what was to keep Emily from nagging him to get rid of them entirely?

Maybe Michael and I should offer to take in his books. Give them a happy home in our library, where he'd be welcome to visit them at any time. I wasn't sure what part of Richmond they'd be living in, but even if it was on the farthest side from us, he'd only be about an hour away from his beloved library. And—maybe it was heresy even to think this—but we could keep a list of the books he'd given us so he could reclaim them if the marriage with Emily foundered on what seemed to be their complete incompatibility.

Probably a good idea to talk it over with Michael before making the offer. So I only wished Harry a good morning and left him to his reading.

Before leaving, I glanced through the French doors at the back of the library into the sunroom. Blaine, the other groom, was there, pacing up and down among the potted plants and wrought iron furniture. He held his phone to his ear with his left hand, and with his right he was squeezing one of those hand-strengthening gadgets. I'd practically worn out a set of those when I'd first started blacksmithing and realized I needed to improve my grip. As I watched, he took the phone away from his ear and tapped it. Then he swapped hands, holding the phone to his ear with the right while he exercised the left. He looked . . . frustrated? Anxious? Definitely some flavor of unhappy. I only hoped whatever he was calling about wasn't something he was trying to take care of for Lexy. As I watched, he stuffed the phone in his pocket, set the hand exerciser on one of the wrought iron tables, dropped to the ground, and began doing push-ups.

I toyed with the idea of going out and talking to him. Asking him if anything was wrong, or if there was anything I could do for him. But something about the expression on his normally bland and cheerful face held me back. I made a mental note to tell Michael about this, too. He and Rob had volunteered to entertain and provide moral support for the two grooms and had spent most of yesterday with them—he'd probably have a better idea whether Blaine was just suffering from ordinary prewedding jitters or whether there was something he needed help with.

I returned to the kitchen and found it empty. I glanced out into the backyard and saw two figures in voluminous black cloaks trudging across the yard, looking just a bit ominous in the eerie gray light. The breeze was making their cloaks flap wildly at the same time that it swept up some of the fallen leaves in our yard and sent them whirling around the two, adding to their air of mystery and menace. Ringwraiths, I thought. Dementors. Darth Vader. The Grim Reaper.

But then Skulk, the larger of our two feral barn cats, broke the spell by trotting up to the two and winding his sleek gray body around their ankles. Skulk might be hell on rats but he held no brief for villains. And next to him I could see that the two figures were rather on the small side for Ringwraiths. One of them reached down a hand to pet him.

Clearly Emily and Lexy were having an unfortunate effect on me. These were no villains out of fantasy. Only two of Rose Noire's Wiccan friends, heading for her combination greenhouse and herb-drying shed in the pasture behind our house, no doubt to help with the Winter Solstice preparations.

I threw on my coat and went out, partly to welcome them, and partly to make sure Rose Noire had recovered from the stress of dealing with the brides this morning.

Rose Noire and her friends were in the greenhouse part of the shed, busily working. Some of them were sewing tiny bags out of gauzy lavender fabric and black ribbons. Lexy's bridal colors. Rose Noire seemed calm and happy, dashing around serving cups of tea and tiny sugar cookies. The herb shed was warm and cozy—if you asked me, "shed" was a misnomer for something that was fully dry-walled and insulated and had electricity, heating, air-conditioning, and running water. And it was decorated to the hilt for Winter Solstice, although to the un-pagan eye it probably looked a lot like Christmas. Same colors—red and green, though without reindeer, wise men, or angels. If anyone enthused to her about how lovely her Christmas decorations were, she would carefully explain that many of the modern Western trappings of Christmas—the red-and-green color scheme, the focus on evergreens, and the significance of stars and candles—had been stolen wholesale from pagan Yule celebrations. But at least this meant that she and Mother were in harmony over the decoration scheme at the house.

And I was relieved to see that all of the dogs were out here with Rose Noire. Spike, the small evil one, had claimed a space right next to one of the heating vents. Tinkerbell, Rob's Irish Wolfhound, was curled up next to the other vent with three—no, four—of the resident and visiting Pomeranians cuddled up next to her. In addition to Winnie, Rose Noire's pup, and Widget, who belonged to Kevin, I was pretty sure I could see Aida's Whatever and Horace's Watson—they often left the dogs with us for company when they were on duty.

I settled down in a disreputable-looking but undeniably comfortable easy chair—one of Mother's thrift shop finds—and wondered if I should give in to the impulse to stay here for a while.

"We're making sachets for one of the brides," one young woman explained. "She wants to give them out as favors to all her guests."

I nodded. And took a deep breath, inhaling the herb shed's pleasing scent. A hint of sage, a small note of rosemary, but mostly lavender. I tried to let the scent work its aromatherapy magic, calming my nerves and lifting my spirits. But a nagging thought kept interrupting the spell. I stepped outside again, pulled out my phone, and called Mother.

"How are you feeling?" I asked, once we'd exchanged greetings.

"Much better, dear," she said. "And with luck I'll stay that way. Your cousins have gone off to entertain themselves for the rest of the afternoon."

"That's good," I said. "Quick question—isn't Emily allergic to lavender?"

"Emily." Mother made the name sound like a sigh. "Emily is allergic to everything."

"But isn't lavender one of her worst allergies?"

"Yes, dear," she said. "Which is why we asked Rose Noire for a moratorium on potpourri this holiday season. Most of her potpourris do contain at least some lavender. And that's also why we have Emily staying over at Rob and Delaney's house. Yours probably does have a certain residual bit of lavender odor by now."

"That's what I was afraid of." I explained about the sachets. "And I suppose it's always possible that Lexy doesn't know about Emily's allergies—"

"Nonsense," Mother said. "Lexy is well aware of them. Have Rose Noire keep the sachets out in her shed for the time being. I will discuss this with the mothers, and we will find a way to keep Lexy from ruining her cousin's day."

"I'm thinking we could have Ekaterina issue a ban on having that much smelly stuff inside the Inn," I said. "For the safety of any guests who happen to have allergies. And then we set up an elegant table at a safe distance outside the Inn's front door, so someone can hand the guests their sachets when they're heading for their cars or waiting for the valet to bring them around."

"That would work," she said. "Good suggestion, dear. I will brief Ekaterina and then issue an ultimatum to the mothers."

An ultimatum? Letty and Betty really must be getting on her nerves. Probably not a good idea to point that out.

"Awesome," I said. With that we hung up, and I went back inside.

Should I tell Rose Noire about Emily's allergies? Not right now. Not when all her friends were so busily—and cheerfully—stuffing industrial quantities of lavender into dozens and dozens of tiny bags. I'd break the news to Rose Noire after they all went home.

Besides, in spite of what Mother had said, I wasn't entirely sure Emily was actually allergic to the stuff or whether she just hated the scent so much that she worked herself into a state whenever she caught a whiff of it.

It had a good effect on me, though. I checked my notebook to make sure I wasn't forgetting about any other urgent tasks, and then spent several peaceful hours sewing and stuffing sachets, often with one or two Pomeranians sleeping in my lap. And chatting with Rose Noire's friends about herbs, aromatherapy, and tarot.

I didn't knock off until it was time to head back to the Inn for Mother's dinner.

Chapter 12

It was dark by the time I headed into town. Several of Seth Early's fake shepherds were equipped with rustic-looking lanterns, complete with battery-powered fake flames. And high above the pasture, the Washingtons' giant star shone brightly over the fields where most of the sheep were now contentedly sleeping. And as usual, a dozen or so tourists were there trying to capture the scene with everything from cell phones to large, professional-looking cameras.

Closer to town I passed the Washingtons' magi. The camels looked much more realistic with their awkwardly shaped legs removed. It looked as if Gaspar, Melchior, and Balthasar had settled their camels down in the pasture and were having a quick confab before marching up the driveway in search of the right stable. Had Isaiah added some kind of animation to make it look as if the camels were chewing their cuds, or was it just an optical illusion created by the flickering LED torches the wise men held? And of course more tourists were roaming up and down the fence, looking for the best angle to capture both the wise men and the star.

Maybe it was time to give careful consideration to the boys' pleas that we follow our neighbors' example and create our own elaborate Christmas display. Josh and Jamie had found a place that sold secondhand store dummies, and had promised that they'd do all the work of creating, setting up, and taking down the decorations. I'd vetoed doing anything that elaborate this year, citing the weddings as my excuse, but I promised we'd start work planning the display in January if they could reach a consensus on what our decorations should be. Since Seth and the Washingtons had the shepherds and wise men covered, Jamie suggested that we complete the trifecta with a life-sized Nativity scene. If we located it properly, he pointed out, we could use hay and treats to lure a few of Dad's heirloom cows and sheep to hang out by the stable—and wouldn't it be nice to include the llamas? To Josh's quibble that llamas were from the New World and wouldn't have been there at the Nativity, Jamie replied that most of the tourists would mistake them for camels anyway. Josh's counterproposal was that instead of a boring old Nativity we have something dramatic, like an animatronic depiction of Herod's Massacre of the Innocents. When Michael and I vetoed this, on the grounds that it would shock the tourists, Josh had protested—but my comment that it would upset poor Rose Noire seemed to have carried more weight. So to my great relief, it looked as if the Nativity theme would win, and by mid-January we'd be busily sewing biblical costumes and repurposing one of our surplus sheds into a stable. And trying—and failing—to convince the boys that no, we didn't have to have the biggest and most elaborate Nativity scene in town. They were now more than happy to serve as tour guides for visiting relatives who wanted to see the town's holiday decorations, since it gave them the chance to take notes on what they had begun referring to as "the competition."

As I drew closer to town, I passed more and more decorations—and, of course, more and more tourists. Thank goodness the Inn wasn't in the center of town. By now most of the locals had learned all the best routes to dart around town without getting caught up in the tourist-driven traffic jams. I picked my way through the outskirts of town and was soon heading back out the road that led to the Inn and, eventually, Grandfather's zoo.

The Inn looked particularly festive after dark, with the light from the lobby spilling out through the tall glass wall that faced the parking lot. A violinist was playing carols in one corner of the lobby, and I could smell cinnamon, ginger, cloves, and oranges—probably from the mulled cider that was a special holiday treat at the restaurant's bar.

Only one thing marred the lobby's holiday perfection. In the little nook to one side, where normally you'd see the enormous Christmas tree blazing in all its glory beside the stocking-decked fireplace, I spotted a large object covered with black tarps. Someone had made an effort to tart it up with several tinsel and evergreen garlands and a red bow the size of a basketball. But it remained an alien object, lumpishly blocking everyone's view of both the tree and the fireplace.

"It is a cage for the eagles."

I started. I hadn't heard Ekaterina's approach.

"I guessed as much," I said, while we performed the customary cheek-kissing ritual.

"Apparently they need their beauty sleep," she said. "And so far we have been unable to free up another space in which to put them. The hotel has never been this full."

"I'll talk to Caroline," I said, "and see if we can't find someplace else for her to keep them. Someplace other than the hotel."

"That would be most appreciated." She smiled, and strode off.

I began turning over the possibilities. Normally, I'd have offered space in our barn, but that probably wasn't such a great idea with all the wedding chaos ramping up. And both Dad and Rob would be delighted to host a trio of eagles, but they, too, were juggling visiting family.

It occurred to me that perhaps Caroline and Ekaterina weren't thinking creatively about where to house the eagles. They were looking for a room. Maybe all we needed was a bit of space someplace other than the lobby.

With that thought in mind, I went through the door that led to the wing of the Inn that contained the meeting rooms. Just inside was a sort of miniature lobby that the hotel called the Gathering Area. During conferences and events like wedding receptions, it served as both a social center for those attending and a place where attendees could take a break from the main event. Right now it was almost empty. Two women sat on one of the settees, knitting in unison, as if practicing for a synchronized needlework competition. And in a far corner, Terri and Frank were sitting on another settee, obviously deep in conversation. I waved to them before starting to look around for a spot where the eagles' cage would be less intrusive.

I came across Hector, one of the hotel's senior bellmen, testing the doors to the Lafayette Room, the smaller of the two conference rooms. He looked up, spotted me, and smiled.

"Merry Christmas, Ms. Meg," he said. "Doubtless you will be pleased to know that the doors to the wedding gift rooms have been properly secured." Although Hector's English was unaccented, something about its rich formality suggested that it might not be his first language—although I'd never figured out what the first would be. So far I'd eliminated French, Spanish, and Russian.

"And a merry Christmas to you," I said. "Which bride does this room belong to?"

"Both," he said. "The Lafayette Room can be divided into two with the folding walls." He gestured grandly toward the doors that led into the two halves of the room. "Ms. Emily's presents are in Lafayette A, and Ms. Lexy's in Lafayette B."

Then he shook his head in apparent sadness.

"What's wrong?" I asked.

"I am worried," he said. "We should have contracted for additional security, with so many valuable things in one place. The way we did when the Inn hosted that gem and jewelry show last year."

"I seem to recall that the organizers of the gem and jewelry show paid a premium for that extra security."

"Yes," he said. "And the brides refuse to do that. A foolish economy. A cousin of mine works as a waiter in an upscale hotel in the District of Columbia. They had a very elegant wedding there—he says it was the wedding of an Indian maharajah, although I think perhaps he exaggerates. Why would a maharajah be getting married in Washington instead of India? But a very affluent Indian family, at any rate, and they had a capacious room full of gifts—much silver and crystal and also jewelry. And wedding bandits pounced upon it and absconded with everything. Well, everything of value."

"That's worrying," I said. "Has someone told the brides that?"

"I'm sure Ms. Ekaterina has told them," he said. "And I have no doubt that the contract they have signed with the Inn makes it clear that we are not responsible if they bring in a vast number of valuable things and fail to take the recommended steps to protect them. But that does not mean the brides will take it calmly if something happens."

"Good point." I winced and closed my eyes at the thought of how Emily and Lexy would react if even one of their presents turned up missing. "Are all the presents there now?"

"Only a few," he said. "Today, they mostly argued about sharing the room, until Ms. Ekaterina came in and ordered us to deploy the dividing wall. And then we had to reconfigure all the decorations to the taste of each bride, and there was much rearranging of the tables. But at last they were both satisfied, and we will be setting out all the gifts tomorrow. And then I will be worried."

"I'll see what I can do," I said.

"Ms. Ekaterina is quite vexed with the brides," Hector said. "And I worry that this might lead her to reject measures that would be helpful in preventing disaster."

I nodded. By this time, Ekaterina was probably thinking that it would serve the wretched brides right if they had all their presents stolen. And part of me agreed with her. But I could well imagine the headaches that would cause. I made a mental note to check with Kevin. He had designed and supervised the installation of a robust system of security cameras for the Inn. All it would take would be another camera or two in each gift room, and we'd at least have proof if any wedding bandits struck. And Kevin could probably find a way to sneak them in without telling Ekaterina, if necessary.

I pulled out my phone and was about to text him. Then it occurred to me that I might need to be persuasive. So I tried calling him. Miraculously, he actually picked up.

Chapter 13

"I'm over at the Inn," I said when Kevin answered. "Any chance you could sneak in a couple of cameras over here to keep watch over the gift tables? Without telling Ekaterina, because right now she's furious with both brides and would probably celebrate if wedding bandits stole all their presents."

"I'd probably celebrate, too," he said.

"Would you still be celebrating when they took it out on your grandmother?"

"Okay," he said. "I'll see what I can do before I leave town."

"That would be great, and— Wait, what do you mean, 'leave town'? I thought you were kidding about that. Your grandmother will never forgive you if you miss Christmas."

"I won't miss Christmas," he said. "I figure I can come back Sunday, or maybe Monday, once most of the brides and their minions are gone."

"You're not going to stay to check out the bridesmaids and see if any of them are hotties?"

"I have. They're not. They're all pretty easy on the eyes, but most of them don't have two brain cells to rub together. And even if they did, now that I've seen Lexy and Emily in action, it's pretty clear the bridesmaids all have lousy taste in friends. Pass."

"Harsh," I said. "But I won't argue with you. Just figure out some way to keep an eye on the wedding loot, so your grandmother doesn't have to take the heat if anything happens to it."

"Roger," he said. "I'll rig something up tomorrow."

With that we hung up, and I realized it was time to head for the restaurant for Mother's dinner.

Which was . . . interesting. At least in Mother's sense of the word. She always used "interesting" whenever she couldn't think of anything positive to say—much the way Grandfather used "fascinating." The guests of honor were the two mothers of the brides, and Mother had done her best to give them completely equal treatment—seating them both at the head of our table, with Mother placed to the left of Emily's mother and me to the right of Lexy's. Or maybe it was the other way around. I'd always had trouble telling them apart—they were both petite and plumply pretty, with similar taste in clothing and hairstyles.

Which was ironic, given how far apart they'd become. Betty and Letty didn't snipe at each other, the way their daughters did, but they either couldn't or wouldn't do anything to end the feud, and no longer seemed to enjoy each other's company.

The eight other guests were Hollingsworth family members chosen for their tact and diplomacy—well, seven family members plus Caroline Willner, who almost counted as family by now. And they'd all been briefed on the subjects to avoid—basically anything having to do with weddings.

An assignment that was proving surprisingly difficult. Mention the holidays and Betty would sigh about how difficult it had been to schedule all the usual family Christmas activities around the wedding. And Letty would sigh and murmur softly about what a lonely Christmas she would be having with Emily off on her honeymoon. Which might have inspired a lot more sympathy if everyone at the table wasn't fully aware that she'd turned down countless invitations to spend the season with one or another of them—including repeated ones from Mother. Mention the possibility that our leaden gray skies heralded snow if the storm currently stalled over the mountains started our way again and they'd both begin audibly fretting over whether it would keep some of the wedding guests from coming. At Mother's suggestion most of us had ordered different dishes, so we could all share . . . but if anyone praised the food, one or both of the mothers would dig out the menu for her daughter's reception to see if that dish was on the menu and fret about it either way.

My attention wandered during one of Letty's monologues—about typefaces, of all things; yet another subject on which the two brides had divergent opinions. Apparently Lexy favored a relatively common serif typeface called Palatino, while Emily had opted for a script typeface so ornate that she probably should have provided the recipients of her invitation with a translation. Each mother was, of course, convinced of the superiority of her daughter's taste in fonts, although they restrained themselves from anything worse than passive aggressive murmurs.

I found my eyes kept going involuntarily to another table, where Terri and Frank were having a quiet dinner for two. I was initially surprised—hadn't Frank said they'd be having a romantic dinner in their room? But perhaps they'd wanted something that didn't travel well and thus wasn't on the Inn's extensive room service menu. Or perhaps they enjoyed the delayed gratification of dining in public and deliberately postponing romance until they were alone. My bet was on that, actually. At first glance they seemed sedate and uninteresting, but if you watched them for more than a minute or two, you knew they were a tight-knit couple. Not because of any public displays of affection—the signs were more subtle. The way Terri smiled fondly at Frank when she thought he wasn't looking. The way he'd occasionally feed her a choice morsel from his plate. The way they laughed quietly together after one of them had said something that must have been sweetly witty. And Terri, in particular, appeared to be watching Betty and Letty with sympathetic interest.

I'd feel a lot better about the upcoming weddings if I'd ever seen either Emily or Lexy interacting that way with her groom. I found myself remembering poor Harry, retreating to our library to get a little reading fix before returning to what I suspected was a strenuous effort to live up to Emily's expectations. And I wondered about Blaine, Lexy's groom. Was his hearty, boisterous manner genuine? Or was he, too, bluffing?

Frank and Terri finished their meal before our group had even gotten around to thinking about dessert, and they stopped by our table on their way out of the restaurant.

"I just wanted to thank you so much," Frank said. "For your guidance on touring the Christmas decorations."

"Absolutely fabulous!" Terri gushed. "I told Frank I want to come back every year. It will be the perfect way to celebrate the holiday *and* our anniversary."

"Glad you enjoyed it," I said.

"And now we can't wait for the nighttime tour," Terri said.

"Meg, you do remember that you're supposed to meet Mr. Luckett at Trinity at eleven," Mother said. "More wedding preparations," she said, in an apologetic tone to Terri and Frank. "I'm sure Meg would be happy to give you her tour of the decorations when she's free."

"Oh, goodness," Terri said. "We weren't expecting her to take us! That would be too much of an imposition, as busy as you all are."

"She drew us a map this afternoon." Frank reached into his pocket and displayed the notebook page on which I'd drawn it. "With all sorts of good advice on what route to take and which streets were more dramatic at night."

"Of course!" Mother beamed at them. "And I hope she told you where to stop for the best cider and gingerbread."

"And we saved room." Frank rubbed his rounded stomach in anticipation.

"Don't forget the Christmas concert on the town square," I added. "I think it's the college orchestra tonight, and they really are quite good."

So after a few more minutes of exchanging thanks and pleasantries, they strolled off, arm in arm.

"Such a sweet couple," Mother murmured, before turning back to Letty with a brave and determined smile. I took a few deep, cleansing breaths—the sort Rose Noire was always recommending to help me keep my composure under trying circumstances—then focused back on the conversation Betty was having with the aunt to her right. They appeared to be discussing wedding-color trends, with Betty making a determined effort to explain the difference between bold, individual, modern color schemes—like Lexy's lavender-and-black theme—and merely loud, gaudy ones. She didn't quite bring up Emily's colors—green and silver with touches of white fake fur—as an example of tasteless color schemes, but she didn't really have to.

We'd only just reached the point of discussing dessert when I realized that it was ten minutes to eleven.

"I should take off now." I stood up and reached for my trusty tote bag. "Or I'll be late letting Austin into the church."

"But the Inn has crème brûlée," Mother pointed out. "Don't you want to stay for that?"

"Maybe I'll ask Ekaterina to save me one," I said. "I don't want to give Austin any grounds for claiming he didn't have enough time to scope out the church. And if I leave now, maybe I can get back here before you're all finished. But just in case I don't, have a great evening, everyone."

Several of the aunts leaped up to give me hugs, so I was already running a bit late by the time I hit the lobby.

"There you are." Ekaterina strode up to me. "How soon do you think you can do anything about those wretched birds?"

She pointed to the alcove where the eagles' cage still obscured the sight of the fireplace and the Christmas tree. I wondered why she was suddenly so upset about the eagles. And then I realized that it probably wasn't the birds that were getting on her nerves. My brother, Rob, and half a dozen of my male cousins who were about his age were sitting or standing around the cage. They'd pulled up one side of the tarp covering the cage, revealing a sleepy- and grumpy-looking eagle. From the look on the eagle's face, I hoped the cage was sturdy.

"All together now!" Rob said. And then a scrap of song wafted across the lobby.

> *Fiiiiive gol-den wiiiiings!*
> *Four calling birds*
> *Three French hens*
> *Two turtledoves*
> *And an eeea-gle in a big cage!*

The eagle emitted an annoyed squeak. I strode over and whisked the cover back down.

"You should be ashamed of yourselves!" I said. "How would you feel if I brought a dozen strangers into your rooms when you were trying to sleep and brayed out silly, off-key songs?"

"We weren't off-key," Rob protested.

"Go find something better to do."

The cousins were already scurrying off in various directions.

"Sorry," Rob said. "I didn't think the eagles would mind. And I just wanted everybody to see how cool they are."

"You can show them off tomorrow, when they're awake," I said. "And see if you can help us find someplace else where they can stay. This isn't really the best spot for them."

"Yeah. Okay." He nodded thoughtfully. "I bet we could find a habitat for them out at Grandfather's zoo. And Caroline's big donor guy might have a blast going out there to see them."

"Excellent idea," I said. "See if you can make it happen."

"Roger." He hurried off.

Maybe, given his curious fascination with the eagles, he'd actually do something about them. If not, I could talk to Grandfather in the morning.

I gave a thumbs-up to Ekaterina. Then I headed for the door and exchanged good nights with Jaime before hopping into my car and heading for Trinity.

Chapter 14

Evidently the upper atmosphere wasn't as frigid as the ground down here where we mere mortals dwelled. No snow yet, but a fine, misty rain was falling, and what didn't freeze into tiny hailstones on the way down was turning into ice on the pavement. I took it slow.

As I drew near my destination I heard a sound in the distance—church bells. Not Trinity's, though, which, apart from being closer, also had a deeper, richer sound. From the direction, I suspected it was the Methodists' bells. Perfectly nice bells, but lighter in tone—like comparing a tenor to a bass-baritone. But why were they ringing now? Were the Methodists sounding the alarm about something? Would the Baptists and Congregationalists follow suit?

And then I realized it was just the college orchestra performing its Christmas concert a few blocks away. Since the Methodist church faced the town square, the orchestra's director usually managed to talk Reverend Trask into ringing the bells to add to the merriment whenever they played a song like "Ring Out, Ye Bells," or "I Heard the Bells on Christmas Day."

I wondered if they'd close with a Christmas carol or, as usual, with one of the music department chair's favorite classical numbers—either the "William Tell Overture" or the "1812 Overture," complete with live cannon booming, courtesy of half a dozen replica Revolutionary-War-era field pieces displayed in the town square. Mayor Randall Shiffley wasn't all that keen on the cannons—as he pointed out, even blank shots could injure someone—but the cannon firing was so popular, both with the tourists and the squad of Revolutionary War reenactors who carried it out, that he hadn't stepped in to veto it.

And no surprise—as I turned into the Trinity parking lot, I heard the opening strains of the "1812 Overture."

To my relief, the parking lot was empty, so my late arrival wouldn't be a source of friction with Austin and I didn't have to feel guilty about leaving Robyn to cope with him alone. Of course, I was only five minutes late, but I'd already noticed that he expected us mere mortals to treat his time with a respect he didn't give to ours. A characteristic he shared with Lexy and Emily, come to think of it.

Chill, I told myself. *Still not your circus, not your monkeys.*

I parked the car and grabbed my big flashlight before heading for the path that led down the side of the building to the door we were supposed to be using. As with the drive over, I took it slow. It was the dark of the moon, or very nearly, and even with the flashlight visibility wasn't great. And the brick sidewalk was tricky enough in daylight, let alone at night under icy conditions.

The graveyard was to my left, although I couldn't really see it—I kept my flashlight aimed at the path. Still, I could sense its presence. Remembering Emily's panic about it made me chuckle to myself. If the Trinity graveyard unnerved her, it was a good thing she'd never attended Caerphilly's annual Halloween festival. I didn't find the graveyard creepy or spooky at all. Maybe I would have if I'd overthought the whole thing when I'd first begun coming here, but not now. It was a quiet, peaceful, beautiful space, redolent of tradition and loving care for the departed parishioners who were buried here. I'd known a few of them in life, and most of the rest felt like old friends by now, thanks to my work on the church history project. If any of their ghosts appeared to me, I'd probably see if they would sit down and have a conversation. Catch up with what the ones I'd actually known had been up to in the afterlife, and interview the rest about the lost details of their biographies. Was Ephraim Burwell drummed out of his family for being a Tory or because he was a known horse thief? Had Hepzibah Belcher actually murdered both of her husbands, or only the one for which they had the seventeen eyewitnesses? Had Ezra Skillern really been the one to fashion George Washington's first set of wooden dentures?

I let myself in the side door and, after a moment's thought, locked it after myself. Austin could knock when he got here. After all, there were vandals targeting Trinity and the other local churches. I planned to stay right here and let the photographer in when he arrived, but what if I got distracted and accidentally gave the vandals entry?

So I paced up and down the hallway, occasionally catching a scrap of the "1812 Overture." But only a scrap during the loud passages—I was on the side of the church that faced away from the town square, and the building was pretty well insulated.

After about ten minutes of pacing I grew impatient. I pulled out my phone and called Austin. His phone rang four times before going to voicemail.

No need to leave a message. He'd know why I was calling.

I continued pacing for another five minutes. It suddenly struck me—what if he was standing outside the front door knocking, in spite of the signs? I might not have heard it if I'd been at the far end of the hall when he'd knocked.

So I peered out the window in the side door. Nothing. I unlocked the door and stepped outside. Still no cars other than mine in the half of the parking lot I could see, and I couldn't think of any reason for him to park at the far end.

"Austin?" I called.

No answer. Should I lock this door and check the front?

I'd try calling him again first. I pulled out my phone and hit redial.

A few seconds later I heard the sound of prolonged farting. It was coming from somewhere nearby.

From the graveyard.

I followed the sound, unlatching the graveyard gate and stepping inside. My call had gone to voicemail, so I hung up and dialed again. The farting sound rang out again. I picked my way through the tombstones toward it.

Austin was lying face up on one of the large slab tombstones—arms outflung, eyes wide open, with a bullet wound in the center of his forehead.

I ended the call and dialed 911.

Chapter 15

"Evening, Meg. What's your emergency?"

Just hearing Debbie Ann's voice made me feel better.

"I need the police at the Trinity graveyard," I said. "I just found Austin Luckett, the wedding photographer. He's been shot."

"Dispatching several nearby deputies," she said. "Do you also need an ambulance?"

I was opening my mouth to say that no, I was fine, when I realized she didn't mean for myself.

"Maybe, just to be sure," I said instead. "He looks pretty dead to me."

"Sending it, and notifying your father as well," she said. "And the chief. Are you in a safe place?"

I wanted to say that of course I was. I was at Trinity Episcopal. I was here every Sunday—well, most Sundays. My sons had been baptized here. Mother was on the vestry. What safer place could you think of?

But at the moment this peaceful place was a murder scene. And the murderer could still be nearby.

I felt a brief surge of anger.

"No one else in sight," I said. "I could go back inside the church, but I left the door open when I came out here to look for Austin, so for all I know the killer could be hiding inside."

"Stay there, then," Debbie Ann said. "Vern's just now pulling into the parking lot."

I heard tires crunching on the gravel. Saw headlights in the parking lot. Heard a car door slamming. A few seconds later, Vern Shiffley, the chief's senior deputy, strode through the graveyard gate. Relief washed over me.

"Vern's here," I said.

"You can hang up then," Debbie Ann said.

"Over there," I said to Vern, gesturing toward where Austin's body lay.

"Damn." He scanned the ground in front of us with his flashlight, then stepped close enough to grab one of Austin's wrists and check for a pulse. "Nothing."

I nodded. I was glad of the limited light. I had a feeling that the neat entry wound in Austin's forehead would be accompanied by a messy exit wound whose details were obscured by the dark. I planned to be elsewhere when Dad and Horace got to that point in their crime scene work.

"Can't have been that long, though," Vern said. "He's still pretty warm. Did you hear the shot?"

"No," I said. "So it probably happened before I got here. I didn't look this way when I arrived—I was too focused on my footing. But even if I was already here when it happened, I might not have heard. I think the orchestra just finished the '1812 Overture.'"

"They did indeed," he said. "With those reenactors firing like crazy. They're definitely getting faster at reloading."

"I was waiting inside, so if I'd heard anything out here I might have assumed it was part of the cannon fire." I wondered if I'd have heard the unearthly screech of the gate if I hadn't gotten Josh to oil it this afternoon. Water under the bridge.

Vern nodded, and began moving his flashlight over the ground around Austin's body. Looking for tracks or other bits of evidence, I assumed. Vern was widely considered the best tracker in the county, so if the killer had left any traces of their passage, he'd be the one to find them.

I realized I was shivering, in spite of my coat.

"I'm going to wait inside," I said.

"Good idea," he said. "Given how the weather's turning, any chance you could get the church coffeemaker going? We could be in for a long, cold night out here."

"Good idea," I said.

I wasn't a coffee drinker myself, but I'd gotten reasonably good at using Trinity's fancy coffee machine. But as I measured out the coffee and water, I found myself wondering if Vern was really thinking of the comfort of the first responders who would soon converge on the graveyard or if he thought I could use something to distract me from the shock of finding Austin's body.

Maybe both.

When the coffee was ready, I filled two mugs—one for Vern and one for whoever else might have arrived—and headed back to the side door. I set the mugs on a small nearby table and peered out through the door's window to see what was happening.

Chief Burke was there, standing just inside the graveyard gate, talking to Vern. As I watched, Dad and Horace arrived, each carrying a bag with his equipment. Although Dad's black doctor's bag looked old-fashioned, it contained everything he needed either to administer emergency care or to fulfill his role as medical examiner. And Horace's CSI kit had grown so large and heavy that he had switched from a large satchel to a pair of the biggest wheeled suitcases he could find.

Just then Vern spotted me and pointed to the door. The chief and I exchanged waves. Vern ambled over to the door, and I handed him one of the coffees.

"More where that came from," I said.

"Good deal." He took a sip. "Chief will be in to see you in a sec."

After he went back out, I pulled out my phone. Robyn had been planning to join Austin and me. Probably a good idea to warn her what she was walking into.

And then I had a moment of panic. What if Robyn had been on time and had encountered the killer? My hand shook, and I almost hit the wrong entry on my contact list. I felt a surge of relief when I heard her voice.

"I know, I know," she said, instead of hello. "I'm running late. I'm just leaving the women's shelter. We had two new arrivals, and I wanted to help them get settled. But I'm not abandoning you to deal with Austin all alone."

"No need to rush," I said. "Someone already dealt with Austin. And just so you know, the police are here."

"The police? Why? Are we talking about more vandalism?"

"No," I said. "But you may have to do another Restoration of Things Profaned anyway. Someone shot him. He's dead. The graveyard's a crime scene."

"Lord have mercy on that poor soul," she said.

The outside door opened and the chief stepped in.

"And Chief Burke just got here," I said. "And he probably wants to interview me."

"I'll be there in five minutes," she said. "Not that there's much I can do, but I want to be there."

With that we hung up.

"Robyn," I said, in answer to the chief's inquiring glance. "She was supposed to meet us here at eleven. I didn't want her blindsided."

"I assume she's still coming?"

I nodded, and gestured to the coffee cup.

"Good." He picked up the cup and took a sip. Followed by a

healthy gulp, accompanied by a pleased expression that I found reassuring—at least I hadn't ruined the coffee. And maybe the parishioner who insisted on donating a supply of gourmet coffee beans was onto something.

"Robyn could have some useful information," he added. "Now let's find a comfortable place to sit and you can tell me why you're down here finding a dead body in the middle of the night."

I led the way to the parish hall, and we sat in two of the worn but comfortable easy chairs. He took out his pen and his pocket notebook and settled into a comfortable position.

"So fill me in."

I did. I explained who Austin Luckett was and related what I knew of his actions during the day, including how the Christmas pageant rehearsal had interrupted his prewedding inspection of the church, which had led to his returning so late. I made sure to mention the conversation I'd overheard while driving him down to the Inn.

"You're thinking this disgruntled client could be a suspect?" he asked.

"I gather from what his assistant said that he's got a lot of disgruntled clients," I said. "If not this one, maybe one of the others. And while I hate to say it, I think you're going to have to put the assistant on your suspect list. Maddie Brown. According to her, he was a horrible boss. Downright abusive." I relayed what she'd said about Austin ruining her reputation with other wedding-industry professionals so she'd be forced to go back to working for him.

"And I'm surprised that she didn't come here to the church with him," I said. "I thought that was the plan, and his van isn't in the parking lot so I'm not sure how he got down here without her."

"We should definitely locate Ms. Brown," the chief said. "And the van. Can you give me a description?"

"It was gray," I said. "I'm afraid I don't know the make and model. Unless— Hang on."

I flipped back through the photos on my phone until I got to the ones I'd taken of the Bestitched mobile dressmaking shop. To my great delight, one of them showed not only Austin's van but also its license plate. I texted it to the chief, and after a few minutes of using our fingers and thumbs to enlarge the picture and peering intently at it, we deciphered the license plate number, and the chief notified Debbie Ann to put out a BOLO on it.

"So," he said. "We have a murder victim with a lot of enemies. Does anyone involved with either of the weddings have any beef with him?"

"In a sane world, I'd say no—why would they?" I replied. "He only got here yesterday, and I don't think most of them had ever met him before. But neither of the brides is operating anywhere near sanity right now. And according to the assistant, Austin was a bit of a lech. Who knows who he might have offended?"

"I do hope we're not going to have to add the whole of both wedding parties to the suspect list," he said.

"Probably not," I said. "Even if he'd managed to offend them en masse, a lot of them should be even now attending various social events that could give them alibis." I explained about the two hen parties, the dinner at the Inn, the crowd Michael had taken to the basketball games, and even Rose Noire's Winter Solstice planning party.

"You're right." He looked pleased. "Those gatherings should account for quite a few of the people here for the weddings. Of course, it will take a lot of careful questioning to make sure they were all where they should have been at the time of the murder. But we should be able to eliminate quite a few of them."

"And don't forget all of Kevin's security cameras," I pointed out. "That should help a good deal."

"True." He pulled out his phone. "And knowing his hours, I assume this is an acceptable time to call him."

"Yes," I said. "He should be awake by now."

The chief chuckled, as if he thought I was kidding. I wasn't. Kevin often kept what I called "vampire hours." Rose Noire sometimes fixed him a bacon-and-eggs breakfast at midnight before turning in herself.

Horace strolled into the parish hall while the chief was enlisting Kevin's assistance. He fixed himself a cup of coffee while he was waiting.

"Good," the chief said when he hung up. "Let everyone know there's coffee here. And it's getting nastier outside. Remind everyone to take breaks inside where it's warm when they need to. No need to court frostbite."

"Will do," Horace said. "Actually I came in to ask Meg something."

Chapter 16

"Ask away," I said, ignoring the sudden irrational surge of tension I felt about answering questions right now.

"Was your photographer guy here to do some kind of photo session?" Horace asked.

"No," I said. "He was going to scope out the church some more. Figure out the lighting and camera angles and such."

"Ah," he said. "If he wasn't planning on taking pictures, maybe that's why he didn't have a data card in his camera."

"No data card in his camera?" I echoed. "That sounds suspicious. He wasn't here for a photo session, but he'd probably have taken test shots while he was planning. Or whenever he saw something that struck his fancy; the man was always taking pictures."

"You're thinking the killer may have taken it?" the chief asked Horace.

"That was my first thought," Horace said. "On top of the missing data card, the door to the compartment where you put it wasn't secured. It was kind of flapping loose. Didn't seem like the way a professional would treat his camera."

"When you find his assistant, you should check with her," I said. "Maybe he wasn't very good at boring things like changing his data cards. I saw what happened this afternoon when the battery ran down on his camera. He shoved it in her face and barked 'new battery!' And then stood there fuming while she took out the old battery, put in the new, and handed him back his camera."

"Are you suggesting that she was here, and he pulled his typical rude maneuver, and instead of just changing the data card she lost it, pulled out her gun, and plugged him?" Horace asked. I could tell from his deadpan face that he was kidding.

"Well, it's a thought," I said. "But I was only suggesting that maybe if she wasn't here, and he had to change his own data card, he might not know how to close the camera door properly and the data card just fell out someplace."

"Always possible." Horace sighed at the thought.

"Searching for something as tiny as a data card will have to wait until it's light," the chief said. "Although I think it's more likely that the killer took it."

"Yeah," I said. "If I'd just bumped off someone who was holding a camera, I think I'd take precautions to avoid leaving any telltale photos behind."

And perhaps, like me, the chief was remembering a local case in which finding a filmmaker's missing footage had helped to solve a crime.

"A little odd, though," the chief said. "That they took the time to remove the data card, instead of just grabbing the camera."

"The camera was hanging on a strap around his neck," Horace said. "No way to get it off without pulling it over his head, and if they did that they'd risk getting blood all over them. But from where it was lying on his chest, they could easily pick it up and get at the card."

"Ah," the chief said. "Then taking the card was the smart move."

Horace nodded.

Just then the chief's phone rang.

"It's Aida," he said as he glanced at it before answering. "What's up?"

He frowned slightly as he listened.

"Keep her there," he said. "I want to talk to her. I'll be there in about fifteen minutes."

He hung up.

"Aida's out at your house," he said to me. "Apparently some ten minutes ago, Ms. Brown, the assistant, called nine-one-one to report that someone had slashed the tires on Mr. Luckett's van. I'm going out to interview her. Perhaps you could meet me there, and help me locate some of the other people I'll be needing to talk to. At least the ones who haven't already gone to bed."

"Can do," I said. "And you can see what Kevin's been able to find out from all his cameras."

"I'll see you there, then." He turned back to Horace. "Keep me posted on what you and Dr. Langslow are finding."

"Roger." Horace nodded. "The Rev is here."

Robyn was bustling into the parish hall, pulling off her coat as she came.

"Meg!" she exclaimed. "Are you okay?"

"I'm fine," I said. "And the chief's letting me go home now."

"Provided you can stay here for a bit," the chief said, turning to Robyn. "In case my officers have any questions that you can answer. And to lock up when they're finished."

"Of course," she said.

"There's coffee." I gestured toward it.

"And I think I'll turn the thermostat up a bit," she said. "It's chilly in here, and your officers might need to warm up occasionally."

"Thanks," the chief said.

I followed him out the side door. He paused by the iron gate to the graveyard. I could see Vern standing just inside the gate, and beyond him, Dad was looking down—I assumed at Austin.

"Meg and I are going out to her house to find some interview subjects," the chief said.

"Good." Dad turned and came over to the gate. "Meg, are you okay?"

"I'm fine," I said. "Although I'm looking forward to putting some distance between me and your crime scene."

"Any more thoughts on the time of death?" the chief asked.

"No." Dad shook his head. "Death would have been pretty close to when Meg called it in. No more than an hour earlier. Probably not that much."

"So either I just missed running into the killer leaving the parking lot, or it happened while I was inside the church, waiting for Austin," I said.

Dad winced slightly and nodded. In addition to being the local medical examiner, Dad was an avid reader of mysteries. I suspected the fascination he always felt when called on to help investigate a real-life murder was dimmed just a bit this time by realizing how close I might have come to being the killer's second victim.

"Call me if you find anything interesting," the chief said.

And we strolled out to the parking lot, both glancing up at the sky as we went, but there were no signs of snow. The chief seemed lost in thought, although I noticed that he didn't get into his car until he saw that I was safely in mine.

The radio came on when I started the car, and I hurried to hit the off button. I'd been listening to Christmas carols on my way here. Normally I'd have left it on—I enjoyed the soft, mostly instrumental selections the college radio station played through the late-night hours. But right now I wasn't in the mood. I was already upset that a killer had intruded into our holiday merriment. Well, to the extent the beastly brides left any room for merriment. I wanted a little space to clear my head of the sight of Austin lying in the graveyard before I tried to regain my Christmas spirit.

At least the sleet had stopped for the moment, and hadn't yet given way to snow. I'd been hoping for the snow to start soon, so we'd have plenty of time to dig out before the weddings. I decided now I should start hoping it held off until Horace had finished working the crime scene.

When I pulled up in front of the house, Maddie Brown was standing beside the gray van, huddled in her inadequate coat—though at least she'd added a hat and gloves from our stash. She looked anxious and agitated. Aida was crouched down by the van's right rear fender, examining the slashed tire. All of this was easy to see in the harsh glow of our outdoor lights, and the huge, flowered bulk of the Bestitched RV made an incongruous backdrop. The chief parked in the empty spot beside the van. I drove to my usual parking spot by the barn and hurried back, hoping to eavesdrop on at least some of his conversation with Maddie.

Evidently Aida hadn't yet spilled the beans to her about Austin's death. And it looked as if the chief was letting her talk for a bit before he broke the news—either that, or he hadn't yet managed to get a word in edgewise.

"—and Austin will be livid when he sees this!" Maddie was saying. "He'll blame me—I know he will, and how could I possibly be out here guarding his van when he also expects me to take photographs of two hen parties going on in two different places, and—"

"So that's what you were doing when this occurred?" the chief asked, gesturing to one of the ruined tires.

"I have no idea," she said. "Since I don't know when it occurred. I was taking pictures of the parties at first, but the women over there kept trying to make me drink with them, and the ones over here kept telling me to get out and one of them almost threw a drink at me, and by nine or ten o'clock they were all passed out anyway, so I went upstairs and had a good crying fit, and then I realized it was time to meet Austin at the church and I came down and found this."

She waved her hands at the tires again. Behind her, I spotted motion in one of the RV's windows. The curtain was pulled back, and a face was pressed against the glass. Make that two faces. Then I focused back on what Maddie was saying.

"Wait—meet him at the church?" I echoed. "I thought you were going to take him there."

"That was the original plan," she said. "But then he decided he needed a break from wedding stuff, and he had me drop him off near the town square so he could take some pictures there, and he said if I didn't hear from him before eleven, he'd walk over to the church and I should meet him there." She looked at me as if seeing me for the first time. "He was meeting with you, wasn't he? Was he furious that I didn't show?"

"What time did you drop him off in town?" the chief asked.

"I don't know. Wait—let me check." She pulled out her phone. "He texted me to hurry up already because he was waiting by the van. That was at four minutes past six. We'd have taken off a few minutes after that."

"And you got back when?" I could tell the chief was working to keep his voice calm and reassuring.

"I guess it was close to seven," she said. "Because there was all that tourist traffic in the center of town, and it would have been much faster for both of us if I'd just dropped him off ten or twelve blocks from the town square, but he wouldn't hear of it, and it was even slower getting back. And he was in a foul mood because of all the traffic—I bet he's even worse now. He'll be furious. He'll insist on taking this out of my paycheck."

"No," the chief said. "I don't think that's going to happen. Unfortunately, Mr. Luckett was killed earlier tonight."

Her mouth fell open, and it must have been half a minute before she spoke.

"Killed?" she said. "Are you sure? What happened? No, don't tell me—I bet he did it again, backed up to get a longer shot and stepped out into traffic. It's happened more than once, and he always yells at me for not warning him."

"No," the chief said. "Someone shot him."

Chapter 17

You always heard about people turning white with shock when they heard bad news, but I'd never actually seen it happen so dramatically. Maddie also swayed a little on her feet, and Aida grabbed her arm to steady her.

"Oh, my God," Maddie murmured. "He actually did it."

"Who?" the chief demanded. "And did what?"

"There's this angry customer," she said. "Well, Austin leaves behind a lot of angry customers, but there's this one who has been calling and calling for days now. Austin was trying to hold him over a barrel and charge several thousand dollars to give him all of the pictures from his wedding instead of just the best fifty. And the guy was making the wildest kind of threats and he knew where we were. I have no idea how, but he did, and he was threatening to come here and force Austin to give him the pictures. He was calling me so often I finally blocked him, but Austin seemed to actually enjoy taunting the poor man."

"Can you provide me with his contact details?" the chief asked.

"His name's Random Wilson," Maddie said.

"Random?" The chief looked up from his notebook. "Not Randall?"

"No, Random." Maddie rolled her eyes. "Random Q. Wilson. And don't make the mistake of calling him Randall or Randy. The guy's got anger-management issues. I've got his number in my phone. Austin would have all the rest in his files."

"The name and phone number will do for now," the chief said. "And eventually we'll need to look at all of Mr. Luckett's customer files. Do you have access to those here, or will we need to send someone down to Richmond for that?"

"He wasn't big on electronic stuff." Maddie had started crying softly. "But it will all be there in his office. I keep his files in good shape." She pulled out her phone and gave the chief the information. While he was writing it down, Aida fished into one of her pockets and handed Maddie a small pack of tissues.

"Thanks," Maddie said. "I don't know why I'm crying. I mean, I didn't actually like Austin. I actually think I hated him sometimes. He was a terrible boss. A terrible human being. But I didn't want him killed. And how am I ever going to get another job?"

At this thought, her soft crying turned into a deluge. I dug into my tote and handed over my spare pack of tissues, since she had already almost gone through the ones Aida had given her.

The chief had pulled out his phone and was talking with someone. Presumably Debbie Ann, the dispatcher. I caught the word "BOLO."

"No, not Randall. Random," he said. "Yes. Your guess is as good as mine."

Then he ended the call and turned back to Maddie.

"Let's go inside." His voice was warm and reassuring. "We don't have to stand out here in the cold. I need to know a lot more about Mr. Luckett if I'm going to figure out who killed him, and you're probably my best source of information."

He stepped up, took a gentle hold on her arm, and began to steer her toward the front walk.

"Aida, can you stay out here?" he asked over his shoulder. "I'd like you to keep an eye on the van until I can get Horace out here to process it. And Meg, is it okay if—"

"The dining room is at your disposal," I said.

"I'm not sure how much useful information I can give you," Maddie was saying. "And I know I'm a suspect. I hate him. Hated him. That's no big secret. Everybody knows how awfully he's treated me . . ."

She went on in much the same vein all the way into the house, and then down the hall. I was relieved when the dining-room door closed behind her and the chief. He was probably enjoying her nonstop, stream-of-consciousness monologue more than I was. Unless she was a great deal more cunning than I gave her credit for, she'd pour out any useful information she happened to possess without much effort on his part.

Of course, he would probably have to sort through an ocean of complaints and self-recrimination to find the useful bits of data. But he was good at that.

The living room was empty, and the fire had gone out. I'd have built it up again for the dogs, resident and visiting, who often spent the evening sacked out in front of it, but none of them were there. They were probably still out with Rose Noire. I could hear music coming from the direction of the library. If I could hear it here, it must be deafening in the soundproofed library. Maybe I'd drop by a little later and ask them to dial it back. I didn't feel up to tackling them right now.

I went out to the kitchen and started our coffee machine.

"Meg? Is something wrong? Why are Aida and the chief here?"

I turned to see Rose Noire coming in through the back door. Evidently her pagan gathering was still going on. Or maybe she'd decided to sleep in her shed to put some distance between her and the partiers. She looked anxious. Should I break the news about Austin, as gently as possible? Probably. But a sudden wave of tiredness washed over me and I realized I was in a rip-the-bandage mood.

"Someone shot Austin," I said. "I found the body."

"Oh, no! Are you all right?"

"I'll be fine," I said. "As long as I get some sleep before too very long. Tomorrow's going to be busy."

She bustled over and took over the work of filling and starting the coffee machine. I sat down at the kitchen table and closed my eyes.

"Don't make too much," I said. "The chief's in the dining room, interviewing Maddie and anyone else who's awake, but I'm not sure how much longer he'll be staying. By the way, are the dogs with you?"

"Yes, they're out with us in the herb shed," she said. "Safer that way. One of the bridesmaids was teasing them—holding up bits of cheese and then eating them herself."

"Lucky for her she didn't try it with Spike," I said.

"She did, but Tinkerbell stepped between them."

I made a mental note to give Tink an extra treat the next time I saw her. Spike's teeth would be harmless against the thick winter coat of an Irish wolfhound, but he could have done some serious damage to the errant bridesmaid's hand. Hard to say whether Tink was protecting the bridesmaid, or whether she knew that Spike's life could be in jeopardy if the bridesmaid tried to brand him as a vicious dog.

"The chief's probably going to want to talk to you and all your guests." I leaned back in my chair and closed my eyes as I said it.

"Except for quick trips in here to use the bathroom, all of us were together all evening," she said. "So if you were worried about whether I'm going to be a suspect, relax."

"I don't think any of you are prime suspects or even useful witnesses for the murder," I said. "But someone slashed the tires on Austin's van. We have no idea if that had anything to do with the murder."

"And we could have done that." She sounded mellow about the prospect. Almost pleased.

"You sound like Dad," I said. "Nothing makes him happier than being a murder suspect, even briefly. Actually, I was thinking that you could have seen or heard something that would give the chief a clue about who did it. And for that matter, when it happened."

"I'll let him know who was here," she said.

I felt her set down something on the table in front of me, and I opened my eyes to find a cup of hot chocolate.

"Thanks," I said. "Why don't you go get some sleep? That's what I'm doing as soon as I unwind. Tomorrow could be a busy day."

"Yes." She fetched her coat from the mudroom and began putting it on. "Where did it happen? Here?"

"No," I said. "Down at Trinity. In the graveyard."

"Oh no! Poor Robyn! Does she know yet?"

"She's there holding down the fort while Horace does his crime-scene thing."

"She must be distraught," Rose Noire said. "And I suppose we'll have to have another restoration ceremony soon." She actually sounded pleased at the idea. The Restoration of Things Profaned had definitely been a big hit with her. Which could be a good thing. Robyn might have to perform it on a regular basis if the chief couldn't find a way to stop the kids who had been vandalizing the local churches.

"Probably," I said. "I'll keep you posted."

She nodded and blew out of the door in a whirl of pink and

lavender. I sipped the hot chocolate and tried to will myself to feel sleepy. No dice so far. Tired, absolutely. Sleepy, not so much.

I decided to make myself useful. I texted my sister-in-law, Delaney.

"You up?"

Then I grabbed my keys, in case the hens had locked themselves in, and headed for the library. Although as soon as I turned in to the long hallway that led to it, I knew the key wouldn't be needed. The library was nicely soundproofed. If they'd had the door closed, I wouldn't be hearing their music blaring quite so loudly.

When I was halfway down the hall to the partly open library door, I got a text back from Delaney.

"Yup. What's up?"

"Can you check your basement? See if all the partiers are there, and what they're up to?"

"Can do."

I arrived at the library door and peered in. The glass bookshelf doors had been a good idea. And first thing in the morning, I'd be calling the Dirty Dogs, the service Mother always brought in to deal with monumental cleaning jobs.

The room's trash can and recycling bin were filled to overflowing and the rest of the room was littered with popcorn, potato chip crumbs, the odd paper plate or plastic glass, and the scantily clad unconscious bodies of the attending hens. The music level was deafening. I looked around, found the small Bluetooth speakers that were pumping it out, and turned them off.

Blissful silence. Well, except for the odd bit of snoring.

I felt a brief surge of anger and closed my eyes until it passed. And I wasn't sure if I was angry at them, or at myself, for not putting my foot down and making them take their party elsewhere.

I checked to see if the sudden quiet had roused any of the young women. Not a creature was stirring. Not even Lexy, who was sacked out face down on one of the sofas, with a disposable plastic martini glass dangling from her limp right hand, dripping its last few drops into the damp rug beneath it.

I counted heads. Six bridesmaids, one maid of honor, one bride. All present and accounted for.

Although there was no telling if that had been true when Austin's murder was taking place. This didn't look like the kind of party whose attendees were in any shape to keep track of one another's comings and goings.

I did a quick pass through the room, picking up some of the worst of the debris—anything that was obviously going to create a bigger mess by morning. I made a mental note to have a word with a few of the bridesmaids when they returned to the land of the living. Mother was vastly proud of the elegant, book-themed Christmas decorations she'd installed in the library, and would not react well when she found out that the hens had dismantled some of them to make headdresses and sashes for themselves. Could I possibly repair them myself, so she'd never know? I wasn't optimistic. Just the thought made me feel tired. But then I was already tired. Maybe I'd feel differently come morning.

Then I grabbed the speakers—to make sure any hens who regained consciousness would have a hard time restarting the noise—and left the library, closing the door gently behind me. Was it shallow of me, feeling upset over the completely predictable chaos in the library, when another human being had been brutally murdered?

I'd sort that out in the morning.

Chapter 18

When I got back to the kitchen, I called Delaney.

"All my hens are down for the count," she said. "And half of them are snoring like buzz saws. Why? Are yours up to something?"

"All out like lights at the moment," I said. "But I have no idea what they might have gotten up to earlier. Someone shot and killed Austin. The wedding photographer," I added, since I wasn't sure Delaney knew the name.

"Oh, no," she said. "That's horrible. " She paused for a moment before asking, "Do we suspect the bridesmaids? Or the brides?"

"No idea," I said. "Given the guy's personality, I suspect anyone who ever met him. He was easy to dislike. The chief will be checking everyone's alibis."

"Ooh, does this mean I'm a suspect, too?"

"First Rose Noire and then you," I said. "Dad's strange fondness for being considered a suspect seems to be contagious. I can't think of any reason why you'd want to kill him, but that's only because you've never met him. Still, I'd be delighted to know that at eleven this evening you were someplace very far away from Trinity, with a passel of deacons and choirboys to alibi you."

"Bother," she said. "I wasn't all that far from Trinity, and you can forget the deacons and choirboys. But at eleven I was still at the second basketball game, watching the Caerphilly Chargers go down to another embarrassing defeat. And so were Rob and your dad and a whole bunch of other highly suspicious characters. They all went out to the zoo for Sleep with the Wombats, but I decided I'd rather come home, spend some time with Brynnie, sleep in my own bed, and make sure the hens didn't burn the house down."

"Wise move," I said. "I hope your game room doesn't look anything like our library. I'm going to call the Dirty Dogs in the morning. Or as soon as the chief says it's okay—he might need to have Horace work both party sites if any of the hens are suspects. You want me to have them put you on their schedule while they're in the neighborhood?"

"Please," she said. "Or I might be tempted to add to the body count."

"You and me both," I said. "Sleep well."

I went back to the kitchen and set out mugs, sugar, and creamer, in case the chief's investigation brought any more visitors who might be in need of caffeine. And then I added some small plates and a tin of Rose Noire's assorted holiday cookies while I was thinking of it.

And as if making preparations for visitors sent some magic signal to the universe, the doorbell rang.

It was Vern Shiffley.

"Got our victim's phone." He held up a brown paper evidence bag. "Chief wants Kevin to get started on it."

"This way." I'd have offered to give the phone to Kevin, but I knew technically that would break the chain of custody, so I just led the way to the kitchen and invited him to help himself to coffee and cookies while I summoned Kevin from his subterranean lair. Which I actually did the old-fashioned way, by opening the basement door, sticking my head in, and shouting.

"Hey, Kevin," I called. "Vern's here with evidence."

And then I realized it had been a while since dinner. And I'd passed up the Inn's divine crème brûlée in favor of an expedition that had ended up with me encountering a dead body—and maybe coming all too close to becoming one myself.

Was this normal hunger? Or do people burn calories faster when they're stressed? I'd look it up later. I'd finished the hot chocolate and was too tired to make more, but I poured myself a glass of milk and began selecting some of my favorite Christmas cookies from the tin.

Kevin appeared, looking disheveled and a wee bit cranky.

"Murder victim's cell phone," Vern said, holding up the bag like a trophy before handing it over.

"Cool beans," Kevin said. "Anything in particular the chief wants me to prioritize?"

"Not that he mentioned," Vern said. "Where he was, who he was communicating with—the usual."

Kevin nodded. But instead of scampering down into the basement with the phone, he poured himself a glass of milk, sat down, and pulled the cookie tin closer. He studied its contents with a persnickety air.

"What's wrong with you?" I asked.

"The chief's counting on me to give him some useful evidence from my security system." He reached in and selected a Toll House marble square, one of his favorites. "And everything's getting in the way."

"Like what?" I asked.

"Well, for starters, that honking big RV the dressmakers came in," he said. "It was quite literally in the way. They parked it in the space closest to the house."

"It kind of needs to be there so we can run a power cord out to it," I pointed out.

"Yeah," he said. "But I think the chief was kind of hoping the camera on that side would show who slashed the tires on that guy's van. And it would have, if the darned RV hadn't been there, completely blocking any possible view we might have had of the van."

"Oh, dear," I said. "I'm sorry. If I'd thought of it, we could have had them park by the barn and run the power cord to that."

"Not your fault," he said. "How were you supposed to know we were having a murder tonight?"

"Only a vandalism incident here at the house," I pointed out. "I can have them relocate it tomorrow."

"Which will be great if we have another murder tomorrow," Kevin said. "Sorry—another vandalism incident."

"Water under the bridge." Vern took a bite out of a chocolate bourbon ball and smiled with pleasure. "Whoever slashed the tires, we'll get them sooner or later."

"It would be sooner if the RV hadn't been blocking that camera," Kevin said, as he selected another cookie—this time a pecan sandie. "And it's going to hinder my ability to figure out what all these bridesmaids have been up to. With that camera out, they could sneak out of the library, waltz through the front door, and drive off without me seeing them—as long as their cars are parked on that side of the house. And I think most of them are, because it's the side closest to town."

I nodded, and fished in the tin. I tried not to resent the fact that Vern had just grabbed the last Beacon Hill cookie. I settled for a chocolate chip bar with black walnuts.

"Meg, the chief suggested maybe you could help me round up people he needs to talk to," Vern said. "Assuming any of them are awake."

"You're going to want to talk to some of the bridesmaids in Rob and Delaney's basement," Kevin said. "They had some kind of drama over there around nine or ten o'clock. Couple of them stormed over here claiming the photographer guy was peeping through the windows and taking pictures of them."

"Isn't that kind of what he's here for?" Vern asked. "To take pictures of them?"

"Yeah, but only when they're fully dressed and with makeup on." Kevin snickered. "That early in the festivities, at least a couple of them were still sober enough to realize it wasn't such a great idea, having their pictures taken when they were half dressed and more than half wasted."

"But Austin wasn't even here at nine or ten, as far as I know," I said. "According to Maddie, he got her to drop him off downtown at around six o'clock so he could take pictures down there. And as far as we know, he stayed there and walked to Trinity for his eleven o'clock meeting with me."

"So that was true?" Kevin asked. "Maddie told them that, but I just figured she was trying to calm them down. And they didn't believe her anyway, and went running through the house shrieking like hyenas, and then the ones who were partying over here got all territorial and tried to chase them off, and the two brides had a screaming match over something until their teams dragged them away."

"Good grief," I said. "Why do those two hate each other so much?"

"Well, I can tell you one reason Lexy hates Emily," Kevin said. "You know Jenna?"

"I know one of the brides has a Jenna in her posse," I said. "But don't ask me to pick her out of a lineup."

"She's on Team Emily," Kevin said. "And that really ticked off Lexy. Evidently what's-his-name, Lexy's groom—"

"Blaine," I supplied.

"Blaine and Jenna used to be an item. So Lexy considers the

fact that Emily made Jenna a bridesmaid like the next best thing to a declaration of war."

"This is sounding a lot like that soap opera my mom and my aunts all watch," Vern said. "If one of them goes away for a few days, they all get together for lunch so the others can bring her up to speed. First time I heard them it was all, like, 'Laura did this, and Jordan did that, and Alexis and Sasha are on the outs again,' and I was going crazy trying to figure out which branch of the family was having that much drama."

"Yeah," I said. "It does sound rather like a soap opera."

"And I'm starting to see why your mother is looking so stressed out," he added. "Chief's probably not going to want to interview the bridesmaids until they're sober. Nothing they say while they're three sheets to the wind would be admissible in court."

"Not to mention that interviewing them will be easier when they're conscious," I said. "Delaney and I checked on them a few minutes ago. All present and accounted for, but all completely blotto."

Vern frowned and seemed to be considering something. I waited patiently, hoping to learn more about how the investigation was going.

Chapter 19

"These parties could make it tough for us," Vern said finally. "If one of these young ladies had murder on her mind, it would be pretty darned easy for her to pretend to be intoxicated and then sneak out once the rest of them had all passed out. And all her buddies would swear on a stack of bibles that she was the first one down for the count."

I nodded.

"And it sounds like there's a whole lot of bad blood between the two brides and their friends," he went on. "Hatfield-and-McCoy-type nonsense. You think it's possible one of them might try to point the finger at someone on the other side of the feud, just to cause trouble?"

"Possible, yeah," I said. "I'm not sure any of them are savvy enough to do a good job of framing anyone on the other side, but they could try, and it would make the investigation that much harder."

"Maybe you could help head them off at the pass," he said. "If you could mention, casual-like, that giving a false report to law enforcement is a class one misdemeanor, and they could get up to a year in jail, or a fine of up to twenty-five hundred dollars, or both."

"Casual-like?" I had to chuckle at that. "Casual might be beyond my capabilities, but I will absolutely make a point of mentioning it a few times tomorrow."

"More like later today," Kevin said.

"And it might also help if I suggested that the sky's the limit when it comes to getting sued for defamation," I added.

"Perfect," Vern said. "Chief's already annoyed at how long he's having to wait to interview them. No sense aggravating him even more. Then again, maybe we'll pick up this Random guy in the meantime. My money's on him."

"Nah," Kevin said, as he selected a couple of Norwegian krumkaker from the tin. "It was Maddie, the long-suffering assistant. And from what I've heard about the way her boss treated her, she'll get off on justifiable homicide."

"Maybe we could round up the grooms for the chief to talk to?" Vern was looking at me. "And—what do you call them? The groomsmen? Unless they're at the parties, too."

"The groomsmen don't start arriving till tomorrow," I said. "And grooms don't get invited to hen parties. They should be out at the zoo, having a sleepover at the Small Mammal House. I could ask Michael to bring them back here to be interviewed."

"Nah, he's having fun with his boys," Vern said. "It will keep till morning."

"I should get started on the phone," Kevin said. "And after that, I'll start reviewing security footage from all my cameras here and next door."

"Want me to help with that?" Vern said. "I'm going to do a quick run through my patrol route before I go off duty, but I could come back here and be a spare pair of eyes on the video."

"That would be great," Kevin said, "if you're coming back anyway. I'll bring up a couple of laptops so you can keep an eye on things up here."

He disappeared into the basement again.

"Not that I'm nagging," I said to Vern, "but shouldn't you be spending your off-duty hours getting some sleep?"

"Wouldn't be able to sleep if I tried right now," he said. "Too keyed up. I figure one last trip through my route will help. I've been cruising by all the churches in town as often as possible, hoping to catch those vandals in the act. The little twerps hit First Presbyterian night before last, you know."

"No, I didn't know," I said.

"Tactical mistake, if you ask me," he said. "Aunt Jane dropped by for a Finance Committee meeting before we got it cleaned up, and it ticked her off something fierce. If they appear in her court, she'll throw the book at them. Anyway, I figure a patrol followed by some boring surveillance video might help stave off insomnia. And maybe I can find a corner to sack out in here, so I'll be available whenever the chief wants to get started again in the morning."

"We can find you a spare bedroom," I said.

"If it's no trouble," he said. "And is it okay if I bring the pup out here to hang with your pack? I figure I'll be putting in some long hours until we solve this, and I don't want him spending too much time by himself."

"We're always glad to have him." It was true—Vern's redbone coonhound was friendly and well-behaved, which was more than I could say for some of our resident dogs. "And you."

"Can Horace let himself in when he gets here?" he asked.

"Yes," I said. "He's got a spare front-door key."

"Good. I gather our murder victim was staying here, and we need for Horace to process his room. Can you tell me which one it is?"

"Second floor, last door on the left." I rummaged in my purse and handed him the master key. "If he locked up, this should open it. And the one next to it's empty at the moment, so feel free to use it if you like."

"Thanks. If I take off on patrol before Horace arrives, I'll leave it where he can get it. Like here." He slipped the key under the cookie plate. Then he picked out a gingerbread giraffe and began nibbling its tiny head.

"Just call if you need anything," I said.

"Will do," he said. Although I knew he wouldn't unless it was an emergency.

As I was trudging upstairs my phone dinged to let me know I had a text.

"Are you okay, dear?" It was from Mother.

I paused halfway up the stairs. Mother would normally have been in bed by now. Always possible she'd done enough napping while trying to shake the migraine that she was now having trouble falling asleep. But why was she asking me if I was okay at nearly one in the morning? Had she heard about the murder?

"Fine," I typed. "Going to bed in a minute."

"Is Chief Burke there?"

Evidently she knew.

"Yes," I said. "And Vern. We're fine here."

A thought occurred to me. The grooms were with Michael, but there were other relatives staying at Mother and Dad's. Lexy's parents, Emily's mother, and a few assorted aunts.

"Did everyone who's staying with you get home safe and sound?" I asked.

"Yes," she texted back. "Except for your father. But I've heard from him. He's still working, so he's fine."

Yes, Dad was probably the only person who wasn't mutinous about losing sleep. He was an avid reader of crime fiction, so nothing made him happier than the chance to get involved in a real-life investigation.

"That's good," I said. "Night."

"Sleep well," she replied. "Lots to do in the morning."

I decided to leave that unanswered. Morning would be soon enough to worry about what needed doing. And she didn't even know yet about the mess in the library. I went up to the bedroom, changed into my warmest pajamas, and crawled into the bed. Which seemed larger than usual and very, very empty. I turned on my side of the electric mattress warmer and pulled out my phone to text Michael.

"You awake?" I typed.

I plugged my phone into the charger cable, but kept it beside my pillow instead of parking it on the nightstand as usual.

A minute or so later, Michael texted back.

"Just barely. Anything wrong?"

I hesitated for a moment between reassuring him and sharing. I decided he'd want to know.

"Tomorrow should be interesting. Someone bumped off Austin." And then, realizing that Michael might not recognize the name, I added, "The wedding photographer."

"Yikes," he texted back. "You okay?"

"I'm fine." And I realized it was true. He was safe. And the boys. And Mother and Dad and all the rest of my nearest and dearest. And Vern and the chief were here, guarding the house and getting started on investigating the murder. Maybe by the time I woke up, the culprit would be locked up in jail.

Should I feel guilty about feeling fine when another human being had just been murdered? Maybe, but I'd exorcise the guilt tomorrow by doing everything possible to help the chief. While staying out of his way. And helping Mother with what would no doubt be the very difficult task of keeping the wedding preparations on course for the next—was it only two more days? Yes—

today was Wednesday. Had been Wednesday—it was Thursday now. I refrained from looking at the clock to see how many hours of the new day had already gone by. I should get some sleep, since Thursday would be another busy day of preparations. Friday would see the rehearsals and rehearsal dinners, plus the arrival of dozens more guests, and I'd be astonished if the brides didn't find—or create—at least a dozen more crises that would need solving. Saturday would be insane, but after that we'd have a few days of relative peace before Christmas.

"Anything I can do?" Michael had texted.

"Keep the boys safe and happy," I replied. "And bring the grooms around tomorrow so the chief can interview them."

"Will do. Sleep well."

"You, too."

And with that I slid my phone onto the nightstand, snuggled a little deeper into the covers that had grown so comfortingly warm, and surrendered to sleep.

THURSDAY, DECEMBER 18

Chapter 20

I awoke to the enticing smell of bacon. And fresh bread. And something involving cinnamon. Rose Noire was on the case.

I checked my phone to see if anyone had tried to reach me. Miracle of miracles, no one had. Of course, it was only seven thirty. Most of my nearest and dearest knew better than to expect coherence from me before nine, and with luck all the brides and bridesmaids who didn't know would still be passed out. I probably hadn't had enough sleep, but enough that I could function, and I didn't fancy my chances of getting back to sleep. Maybe I'd manage a nap later.

And a glance out the window showed that the snow hadn't started yet. That was good for the chief's investigation—and probably also good for Mother's sanity. I suspected my aunts Betty and Letty would go into full panic mode at the first flake, no matter how much we'd done to reassure them that there were enough snowplows and snowmobiles in Caerphilly to make sure everyone got to the church on time.

When I was dressed and felt ready to tackle the day, I texted Michael.

"How did Sleep with the Wombats go?"

A minute or so later, my phone rang.

"You're up early," he said.

"Said the pot to the kettle," I replied. "My body wanted more sleep, but my brain wants to find out how the chief's investigation is going. I decided to go along with the brain."

"I figured as much," he said. "Sleep with the Wombats was enjoyable, although I don't think anyone got an optimal amount of sleep. I'm planning a nap later. The boys are going to stay here with your grandfather for the rest of the morning. He's got some educational projects on tap."

"Not another look at the mating habits of the naked mole rats, I hope," I said.

"Oh, no." Michael was chuckling. "He learned his lesson on that. I think he's going to have them working on dissecting owl pellets. Right now we're down in the employee café having breakfast. After that I'm going to bring Blaine over to talk to the chief, just so we can get it on the record that he's in the clear and the chief can take him off the suspect list."

"And Harry," I reminded him. "The other groom," I added, in case he was having as hard a time as I was remembering their names.

"No idea where Harry is," he said.

Uh-oh.

"I thought he went to the games with you," I said. "And slept with the wombats."

"He came with us to the gym," Michael said. "But maybe ten minutes before tip-off for the first game he said he was getting a headache. I offered to run him back to your parents' house, but he said no, he just needed to get some fresh air. Said he'd walk around for a while, come back if his head got better, or catch a taxi home if it didn't."

"Did you explain about how few taxis we have in Caerphilly?"

"I did." Michael laughed. "Not sure he believed me, so I made sure he had my number in his phone so he could call if he needed a ride. He never called, never reappeared."

"Did you believe him about the headache?" I asked.

A short pause.

"Actually, yes," he said finally. "He looked like death warmed over. Of course, he's been kind of . . . morose ever since he got here."

"You think maybe he's having second thoughts about getting married?"

"Could be. Or maybe just getting the jitters about how the whole thing has turned into such a big production. I can think of more than one of my guy friends who reacted that way—in love with the fiancée, looking forward to their life together, but seriously tempted to turn tail and run at some point during the wedding planning."

"I can understand that," I said. "Would now be an appropriate time to mention how glad I was that we saw eye-to-eye on eloping?"

"It would," he said. "I think right now both grooms are looking at me a little enviously. Especially Harry. Do you know what he told me last night? Emily was trying to get him to change his last name before she'd agree to marry him."

"Yes," I said. "I heard about that from Mother. Emily didn't think Koenig was elegant enough for her taste."

"That seems to have blown over," he said. "So I gather she figured out she could keep her own last name. Plenty of women do these days."

"Actually Mother and I pointed out that Koenig means 'king' in German," I said. "Emily liked the sound of that. And speaking of Harry—we should check to make sure he got safely back to Mother and Dad's. I asked Mother last night if everyone who was staying there had gotten back safe and sound, and she said yes, but she might have assumed Harry was with you down at the zoo. And Emily will have a cow if she thinks we've misplaced her groom."

"On my to-do list," he said. "But I didn't want to wake anyone up too early. I assume your dad was out late with the murder investigation, and I know your mother's having a hard time coping with the brides. I sent Harry an email, and I figured if he hasn't checked in by nine thirty or ten, I'll call him."

"Good thinking," I said. "Of course, this means he was out wandering by himself downtown at the very time Austin was getting bumped off."

"Is there some reason why you suspect him?" Michael asked. "He seems pretty harmless to me."

"Harmless?" I echoed. "I can't figure out if that's a compliment or an insult."

"You know what I mean," he said. "Quiet. Mild mannered. Goes out of his way not to be a bother."

"Isn't it the quiet ones you have to watch?" I said. "And that was a joke. I don't know of any reason to suspect him. I just wish he'd stayed at the game with you. I want everyone in both wedding parties in the clear, so the show can go on this Saturday, even if the chief hasn't yet caught the killer."

"You might get Kevin to check whatever video feeds he has access to from downtown," Michael said. "Looking back, maybe I missed a signal—maybe Harry wasn't all that keen on basketball and would rather have gone to the concert in the town square. Maybe he pretended to have a headache so he could go and do that."

"That would be in character," I said. "The man reads. Real books. I found him in our library yesterday, happily immersed in *David Copperfield*."

"Sounds as if he'll be a nice addition to the family."

"Yeah," I said. "I just wonder what he sees in Emily."

Michael didn't answer immediately, and I wasn't surprised. He was a big believer that if you couldn't say something nice, maybe you shouldn't say anything at all.

"I doubt if we're seeing her at her best," he said finally.

"It sounds to me as if she's going to pressure him to get rid of his library," I said. "By claiming to be allergic to book dust. Would it be okay if I let him know he can rehome his books with us? At least until he can work out a compromise with her?"

"Good God," he said. "What is she, a barbarian? Absolutely. Look, I should sign off—Blaine's impatient to get his visit with the chief over with. See you soon."

He was right, I thought, after we said our goodbyes. We weren't seeing Emily at her best. And was it unkind of me to think that maybe even her best wasn't good enough for a nice guy like Harry?

Assuming he was a nice guy. It occurred to me that maybe I should check with Mother to see if she knew where Harry was.

She was probably up, but in case she wasn't . . .

"Is Harry at your house?" I texted her.

"Let me look," she texted back.

I sat, staring at the screen for the several minutes it took her to reply.

"Yes. But still asleep. Why?"

"Just worried when I found out he never made it to the zoo."

"He got here very late, but he's fine. We'll talk later."

I felt reassured. I could banish the vision I'd had of Harry on the lam, making good his getaway while Mother and Dad assumed he was out at the zoo and the Sleep with the Wombats crew thought he was just a party pooper who'd wimped out and gone home.

Of course, the fact that he was currently fast asleep at Mother and Dad's didn't mean he wasn't the killer. What if—

I shoved the thought aside, grabbed my trusty notebook, and headed downstairs.

In the kitchen I found Rose Noire busily fixing bacon, sausage, eggs, French toast, cinnamon rolls, and biscuits, accompanied by a vast quantity of yogurt and fruit salad. Kevin and the chief were sitting at the kitchen table, digging in. I confess, I did a double take when I saw Kevin. He was the original night owl.

"So are you up already, or still up?" I asked.

"Still up," he said, through a mouthful of toast. "Going to catch some Zs pretty soon."

"Kevin and Vern have been looking at video all night," the chief said.

"Well, Vern turned in around three a.m.," Kevin said. "He sacked out in one of the spare bedrooms upstairs, with orders to wake him when the chief needs him."

"We'll let him sleep a little longer," the chief said. "It's not as if any of the people I need to talk to here are conscious yet."

"That reminds me," I said, turning to the chief. "Michael was out at the zoo last night with a bunch of the out-of-town kids."

"I know," he said. "And thanks again for inviting Adam. From what I've heard, he's been having a great time."

"Good to hear." Adam, the youngest of the three orphaned grandchildren the chief and his wife were raising, was the boys' best friend, and Josh and Jamie would have mutinied if he hadn't been invited to Sleep with the Wombats. "Michael's coming over soon," I went on. "He can bring you up to date on all the people he can vouch for between whenever the basketball games started and midnight, when they headed out to the zoo. And he's bringing one of the grooms. But the other groom went walkabout during exactly the time period when we'd like to know where he was. Not that I know of any reason why he'd have a grudge against Austin, but you never know."

Neither the chief nor Kevin said anything immediately, and I felt a sudden surge of anxiety. I had to remind myself that it wasn't my fault Harry didn't have an alibi.

It didn't erase the slight and wholly irrational guilt I was feeling about pointing out that fact to the chief.

Chapter 21

"I was already aware that Mr. Koenig went AWOL from Sleep with the Wombats," the chief said finally. "Can you give me his contact information?"

I flipped through my notebook until I found my list of Emily's wedding party members and shared Harry's cell phone number. And then, while I was at it, I took pictures of both wedding party lists and sent them to him.

"Thank you," he said.

"Michael thinks Harry's harmless," I said. "And he might have just bailed on basketball so he could go to the concert in the town square." I turned to Kevin. "Any chance you might be able to spot him in some of the video feeds you have access to downtown?"

"I'll put it on the list." Kevin yawned. "Can you get me a picture of him?"

"There's probably one on Emily's wedding website." I pulled out my phone and looked for the link I had somewhere.

"She has a website about her wedding?" The chief sounded surprised.

"Lots of brides do these days," I said. "Sometimes they set it up themselves, and a lot of the time their wedding planner does it for them. Here you go. Sending you his picture."

"Thanks." Kevin yawned again as he said it.

"Can you send me a link to that site?" the chief asked. "Because it just might answer one question that's been puzzling me—how this Mr. Wilson, the disgruntled client, could have known Mr. Luckett was here in Caerphilly. I was thinking that he'd have to have been a pretty dedicated stalker to track him down here. But if the brides' websites give details of who the wedding vendors are—"

"They absolutely do," I said. "I've been meaning to ask whether they give the brides a discount for doing that, or if the brides are just hoping they will. But both Emily's and Lexy's sites definitely credit Austin."

"So if the guy's smart enough to do an online search for Austin's name, their websites would pop up," Kevin said.

I sent the chief links to the two websites, so he could see for himself.

"Thank you," he said.

Someone knocked on the back door, then opened it.

"Meg? Okay if I come in?"

We all turned to see Nikki standing outside peering in.

"Of course," I said. "Come in and have some breakfast. And tell the ladies to do the same."

"I'll invite them when I go back," she said, shedding her coat as she came in. "But I think they're already dishing up bún chả giò and phở for themselves. Vietnamese comfort food."

"And you prefer bacon and eggs?" The chief sounded amused.

"I'm an equal opportunity eater." Nikki, never shy, had picked up a plate and was holding it out for Rose Noire to fill. "I'll have bacon and eggs with you guys and bún chả giò and phở with them if there's any left over, which there almost always is, because Vietnamese aunties don't know how to cook small quantities. Look, I wanted to tell you about something that happened yesterday. Something that photographer guy did. Aida told us about him getting knocked off, and I have no idea if this had anything to do with it—"

"You never know what could be relevant." The chief pulled out his notebook. "So what happened?"

"We were doing some fittings out in the trailer." Nikki slid her plate onto the table and sat down. "And it was pretty hectic, because we had both Team Lavender and Team Silver at the same time."

"Team what?" The chief looked puzzled.

"Those are the wedding colors," I explained. "Lexy's colors are lavender and black, and Emily's are silver and green."

"Silver and *moss*," Nikki corrected. "Don't let her hear you calling it green. Moss is elegant. Green is tacky. According to her. Anyway, things were a little chaotic, because most of them were going all mean girl on each other, and then suddenly half of them started shrieking, and the ladies and I thought they'd escalated from verbal sniping to actual combat, and I rushed outside to break things up and guess what I found?"

She popped half a slice of bacon into her mouth and chewed on it.

"Something to do with Mr. Luckett?" the chief asked.

"Wait," I said. "Let me guess. They caught him taking pictures of the bridesmaids while they were running around half naked."

"I guess they already told you." Nikki looked disappointed. "Or was that a lucky guess?"

"An informed guess," I said. "Remember, I had the dubious pleasure of his company for quite a while yesterday. So why didn't

I see any claw marks on him later that day? Some of those bridesmaids have nails so long they could probably take on a grizzly."

"He outran them," Nikki said. "Hopped into his van and laid rubber. And then his assistant said not to worry, because eventually when he filled up the data card he'd hand it to her to upload the photos into the cloud, and she'd delete all the embarrassing ones."

"I bet she's had to do that before," I said.

"Yeah," Nikki said. "She definitely had that 'here we go again' vibe."

"What time was this?" the chief asked.

"Around four thirty in the afternoon. Maybe five," Nikki said. "It had just gotten dark, whenever that would be."

"Was that the last time you saw him here at the house?" the chief asked.

"He came back maybe an hour later and made his assistant drive him somewhere before any of the bridesmaids could catch sight of him. And good riddance. Sorry—I didn't mean that the way it sounds."

"You were just glad he didn't stick around and cause more trouble," I said.

She nodded.

"Do you know which bridesmaids were angry at him?" the chief asked.

"Sorry." Nikki gave a tight shake of her head. "They were pretty much all swarming us at the same time. But if you check the photographer guy's camera, you should be able to tell who he was doing his Peeping Tom number on."

"Good idea." The chief glanced at me as he said this, and I deduced that perhaps he didn't want to reveal the fact that the data card was missing from Austin's camera. So I just nodded sagely.

Just then the doorbell rang. I shoved back my chair, ready to head for the front door.

"You stay put," Rose Noire said. "I'll answer it."

"Probably one of my deputies," the chief said. "With one of my interviewees. I want to talk to the various brides and bridesmaids as soon as they're awake, so I'm having the rest of the possible witnesses brought here."

"So you're ready to pounce on the unwary bridesmaids as soon as they stagger into the kitchen," I said. "Very reasonable."

"Let me know as soon as they're stirring," Rose Noire said as she headed for the door to the hall. "I've got a different menu planned for them."

"You think they'll turn up their noses at this?" I asked, gesturing to my plate, which still had a few bits of scrambled egg, along with the greasy spot from which the bacon had disappeared—locally produced bacon from one of Dad's friends who ran an organic, free-range pig farm.

"Greasy foods aren't optimal for anyone with a hangover," she said. "I've been working on a more restorative menu for the bridesmaids." With that she left the kitchen.

"Could also be Horace," the chief said. "He was up so late at the graveyard that I just sealed Mr. Luckett's room here and told him to go home and get some sleep. I should go and see."

With that he strode out. I glanced over at Kevin and caught him yawning again.

"You should get some sleep," I said. "The chief's probably going to be keeping you pretty busy."

"I know." He grabbed a last slice of bacon and disappeared into the basement.

"Gotta run," Nikki said. "Mrs. Nguyen and Mrs. Giap want us to get some work done before the bridesmaids show up."

"That could take a while," I said. "But go on, before the bún chả giò is all gone."

She grinned, grabbed her coat, and went out the back door.

I pulled out my notebook and began planning my day.

Or trying to. I found myself thinking about what Nikki had just told us, and connecting it to something Kevin had mentioned last night—about the bridesmaids at Rob and Delaney's house going on the warpath because they thought Austin was playing Peeping Tom again. Was it Austin doing that? And if so, how had he gotten out to the house and then back to town in time to meet me—and his killer—at the graveyard?

And if it wasn't Austin peeking into the basement windows at Emily's party, who was it? Possibly someone who was looking for him. Someone who finally caught up with him in the Trinity graveyard. But apart from Robyn and me, who could possibly know that he was supposed to show up there at eleven?

Maddie knew, of course. And she wasn't shy about complaining when she felt put upon, so anyone who'd run into her would have known. Of course, from what I'd seen, she *was* put upon, and had every right to complain. Had she always been like that, the whole time she'd been working for him? Or had his mistreatment of her—and her resentment of it—only recently reached the point where she could no longer hold it in, and it spilled over into every conversation about him?

And what if it had also spilled over into violence?

I hoped not. I liked Maddie. I didn't want to find out she was a killer. Because if she was, it would probably turn out that she'd been driven to it by his abusive treatment of her. And yet, even if he'd done everything she claimed he'd done—ruined her attempt to start her own photography career, belittled her physical appearance, and treated her abominably—it didn't make killing him okay. Understandable, maybe, but not okay. Not grounds for justifiable homicide and probably not even for voluntary manslaughter.

I made a mental note to make sure either Vern or Kevin had told the chief about the second alleged Peeping Tom incident and tried to focus on my notebook.

Which wasn't working all that well.

Rose Noire returned.

"The whole force will be here before long," she said. "Here, you take the rest of this." She deposited three slices of bacon, a sausage, and a small amount of cheesy scrambled eggs on my plate. "I'm going to switch over to my hangover-healthy menu."

I didn't argue. As I was savoring the last slice of bacon, I heard a car pulling up outside, and since Rose Noire was cooking and could do without more interruptions, I headed for the front hall, so I could open the door before the latest arrivals rang the bell.

To my relief it was Michael, accompanied by Blaine, Lexy's fiancé.

Chapter 22

"How's it going?" Michael asked, coming over to give me a quick kiss.

"Slowly, from what I can tell."

"How's Lexy?" Blaine asked.

He didn't really want an honest answer to that, did he? I'd planned on doing my best to avoid interacting with Lexy or Emily or any of their minions until they'd gotten past their hangover and whatever noisy reaction they had to finding that someone had bumped off their carefully chosen photographer. From what I'd seen and heard, I could probably have answered his question, but the answer wouldn't be very complimentary, so I kept it to myself.

"I haven't really talked to her this morning," I said. "They were all up rather late last night."

"And tied one on, I bet." Blaine chuckled. "I should stay away from her until the morning after wears off." He didn't sound wary or disapproving. Indulgent, and maybe a little proud. No accounting for taste.

I heard the dining-room door open.

"Morning, Chief," Michael said.

I turned to see my friend Aida, one of the chief's deputies, striding toward the front door and the chief standing in the dining-room doorway. Aida waved at me before exiting, but she was clearly a woman on a mission.

"Good morning," the chief said. "From what Adam texted me this morning, I gather a fine time was had by all out at the zoo last night. And I see you have a witness for me."

Michael introduced Blaine and the chief, and the two of them disappeared into the dining room.

"Weird night," Michael said when the door had closed behind them.

"At least we know he had nothing to do with the murder," I said.

"Yeah, but he was acting pretty weird last night."

"Weird in what way?"

Michael glanced at the dining-room door, then strode into the living room. I followed him.

"Okay, here's what happened," he said, taking a seat on the raised hearth. "During the women's game, just before the end of the second quarter, Blaine got a phone call. He didn't answer it, but he said he was sorry, he had to go return the call. And he left the stands and wandered around a bit—I thought he was looking for an exit, but he ended up pacing up and down along one end of the gym—I was surprised the referees didn't shoo him away. They usually try to keep that area clear so players won't run into anyone if they run off the court. But I guess he did a good job of staying clear whenever the play got close to him."

"Pretty noisy place to make a call," I said.

"Definitely." He held out his hands to warm at the fire. "He had the phone in one hand and the other hand over his ear the whole time. And I didn't get the idea it was a cheerful phone call. He looked . . ." He frowned as he searched for the right word.

"Angry?"

"No." He shook his head. "But not happy. Stressed, maybe. And the phone call lasted over an hour. Closer to two. The rest of the women's game, and all through the short break, and then nearly to the end of the first half of the men's game."

"Weird," I said.

"I figure he didn't want to take it outside because it was so cold," he said. "But I have no idea why he didn't go out into the hallway. He could have shown his ticket stub to get back in—I made sure everyone had their stubs in case they needed to make a bathroom run. It doesn't make sense."

"Unless he wanted to be seen for some reason," I suggested. "Like maybe he knew something was going on that he'd want an alibi for?"

Michael thought about that for a minute or so.

"That's a little hard to believe," he said. "I mean, the guy's not a rocket scientist, but he seems like a nice guy. Was a good sport about Sleep with the Wombats—in fact, he seemed to enjoy it, and he was a big help with the younger kids. Admits to being a little nervous about all the upcoming festivities—joked about needing cue cards for the ceremony. But if he had anything to do with the murder . . . well, he's a better actor than most of the Drama Department."

"You should tell the chief about it," I said. "Maybe there's an innocent explanation, but it's weird."

"I will. And of course, you know what your dad would say."

"I can imagine," I said. "In his beloved mystery books and movies, you always want to look closely at any character who has a perfect alibi. They always turn out to be the killer."

"A good thing for Blaine that the chief doesn't share your dad's addiction."

I nodded.

"I'm going to take a shower while I'm here," he said. "Might even put my feet up for a few minutes before I have to go back to entertaining the visiting friends and family. Unless there's something useful I could do here?"

"Keeping the grooms out from underfoot is highly useful," I said. "Plus, I think the groomsmen or ushers or whatever you call them will be turning up later today, and you'll have to entertain them while I help Mother with the brides and bridesmaids. Get some rest while you can."

"Can't say I'm looking forward to hanging out with Blaine's buddies," he said. "At least if they're all like him. Not that he isn't perfectly pleasant, but we don't seem to have much in common. But meeting Harry's might be interesting. Speaking of Harry, do we know where he is?"

"At Mother and Dad's," I said. "Mother said he got in very late."

"Good," he said. "I'd have gone looking for him if I didn't have a whole herd of other guests on my hands." With that he headed for the stairs.

"He's a grown-up," I called after him. "Evidently he coped somehow."

Would we get to meet Harry's friends, I wondered? Maybe I was doing him an injustice, but while I wasn't doubting that he had half a dozen friends, I had a hard time imagining he had that many friends who would pass muster with Emily as presentable enough to appear in her wedding. Their wedding.

No, *her wedding* was probably accurate. And Harry's groomsmen would probably turn out to be her picks rather than his. Depressing thought. Especially when I remembered that the head count for her wedding was much smaller than Lexy's, mainly because Harry's parents were deceased and he could only think of half a dozen people he wanted to invite.

"Stop depressing yourself," I muttered. I decided to go back to the kitchen, where it would look less as if I was trying to keep track of who the chief was interviewing.

I sat down at the kitchen table and had just pulled out my notebook when—

"Meg, dear." I looked up to see Mother entering the kitchen. "Are you all right? You've had a difficult time."

She came over and planted a kiss on my cheek, more soundly than usual. And I could see her studying me, briefly, and then nodding slightly, as if her inspection had confirmed that I had survived last night in good shape.

"I'm fine," I said. "Not looking forward to dealing with how the brides are going to react to all this."

"Or their mothers." She gave a slight sniff that I knew was a sign of mild displeasure. "They don't seem to be able to look past the inconvenience this will cause their daughters. Of course, it has distracted them from worrying quite so much about the threat of snow."

"And I'm sure their daughters will behave as if this, like the snow, were something we'd organized on purpose to spite them," I said.

"'Will behave'?" Mother raised an eyebrow. "They haven't already expressed their displeasure?"

"At this hour?" I glanced at the clock. Only nine-thirtyish. "They're all still comatose after last night's festivities. With luck they'll sleep a few hours longer—I'm not looking forward to dealing with those two when they're under the influence of a grudge on top of their hangovers."

"So trying," Mother murmured. "But at least that gives us some time to do a little damage control before they're awake."

"If by damage control you mean putting our library and Delaney and Rob's game room to rights, let's not worry about that just yet," I said. "For one thing, most of the bridesmaids are still sacked out there. And for another, I'm calling the Dirty Dogs in as soon as the chief says it's okay, and you're not allowed to look at either room until they're finished."

She closed her eyes long enough to take a deep breath. Then she opened them again and her face took on a determined expression.

"Thank you, dear," she said.

I wasn't sure if she was thanking me for organizing the cleanup or for warning her that damage had been done.

"The decorations might need a little touching up," I added. Probably good to start breaking the bad news to her gradually.

"You mean they didn't ruin everything? That's encouraging. Nice that something is. Does the chief really need to interview Betty and Letty and all the very respectable ladies who were with me at last night's dinner?"

"The Inn's not that far from Trinity," I said. "Maybe a five-minute drive at most."

"Yes, dear," she said. "But not a single one of them left the table for more than a five-minute trip to the bathroom—they couldn't possibly have gone over to Trinity, killed Mr. Luckett, and gotten back before we noticed they were gone. Can't he take my word for it that none of them left the hotel?"

"I'm sure he would be happy to take your word for it," I said. "But remember, he has to look ahead to when he's caught the killer and their defense attorney is trying to cast doubt on their whereabouts. After all, they're all relatives except Caroline, and she might as well be by now. A jury might suspect that you'd cover up for them."

"Not a Caerphilly jury, surely."

"No, but what if the defense asks for a change of venue? And gets a jury that has never heard of any of us? He needs to be prepared for whatever could happen."

"Well, that makes sense." She finally sounded less annoyed. "And at least half a dozen of the Inn's staff can vouch for all of us. They were very attentive. Anyway, right now we have something else to do."

She pulled out the tiny notebook that was her equivalent of my notebook-that-tells-me-when-to-breathe. I could never figure out how she got along with such a minuscule notebook. Granted she did a lot more delegating than I did, but she still had to keep track of the projects her minions were performing for her, didn't she?

And then something occurred to me that I'd never thought of before, as often as I'd seen Mother's notebook. Maybe its tiny size was her way of setting a reasonable limit to how many tasks and projects she took on. After all, just the sight of it had made me postpone asking her to help organize staking out the town's churches to catch the vandals. That project could stay on my to-do list for the time being.

Meanwhile I pulled out my own notebook and braced myself to hear what Mother thought we had to do.

Chapter 23

"First of all, we need a new photographer," Mother said. "I know that sounds cold, but the show must go on."

"We've got Maddie. Austin's assistant," I added, seeing from her expression that the name didn't ring a bell. "She's a photographer in her own right, you know. In fact, she'd be running her own wedding photo business if Austin hadn't sabotaged it."

"Sabotaged it?" Mother frowned. "How?"

"By blackening her reputation to the entire Richmond wedding vendor community so she'd have to come back to work for him."

"Yes." She nodded. "That sounds like his style. But are you really sure we can rely on her being available by Saturday? From what I've heard she looks like one of the most likely suspects in his murder. What if Chief Burke arrests her the night before the wedding? We need to have a backup plan."

"Don't we have a few photographers in the family?" I asked.

"Of course, dear." Was there just a note of reproach in her tone? "Several very good ones. The challenge will be finding one who isn't already booked for this weekend."

After much detailed scrutiny of the family tree, we settled on two likely prospects. One was a twentysomething cousin who had put her photography business on hold a year ago when she gave birth to twins. The other was a teenage cousin who was still in high school, but had recently been accepted to the Digital Photography program at the Savannah College of Art and Design, and might well be interested in earning a little extra money toward his tuition.

"Which one should we try first?" Mother was frowning pensively at the page in her notebook on which she'd entered their names and numbers.

"Let's try them both right now," I suggested. "Better to have too many photographers than none at all. How about if you call the mother of twins, and make sure she understands how much expert twin-savvy childcare help we can provide. And in the meantime—"

Just then my phone rang.

"In the meantime, I will see what Ekaterina needs this morning," I finished.

I answered the phone and put it on speaker, which might save time if Mother needed to know about whatever Ekaterina had to say.

"Good morning, Meg," Ekaterina said. "Could you possibly drop by the Inn this morning? We have a situation in which your expertise would be helpful."

"Sure," I said. "Do you—"

"No! Put that down this second!" Ekaterina shouted. "Sorry, Meg. That was not for you, but I must go. Please come."

With that she hung up.

"I think Ekaterina needs me," I said.

"It definitely sounds that way." Mother shook her head wearily. "You should go right away. We could have a real problem if the brides wear out their welcome at the Inn."

"From what I can tell, it's a dead heat between the brides and Caroline's eagles for who Ekaterina throws out first. I'll keep you posted."

When I arrived at the Inn, Jaime, the doorman, looked happy to see me. No, make that relieved.

"So glad you came," he said, bowing me in more elaborately than usual. "Things are a bit difficult this morning."

I was tempted to suggest that however difficult things were here at the Inn, they couldn't begin to match stumbling over a dead body in a graveyard close to midnight. But then I reminded myself not to take out my lack of sleep on him. And besides, I could see he was genuinely upset.

"What's wrong?" I asked.

"It is about the eagles," he said. "Perhaps you can restore harmony."

He gestured toward the alcove where the eagles were being kept. I could see Caroline and Ekaterina standing there. Neither looked happy. Nearby stood an anxious-looking young woman in a crisp beige-and-white staff uniform. I recognized Sonia, a longtime member of the Inn's housekeeping staff.

I hurried over. Sonia stepped back with a look of relief on her face.

"What's going on?" I asked.

"Someone's been mistreating my eagles," Caroline said.

"I said last night we should have moved them," Ekaterina said.

"No argument from me, but where?" Caroline turned to me. "There's no room here at the Inn."

"The only other spaces where we could possibly set up the cage are some of the storage rooms," Ekaterina said. "And they are not heated. We could bring in space heaters—"

"But that would be a fire hazard, and not very effective to boot," Caroline said. "But we do need to relocate them. It's pretty obvious that someone has been mistreating them. Nathanael has become very reactive—that was never a problem before."

"Nathanael?" I echoed.

"Nathanael Greene, like the general." She pointed to the largest of the eagles. "We name the eagles after Revolutionary War heroes."

"And someone has been feeding them junk food," Ekaterina said. "Sonia, show them what you swept up from in and around their cage."

The housekeeper looked startled, then stepped forward to hold out a dustpan. It was, indeed, full of junk food. I recognized popcorn, Cheetos, and possibly Doritos.

"You're right—we need to move them," I said. "And I'd offer them a place at my house, but we're also full to the brim. Plus there's no guarantee that whoever has been mistreating them here at the hotel isn't part of the crew we're hosting for the wedding."

"Good point," Caroline said.

"What about asking Grandfather if he can find a suitable place for them?" I suggested. "After all, whenever he and Dad rescue a wounded raptor around here, he's generally able to find a vacant habitat to keep it in until he can send it down to you. And the zoo's just five minutes down the road from here, so it wouldn't be a big deal to take your donor guy down there to see them. Heck, he might actually get quite a kick out of it." I felt slightly annoyed. Hadn't I suggested that very thing yesterday? And then I remembered that I'd suggested it to Rob, who had probably forgotten about it five minutes later. Mother and I had given up trying to convert Rob to the Way of the Notebook.

"That sounds quite reasonable," Ekaterina said. "I would even be happy to put the hotel shuttle at your disposal, whenever he wants to visit them."

Instead of leaping at the suggestion. Caroline frowned slightly.

"And he has trained zoo staff who can take care of them," Ekaterina added. "I tasked our bellhops with watching over them, but they were required to assist customers when called, so they could not guard them constantly. And who knows? Perhaps they were unaware of what the eagles' proper diet would be."

"You think your bellhops fed popcorn and Doritos to my eagles?" Caroline demanded.

"Of course not!" Ekaterina exclaimed. "They were under orders not to interfere with the eagles in any way."

"But they might not realize that they should keep a guest from feeding them junk," I said, turning to face them. "Or they might be shy about challenging a guest, even if they know it's a bad idea. And another thing—"

Just then I heard a disquieting sound from behind me. The housekeeper gasped and covered her mouth with her hand. Ekaterina muttered something in Russian. Caroline blinked and sighed.

"Maybe you're right," Caroline said. "We should call Monty."

I turned to see that the smallest eagle had projectile vomited all over the lower third of the elegantly decorated Christmas tree.

"How about if I call Grandfather now?" I said. "And while I'm doing that, maybe you could get Clarence Rutledge to drop by and check out the eagles. Make sure whatever people have been feeding them hasn't caused any serious problems."

"Sonia," Ekaterina said. "The veterinarian will be arriving soon. We should probably allow him to see the . . . evidence of the birds' unwellness. But perhaps you could assemble a crew to clean up the damage once he is finished. It has become more than I would expect you to do by yourself."

Sonia murmured her assent and raced off. I braced myself and craned my neck so I could see exactly what the eagle had been eating.

Yes, Cheetos and popcorn.

"Let's ask Kevin if any of his cameras would let us identify the culprit," I suggested to Ekaterina.

"A good idea," she said. "And if this General Greene has come to any harm—"

"General Greene's the big one," Caroline said. "The one who puked is Sybil Luddington. We named her after the sixteen-year-old girl who completed a daring ride just like Paul Revere's, only twice as far. And in the rain."

Trust Caroline to use her rescued raptors to teach not only history but feminism.

"So let's get poor Sybil into a more suitable habitat." I pulled out my phone and called Grandfather.

"Josh and Jamie are fine," he said. "Got a couple of budding biologists here if you ask me."

"Great," I said. "Any chance I could enlist you for another ornithological project?"

I began to explain the plight of Caroline's rescued eagles and, to my relief, he didn't need any persuading.

"No problem," he said. "I've been wondering how soon the birds would wear out their welcome at the Inn. Got a couple of habitats that will suit them just fine. I'll head over now while we've still got all my pupils. Give them a lesson in wildlife rehabilitation. Manoj! Bring the truck around."

With that he hung up.

"Grandfather would be happy to shelter the eagles," I said. "He's on his way."

"Excellent!" Ekaterina said. "Call me if you need any assistance in moving them."

With that she hurried off. I could actually understand why. Not only was the sight of the vomit-splattered Christmas tree depressing, but the whole area reeked. I put another six or eight feet between me and the eagles.

Caroline looked glum.

"Don't worry," I said. "Grandfather's staff can take great care of the eagles. And your donor should have a lot of fun visiting them."

"Maybe too much fun," she said in a disgruntled tone. "What if the old goat tries to poach my donor?"

That took me by surprise.

"Why would he?" I asked. "I mean, Grandfather's not really in need of funds, is he?"

"He doesn't need funds nearly as much as I do," she said. "But when did you ever hear of a nonprofit that couldn't use more funds? And don't tell me he'd refuse a honking big donation if one fell into his lap?"

"I'll keep an eye on him," I said. "And give him hell if he tries to snake your donor. But I can't believe he'd actually do that."

"Thanks." She still looked glum. "And you're right, I know. He wouldn't deliberately steal my donor. But what if his zoo overshadows my refuge? What if my donor decides he'd get more bang for his bucks at the zoo? It wouldn't be Monty's fault if that happened. But I need to stop worrying about it. Right now, we need to keep the eagles safe."

"Are they going to be okay?" came a voice from behind us.

Chapter 24

I glanced up to see that Frank and Terri—the normal wedding couple, as I'd mentally dubbed them—had joined us. I noticed they were keeping their distance from the eagles, and trying not to look at the besmirched Christmas tree.

"They should all be fine," I said. "And any minute now we'll be relocating them to a habitat out at the Caerphilly Zoo."

"Oh, thank goodness," Terri said. "Not that we have anything against them, of course. It's been interesting having them."

Clearly she, like Mother, used "interesting" when she couldn't think of anything nice to say.

"But I don't think this is a safe place for them," Frank said. "There's just no way the staff can keep people away from them. And people were teasing them."

"We tried to stop them," Terri said. "And were ignored."

"What's wrong with people, anyway?" Caroline muttered.

"That young man with the camera was the worst," Terri said.

"He was teasing them so he could get more dramatic pictures of them."

"What?" Caroline exclaimed.

"Austin?" I asked. "The one who was here with the brides?"

"Yes," Frank said. "I'm afraid we had a few testy words with him."

"Such a rude young man," Terri murmured.

"I could murder him," Caroline said. "If I'd known he was doing that—"

"Be glad you didn't know," I said. "Or you'd be at the top of the chief's suspect list."

"Suspect list?" Frank echoed. He and Terri looked worried.

"I'm going to call Clarence," Caroline said. "Get the eagles checked out."

She strode off to find a quieter spot for calling.

"Do you remember what time it was that you saw Austin?" I asked.

They exchanged a look.

"Was it after we came back from seeing the decorations by daylight?" Frank asked.

"No, I think it was just before we went down to dinner. Does it matter?" she asked, looking at me.

"It could help the police trace his movements."

From the looks on their faces I realized they hadn't heard the news.

"Trace his movements?" Frank said. "Has he . . . has he done something?"

"He's dead," I said.

Terri gasped and covered her mouth with her hands, and Frank flinched as if the words had struck him.

"Dead?" he said. "How?"

"Someone shot him," I said. "Not here," I added. "And hours after you saw him—although our police chief would probably like to talk to you. He'll be talking to the hotel staff and any guests who might have seen him. I gather he's trying to reconstruct Austin's movements in the hours leading up to the murder."

"We'll be here for the next few days." Frank had put his arm around Terri, who seemed shaken by the news. "And of course we'd be happy to give the police what little information we have."

"Maybe you could let me know your cell phone number," I suggested. "And he can contact you to set up a time to interview you."

"Of course." Terri reached into her purse and pulled out a small leather-bound three-ring binder. A woman with a notebook. I nodded my approval as she jotted down his and her cell phone numbers in a small, neat hand.

"So sad," she murmured as she handed me the paper. "He was so young, and now cut down in his prime. Will there be services? We didn't exactly know him, but since we were among the last to see him alive . . ."

"He's not local," I said. "He lives in Richmond, so whatever services they have for him might be held down there. Unless his family lives someplace else." I realized that I knew nothing about Austin. Did he have family, in Richmond or wherever? Did he have a girlfriend or even a wife? The chief probably knew by now—I couldn't imagine Maddie holding back any information she possessed. And I had no real need to know any more about him than I already did, so why did I suddenly feel an almost irresistible impulse to go and pump Maddie for information? Or, better yet, ask Kevin what he'd learned.

"Well, if you hear of anything happening locally, do let us know." Frank had taken Terri's arm and was gently steering her away.

"And if the chief needs us, we'll be back in an hour or so," Terri called over her shoulder. "We're going to do a little present shopping and then try out another restaurant downtown."

I thought of asking which restaurant. Not that it mattered.

Bad restaurants occasionally opened their doors in Caerphilly, but they didn't usually last long. Some of the current crop were better than others, but I couldn't think of one that I'd warn them away from. Well, maybe Chez Maurice, whose pretentious attitude somewhat spoiled its excellent (though overpriced) French haute cuisine. And I could never understand the appeal of the Frilled Pheasant, a tea shop that catered to a clientele who liked antimacassars, tiny portions, and raised pinkies. But neither of them was actually bad. Just expensive and annoying.

I waved to Terri and Frank and watched as they made a beeline for the door.

"If you don't mind, Meg."

The cleanup crew had arrived—half a dozen uniformed staff members armed with mops and buckets and a rug-shampooing machine that they seemed to want to park where I was standing. I moved out of their way, but clearly they weren't going to make much progress in their cleanup until the eagles left.

I decided to stick around until Grandfather arrived to collect the birds, just in case. I could intervene if Grandfather tried to do anything that would upset Ekaterina, and I could protect the cleaning staff if he got the idea into his head that the staff had been responsible for trying to poison the eagles.

And I could serve as a buffer if tension arose between Caroline and Grandfather over her potential donor. Normally the two of them were staunch allies, battling anything and everything that threatened the welfare of animals and the health of the planet. I was determined to do whatever I could to ensure that any tension over their potential donor didn't spoil that.

Clarence Rutledge arrived and began checking out the eagles and tut-tutting over their treatment while Caroline hovered nearby, looking anxious.

And not long afterward, Grandfather turned up—a lot sooner than I expected. Was that a good sign? Was he eager to give the eagles a proper habitat to please Caroline? Or just excited about adding three more interesting specimens to his zoo, even temporarily? He was accompanied by three uniformed zoo staff and a swarm of a dozen grade- and middle-school-age kids—including Josh and Jamie.

"Good!" he exclaimed. "Clarence, you can ignore the voicemail I left you—I was calling about the eagles."

"Don't worry," Caroline said. "I called him as soon as I knew that they might be unwell."

"I should have mentioned that when I called you," I said.

"You should have come last night, Mom," Josh said, racing up to me. "We've been doing this really cool project for Great," he added, using the nickname the boys had for their great-grandfather.

"And if you'd come with us, maybe someone else would have found the dead guy," Jamie said, giving me a hug.

"We've been feeding bugs to frogs," one of the boys' smaller cousins piped up. "And watching them come out the other end."

If I'd thought about it, I might have predicted that Grandfather's project would include something like frog poop.

"Not bugs," Josh corrected. "Beetles."

"Japanese water scavenger beetles," Jamie added.

"Yes, *Regimbartia attenuata*," Grandfather said. "A fascinating species."

"So you've been spending your morning watching frogs digest beetles," I said. "That sounds . . . um . . ."

"No, they don't digest them," Josh said.

"The beetles escape," Jamie explained. "As soon as the frog swallows them, they start crawling, and eventually they come out of . . . the other end."

To my relief, Grandfather refrained from providing the scientific term for the beetles' escape route.

"We feed the beetles to Japanese pond frogs," he said. "*Pelophylax nigromaculatus*. They're both part of the same ecosystem, and we used to think that the beetles formed a significant part of the frogs' diet. But the beetles carry a supply of oxygen underneath their exoskeletons—which lets them breathe while traveling underwater. And the exoskeletons are hard enough to resist the frogs' digestive juices. Not indefinitely, of course, but long enough. In our studies, ninety percent of the beetles eventually escape undigested and go on to live out their lives."

"Usually it takes a couple of hours," Jamie said. "But we had one that made it out in nine minutes."

"Which must have been quite exciting for the frog," Grandfather remarked.

"All, um, out the other end?" Caroline asked. I was glad to see her momentarily distracted from her worries. "Do any of them manage to escape from the frog's mouth?"

"Not that we observed," Grandfather said. "You're thinking of bombardier beetles." He turned to the boys. "When consumed by toads, bombardier beetles often release a mix of noxious chemicals that causes the toad to vomit, enabling the beetles to escape."

"Cool," Josh said. "Can we do bombardier beetles next?"

"I don't see why not," Grandfather said. "Manoj, get on the horn with whatever supply house carries bombardiers and lay in a good stock of them."

Manoj was a diminutive zoo staffer who had risen to the unenviable position of Grandfather's chief assistant, due largely to his mild temperament and his ability to keep Grandfather happy and out of trouble. He pulled out his phone.

"You mean there're places you can just call up and order insects?" Josh asked.

"Only for zoos," I said, with a stern look at Grandfather in case he felt inclined to contradict me.

"Yes, I think we'll be doing a lot more observations of various beetles," Grandfather said. "Good project for the kids to learn about the scientific method."

I had to give Grandfather credit—he was very good at finding ways to make science appealing to the preadolescent mind. Of course, that was probably because his sense of humor greatly resembled that of a preadolescent boy.

Just then another of the eagles vomited.

"Dammit," Grandfather muttered. "Clarence, have you been able to figure out what's going on with those birds?"

"I think it's only indigestion," Clarence said. "Under normal circumstances, I'd suggest just covering their cage and letting them get over it."

This caused a visible murmur of unhappiness among the waiting housekeeping staff.

"But given how close the zoo is," Clarence went on, "and how unsuitable their current location is for getting the kind of peace and quiet they should be having for their recovery, I recommend that we relocate them now. Get them settled in a nice, comfortable habitat. And I'll stick around until I'm sure they're calmed down after the trip."

"You heard the man," Grandfather said. "Operation Eagle Rescue!"

The waiting zookeepers snapped to attention. Several ran outside and returned pushing large, wheeled cages. Well, they'd have been large for canaries—they didn't even give the eagles room to fully open their wings.

"Don't worry," Grandfather said, when Jamie pointed this out. "This is only for them to travel in. We have nice, big, adjoining habitats waiting for them out at the zoo."

About that time I noticed that in addition to the kids and the zookeepers, Grandfather's party included a middle-aged man in a red plaid flannel shirt. Caroline frowned when she noticed him, and the sight of him seemed to send her back into a bad mood. Was he someone she disliked? An environmental malefactor who had somehow wormed himself into Grandfather's good graces?

When the man in red plaid saw Caroline, he came over to talk with her.

"We had quite a time out there last night," he said.

"Glad you enjoyed it," she said. "I was going to suggest taking you for a tour of the zoo while you're here, but I suppose Monty already did that."

"Haven't had much time yet." The man chuckled. "What with the kids and the beetles and all. Great time, though."

That was when it hit me—this must be Caroline's donor guy. And not only had he joined Sleep with the Wombats, giving Grandfather ample opportunity to charm him, but now he was witnessing what Caroline probably considered her failure to keep the eagles safe. Which I would have protested was the brides' fault, not hers. But I knew that wouldn't fly with her. She'd be blaming herself.

And looking daggers at Grandfather as we watched the zoo staff carefully bundle up the eagles and wheel them out to the waiting zoo truck, with Clarence hovering over them.

Donor Guy seemed to be enjoying the whole thing. The last sight I had of him, he was strolling out of the lobby, flanked by Grandfather and Caroline.

"Can't wait to see those bombardier beetles," he was saying.

Behind me the housekeeping crew had sprung into action. Two of them were disassembling the cage. Others were vacuuming the rug. Several were carefully removing soiled Christmas ornaments from the tree.

Ekaterina appeared.

"Thank goodness," she said.

"Sorry for all the trouble," I said.

"Not your fault," she said. "And not Caroline's obviously. We have never previously had trouble with the animals she brings to display to important donors. Well, except for that time one of my staff startled her opossums and did not realize they were only playing dead. Luckily we enlightened him before he could carry out his plans to bury them. Normally her animals cause no problems. But normally we have a safe place to put them."

"Blame the brides," I said. "That's what I'm doing."

"Yes." She looked preoccupied. "I do not think we will be able to restore the tree to its original glory without the assistance of your mother."

"I'll break the bad news to her," I said. "And see if there's anything I can do to help. Have you talked to her yet today?"

"She came in a little while ago and collected two of your aunts who are staying here," she said. "I believe she was taking them out to your house for the chief to interview them, so we didn't have much chance to talk. If you don't mind, I will go and assist my staff in the cleanup."

She bustled over to the alcove.

I pulled out my phone to call Mother. Then I changed my mind. Maybe I should break this news to her in person. She hadn't seemed too distraught over my hint that the hen party had damaged the library decorations, but the Inn's Christmas tree was a much bigger deal.

I put my phone in my pocket and trudged back to my car.

Chapter 25

I spent the drive home working out the most tactful way to break the news about the Inn's Christmas tree to Mother. By the time I arrived, about the only bright idea I'd had was to pitch it as something that would give her a perfectly valid reason to leave the brides to their own devices.

Of course, that would probably leave me to deal with them.

As I was parking my car by the barn, my phone rang. I glanced down warily before answering, then relaxed when I saw it was Robyn.

"Morning," I said.

"Where are my angels?" she demanded.

"Angels?" It took me a second. "The Barbie angels in the sanctuary?"

"Of course," she said. "I came in just now to get everything ready for the Advent carol service later this afternoon, and when I went into the sanctuary, I found someone had stolen six of the twelve angels—the ones clustered over the altar."

"Oh, no," I muttered.

"And did considerable damage to the surrounding decorations in the process. And we both know who's probably behind it."

"Emily," I said. "The wretch."

I decided I didn't want to have this conversation in the house. The chief might like to surprise Emily with his knowledge of her misdeeds. But it was too cold to stay outside, so I let myself into the barn and headed for my office, at the far end.

"I'm putting out a call to the Decorations Committee, in the hope that we can patch things up before the service," Robyn said.

"Do you have anyone willing and able to climb up on the ladders?" I knew most of the Decorations Committee members were senior citizens. "Because I could probably bribe the boys to come and help."

"Thanks," she said. "I'll let you know. A couple of the committee members are seeing if they can recruit their children or grandchildren. Getting back to Emily—there will be several dozen people from Trinity at her reception. She can't possibly be stupid enough to think she can use them there, can she?"

"She might be." I sat down in my office chair and propped my feet up on one of the copier paper boxes that served as my storage system. "Especially if she was somewhat inebriated when she took them. Do you have any idea when they were taken?"

"Probably last night," she said. "Sometime between eight p.m., when I locked up and went home, and just now, when I came in to make sure everything was ready for the service."

"You didn't go into the sanctuary last night, while the police were there?"

"I'd have reported the theft to them then if I had," she said. "I was focused on keeping the coffee flowing and answering whatever questions they had. I didn't go into the sanctuary. Although— Wait a minute. Let me check something."

She broke off. I waited for a few seconds. A minute. I heard footsteps.

"Aha!" she exclaimed.

"'Aha' what?" I prodded.

"I had to jack the thermostat up last night," she said. "And it never quite got warm enough for me to feel comfortable taking off my coat. Still chilly this morning, in fact. I just assumed maybe we needed to have some more maintenance on that old furnace but then something occurred to me, and I went around checking windows. Someone broke that small window in the sacristy. They must have gotten in that way."

"That makes sense," I said. "If I were going to break into Trinity, I think that's the window I'd choose."

"Is this something you've actually been considering?" Robyn asked. I wasn't sure if she was joking.

"Of course not," I said. "But think about it—that window's way at the back and screened by a lot of bushes. Plus the sacristy is on the opposite side of the church from the graveyard. Emily was terrified of the graveyard. It makes sense that she'd go after the other side of the building. Have you called the theft in to the police?"

"Next on my list," she said. "I thought I'd call you first. Warn you that you might be harboring a thief and a vandal."

"I know how you feel," I said. "The chief is here, interviewing witnesses—if you like, I can let him know."

"Thanks," she said. "I'd appreciate it. I'm going to call it in, then stay here and guard the crime scene—it is a crime scene, right?"

"Definitely. Dammit—if they weren't family, Emily and Lexy both would be out on the sidewalk by now. Although when Mother hears about this, she just might banish them from the Hollingsworth clan."

"I guess my people-reading skills aren't as good as I thought they were," she said. "I thought they were both just fairly typical brides. Maybe a little toward the high-maintenance end of typical, but nothing in our counseling meetings raised any red flags."

"So you had meetings with them before you agreed to perform the weddings," I said. "I was wondering how that worked."

"Oh, yes," she said. "Standard procedure. I always have several counseling sessions—at least one with each partner and then with the couple together. These days we can do it over Zoom, which makes it a lot easier for out-of-town couples, and if I'd had any reservations I'd have insisted on more counseling. I thought the worst thing we'd have to deal with was the groom who's Catholic and feeling a certain amount of guilt over getting married in an Episcopal church."

"We're talking Harry, right?" I couldn't imagine Blaine feeling guilty over anything, with the possible exception of abandoning one of his sports teams when they were having a bad year.

"Yes, Harry. Nice guy." She sighed. "They both seem to be nice guys, and I'm sure the brides aren't normally quite so . . . high maintenance. And I should have realized what a problem it was, having two weddings here this Saturday. Having any weddings here less than a week from Christmas. Actually, I did realize it and tried to talk them into any other Saturday in December, but they were so insistent and I hated to feel I was spoiling their plans."

"Talk to the vestry," I said. "Get them to pass a rule about how close to Christmas you're allowed to have weddings. Then you're not spoiling anyone's plans—just enforcing church policy."

"An excellent idea." The idea seemed to cheer her. "Well, I should go."

We said our goodbyes and hung up. I sat there for a minute or two, thinking. I had no doubt that Emily had either stolen the dolls or talked someone else into stealing them for her. And whoever stole the dolls might have seen something while burgling the church.

Maybe the killer.

I headed for the house.

I found Vern sitting at the kitchen table, which was covered with brown paper evidence bags. He was staring at the screen of a laptop with a cup of coffee at his elbow. Rose Noire was sitting nearby peeling vegetables.

"I see Horace has been busy," I said. "Is the chief tied up? Robyn Smith just called me to report another problem down at Trinity."

"Those vandals didn't hit the graveyard again?" Vern sounded alarmed. "The chief will go ballistic if they've messed up his crime scene."

"No, this was inside the church," I said.

"Tell me about it." The chief appeared in the kitchen doorway.

So I filled him in on what Robyn had reported. When I'd finished, he looked thoughtful.

"Horace is processing Mr. Luckett's room," the chief said. "I'll send him over to Trinity as soon as he's finished with that."

"You don't want us to start looking for the missing angels?" Vern asked.

"If we didn't have a murder on our hands, I'd say of course," the chief said. "But under the circumstances . . ."

"I get it," I said. "The dolls aren't that valuable. What's important is whether the theft had anything to do with the murder."

"But we should still keep our eyes open for the angels," Vern said.

The chief nodded.

"Feel free to say no," I said. "But Emily's staying over at Rob and Delaney's house, and the last I heard she and all the rest of them were still passed out. Would it be okay if Delaney and I check to see if she has hidden the angels over there?"

The chief frowned for a moment.

"If I weren't short-handed," he muttered.

"But we are," Vern said. He turned to me. "Aida's gone down to Richmond to check Luckett's office. See how many other angry customers might be gunning for him. She left her pup here for company, by the way. And Sammy's checking with all the local bed-and-breakfast places to see if this Random guy is staying in one of them, and I'm about to go over to search the graveyard by daylight."

He didn't mention what he'd be searching for. I assumed he'd be looking for the data card—and also that the chief wanted its absence to stay a secret for now.

"Look," the chief said. "But if you find anything, don't touch it. Call me."

"Can do," I said.

I threw on my coat, and as I went out into the backyard I called Delaney.

"What are your houseguests up to?" I said.

"Still snoring, last I checked," she said. "I'm standing guard, with orders to notify Vern as soon as any of them wake up, so he can drag them over for interrogation."

"Interview, please," I said. "The word 'interrogation' might upset them."

"That's why I'm using it," she said. "I might even escalate to 'third degree' if those bimbos wake up cranky. What's up?"

"I'm heading over to your house. We need to search for something—preferably before Emily and her troops wake up." As I walked along the path through the woods from our house to Rob and Delaney's, I filled her in on the theft of the angels. And my reasons for suspecting that Emily—or one of her bridesmaids—was the thief.

By the time I reached their back door, Delaney was waiting for me.

"I've got the keys," she said. "Let's rock and roll!"

"Remember," I said. "If we find anything, we don't touch it. No disturbing the evidence—we call the chief. And we do it together, so we have a witness if we find anything."

"Got it," she said. "Let's start with the blushing bride's room."

Chapter 26

Delaney winced when she opened up the door to Emily's room. It was a hot mess. The bed was unmade—in spite of the fact that Emily had spent the night passed out on one of the couches in the game room. The floor, the bed, and every other horizontal surface in the room were strewn with dirty clothes, food wrappers, soiled dishes and glassware, cosmetic bottles, and every other kind of detritus.

"How can anyone make this much of a mess in only two days?" Delaney muttered.

"Relax," I said. "The Dirty Dogs will handle it."

And we got excited, at first, when we found several traces of gold glitter on the floor by her bed. But no angels.

"Still, the glitter's suspicious," Delaney said.

"Don't touch it," I said. "We might want to get Horace in to do forensics on it."

"Yes," she said. "But let's take some pictures of it."

We both pulled out our phones and documented the glitter, then went on to the rooms occupied by the maid of honor and the six bridesmaids. Their rooms weren't quite as bad as Emily's, but none of them was going to win any awards for good housekeeping. And none of the others showed any trace of glitter.

We descended into the basement game room and searched that, ignoring the snores from the still-slumbering bridesmaids and the curses from those who were awake enough to resent our intrusion. Alas, we found no dolls, and no traces of glitter. Only a mess so astounding that I had to keep reminding Delaney that the Dirty Dogs would be handling it.

"Where in the world could she have hidden them?" Delaney said, as we emerged from the basement into the kitchen.

"Where in the world could who have hidden what?" Rose Noire had just arrived, and was unbuttoning her coat.

"Is Brynn okay?" Delaney asked. Most weekdays Rose Noire took care of Brynn, Rob and Delaney's one-year-old daughter, while they were at work.

"She's fine," Rose Noire said. "Two of my friends are playing with her out in the herb shed. I just came over to get her a change of clothes. She managed to spill a sippy cup full of juice all over herself. What's wrong?"

"We suspect Emily of stealing some of the angels from Trinity's holiday decorations," I said. "And there are telltale signs of glitter in her room, but no sign of the angels."

"Do you suppose she took them with her?" Rose Noire asked.

"She hasn't gone anywhere yet," Delaney said.

"Oh, dear." Rose Noire looked anxious. "I thought they were due at the beauty shop this morning. To get their nails done."

"All of them?" I asked.

"Yeah, all eight," Delaney said. "But I think their appointments are for this afternoon. I feel sorry for Angel and Ruth and their staff. One cranky, entitled, hungover client would be a lot to handle. Eight of them? Yikes. But getting back to the angels—if Emily took them, I bet we'll find traces of glitter in her car."

"I'll go look," Rose Noire said.

"If you see any, don't touch it," I called.

"I probably won't be able to get in," she called back. "I'll just look through the windows."

"If I were Emily, I'd hide them at your house," Delaney said. "That way if anyone found them she'd have plausible deniability."

"If by plausible deniability you mean the ability to dump the blame on Lexy, that definitely sounds like something she'd do," I said. "I'll go back and search at home."

"And I'll do a little more searching here," Delaney said. "Just in case she found what she thought was a good hiding place somewhere other than the bedroom she or one of her friends is occupying." She headed for the stairs.

I was in the mudroom, putting on my coat, when I noticed something. Glitter on the floor. I pulled out my phone and took a few pictures of it.

Rose Noire appeared in the doorway.

"No glitter in the car that I can see," she said.

"But glitter here," I said.

"The plot thickens!" she exclaimed.

I went out the back door and joined her. But having seen the traces of glitter in the mudroom, I kept my eyes glued to the ground.

"More glitter," I said.

We followed a faint trail of glitter that ran along the side of the house, leading up to where the trash can and recycling bin stood.

"She didn't," I muttered.

I lifted the lid of the trash can. There, lying atop the rest of the trash, were the Barbie angels. What was left of them. Their robes, wings, and halos had been ripped to shreds, and several of the dolls' heads and limbs had been wrenched off.

"I'll kill the bimbo," I muttered.

"Oh! Those poor things!" Rose Noire reached out as if to pick up one of the dolls to comfort it. I grabbed her arm.

"Evidence," I said. "The chief told me to call him if I found the angels. He's going to have Horace do forensics."

"Oh, very good."

"Can you go tell Delaney so she can stop searching?" I was taking out my phone to call the chief. "I'll stand guard here."

As luck would have it, Horace was still working on Austin's room. Within fifteen minutes, he was happily photographing the contents of the trash can, while Rose Noire and I looked on.

"Are you going to take all of them away as evidence?" Rose Noire asked.

Horace looked surprised, and I found myself wondering if he'd planned to take any of them as evidence.

"We don't really need them all," Horace said eventually. "One will do. Why?"

"Then let me have the rest." Rose Noire was looking at the dolls with much the same expression she normally wore while tending sick animals. "We can fix them. It will be a wonderful project that we can do with some of the visiting little girls."

"Works for me," Horace said.

We watched solemnly as he bagged one of the dolls—a Ken whose detached head still wore a cheerful grin. Then he helped us gather up the rest of the remnants and tuck them neatly in the wicker basket in which Rose Noire was already carrying clean clothes and diapers for Brynn.

"We also found traces of glitter in the house," I said. "Including the room where Emily's staying."

"Show me," he said.

So while Rose Noire headed back to her herb shed with the dolls, I led Horace into the house and showed him all the spots where I'd found glitter.

"You're sure you won't need all the dolls?" I asked, as I watched him photographing the glitter in the mudroom.

"One should be enough," he said. "No offense to the Sunday school kids, but the window they broke down at Trinity's worth more than all the dolls put together. At least monetarily speaking."

"Did you factor in the fifty pounds of glitter they used to make the things?" I asked. "That stuff doesn't come cheap."

"Cheaper than reglazing a window." He had collected a bit of glitter on a swab and was tucking that into an evidence bag. "And when you add up that plus the damage they did to your mother's decorations in the church, I'm pretty sure it's going to total well over a thousand dollars, which takes it from a misdemeanor into felony territory."

"Why does that make me so happy?" I said.

"Because you're a sane, law-abiding citizen," he said. "Not an entitled, self-centered sociopath."

"I didn't realize you'd already met the brides," I said.

He was still laughing about that when we said goodbye to Delaney and headed back through the woods to my house. In the kitchen we found Vern guarding the collection of brown paper evidence bags, which had more than doubled in size since the last time I'd seen it.

"Meg gets the prize for finding things," Horace said. "Well, you and Meg both."

"What did you find?" I asked. "If you're allowed to say," I added.

"The missing groom." Vern poured himself another cup of coffee from the pot and sat down at the kitchen table. He seemed to be doing some kind of inventory of the brown paper bags, or maybe just putting on a show of being attentive to them, to please Horace.

"The one who's downstairs pumping iron?" Horace asked.

"Again?" I muttered.

"No," Vern said. "The one who skipped out on the basketball games so he could roam around town all evening. He's in with the chief now," he added to Horace.

"You only just found him?" I wasn't sure I liked the sound of that.

"Found him around one-thirty last night, when I was doing that last sweep through town," Vern said, reaching for the cookie tin. "Or this morning, if you want to be technical about it. He was sitting on a bench by the town square. Seems he'd left a message on the taxi company's voicemail and was waiting for them to come and fetch him."

"Good grief," Horace said. "He's lucky you found him when you did."

"Yeah." Vern shook his head. "City folk. Guy was half frozen by the time I found him."

"And he's only got himself to blame for that," I said. "Michael told him how little taxi service there was. And also told him to call if he needed a ride."

"He mentioned that," Vern said. "And said he didn't want to be a bother."

"And it never occurred to him that worrying about what the devil had happened to him might be at least as much of a bother?" I asked.

"I guess not," Vern said. "And he wasn't all that eager to say where he'd been all evening. Claims he was just walking around downtown. I know he wasn't sitting on that bench for more than half an hour. Town square was part of my patrol area last night. I went by that very bench about every twenty minutes up until Meg's call about the murder came in and I went over to Trinity. I'd have spotted him. And even when I went back out, I didn't see him there the first time I passed the town square. Didn't see him anywhere downtown until he popped up on that bench at one-thirtyish."

"Kevin's going to see if he can spot him on any of the downtown security cameras," Horace said.

"So what did you do with him when you found him?" I asked.

"Let the chief know," Vern said. "And the chief was already on his way home and said morning would be soon enough to talk to him, so I dropped him off at your mother and dad's farm, with orders to stay put until I came to pick him up this morning."

"The chief didn't trust him to come in under his own steam?" I asked.

"He doesn't have a car," Vern said. "Lives in downtown Richmond and just Ubers everywhere."

"The poor guy," I said. "So he's been stuck out here in the country with no way to get anywhere. If I'd known that I'd have suggested finding him someplace closer to town."

"He doesn't seem to mind," Vern said. "Says it's real peaceful there at the farm. Been spending his time hanging out in the pasture with the sheep, reading a book. Your daddy's livestock dogs seem to have taken quite a shine to him—they came running up to lick his face when he got out of my patrol car."

Horace nodded, and I wondered if he was thinking the same thing I was—that dogs were good judges of character. Especially livestock guardian dogs like Nigel and Sebastian, the Great Pyrenees Dad had recently adopted to watch over his heirloom-breed cows and sheep. It was the dogs' job to deal with predators, whether two- or four-legged. As Dad was fond of remarking, they had good radar for bad eggs. I made a mental note to ask Mother what the dogs thought of Blaine.

Vern started chuckling.

"What's funny?" Horace asked.

"Mrs. Langslow and some of her ladies were having hot chocolate and cookies when we got to the farm," he said. "Insisted on serving me a cup and a slice of cake, which was kind of them, 'cause it was pretty obvious that they were all dog-tired and ready for bed. And when I got up to go, I reminded Harry that I'd be by in the morning to take him down to see the chief. And I warned him not to leave town—kind of joking, like, because we'd already discussed the fact that he didn't even have a vehicle. And he said there was no chance of that—if he ran off, Emily would hunt him down and drag him back by the . . . hair. I had a feeling he was about to say something a little saltier and changed course when he remembered there were ladies present. And he blushed as if maybe they could guess what he hadn't even said."

Horace and I laughed at that. Yes, I had a hard time imagining Harry saying anything off-color in front of women. Maybe I'd check with Rose Noire and see what she thought of Harry. Although I'd bet anything she'd have complimentary things to say about his aura. I had a hard time myself, seeing him as a suspect.

I turned the idea around in my head. Could Harry possibly be the killer? If Austin had done something truly awful, I could maybe—just maybe—see Harry taking action against Austin. Or, more likely, if Austin was threatening or planning something nasty. Harry as knight errant? Maybe. Even that was a stretch. Harry registering a stern and well-articulated formal protest with the proper authorities sounded more likely.

"And sorry," Vern said. "I guess no one told you he'd been found. Hope you weren't too worried."

"I wasn't really worried," I said. "Mother already told me he was back. I just hadn't heard how he'd been found."

"Horace," Vern said. "I need to head over to search the graveyard—can I turn all this back over to you?"

He waved his arm to indicate all the brown paper evidence bags.

"No problem," Horace said.

Vern seemed relieved to have handed all the brown paper bags back to Horace. Horace, on the other hand, seemed pleased to be reunited with his evidence. He fingered some of the bags, shifting a few of them slightly so they lay in pleasingly even rows and columns.

"While you're searching," I said, "keep your eyes open for glitter."

"Glitter?"

"You know, those little bits of shiny gold and silver—"

"I know what glitter is." Vern sounded amused. "Just not sure why I should be looking for it in the graveyard. Unless the vandals have escalated to glitter bombs."

I explained about the trails of glitter we'd found over at Rob and Delaney's.

"Yeah, I guess if someone stole the angels and then shot Luckett, there'd be some glitter in the graveyard, too. I'll keep my eyes open."

He nodded to us and strode out, passing Rose Noire on her way in.

Chapter 27

"Oh, dear," Rose Noire said. "The chief's still using the dining room, and Delaney's about to send over the first batch of bridesmaids for breakfast."

"More like brunch," Horace said. "It's a little past noon, you know. I should be taking all this down to the station anyway. Meg, you don't happen to have any cardboard boxes you could spare, do you?"

"Are you kidding?" I said. "This close to Christmas, with all the online shopping everyone in the household has been doing? We're drowning in boxes. I'd love for you to thin the herd. Let me fetch you a few."

"Two or three decent-sized ones will do." He was still rearranging his evidence bags—evidently, however Vern had organized them didn't meet with his approval.

I went down into the basement. On my way to the storage area where we stashed boxes, I passed by Kevin's lair. He was staring at one of his dozen monitors, which appeared to be showing a still picture of our backyard.

No, evidently he was fast-forwarding through a video of our backyard. It just looked like a still picture until Skulk, the larger of our two feral barn cats, raced across the screen in comically sped-up motion. I'd never seen him move that fast—not even in pursuit of a fat, juicy rodent.

Kevin smiled briefly at the sight, then returned to scowling at the screen.

"Not finding anything useful?" I asked.

"Not as much as I'd like," he said. "Which one is this?"

He paused the surveillance video and called up a picture on another nearby monitor.

"That's Emily," I said. "One of the brides."

"The one who's staying with Delaney and Rob?"

"Yes," I said. "Why?"

"Any idea why she and one of her buddies would be spending more than two hours over here last night when her hen party was supposed to be going full steam?"

"No idea at all," I said. "When was this?"

He glanced down at a notepad on his desk.

"Between nine forty-seven and three minutes past midnight."

"Are you sure she was over here?" I asked. "Because we're pretty sure she was over at Trinity sometime last night, stealing some of the Christmas decorations."

"That could be it," he said. "Five or six of them raced over here and got into some kind of argument with the ones in the library. Most of them went back about half an hour later, through the backyard, but I can't pick up Emily and her sidekick leaving that way until midnight. I just thought they were up to some kind of mischief here."

"For someone who's been trying to avoid having any interaction with the visiting bridesmaids, you've certainly managed a pretty accurate assessment of their character," I said. "So if they went out our front door and took off for town from there, the Bestitched RV would have kept your cameras from seeing them. That could explain a lot."

"Not necessarily," he said. "My camera covering the other side of the house was working just fine. If they took off from here for town, how come I didn't see them going back to Rob and Delaney's for a car?"

I reminded myself that Kevin didn't get out much.

"Because the county is redoing the drainage ditches along that part of the road," I said. "They started down by Caerphilly Creek, and they got to the part in front of Rob and Delaney's before they knocked off for their Christmas break. Between the heavy equipment, the piles of building supplies, and the mud, there's not really any place you'd want to park down there. So unless they got one of the few spaces in Rob and Delaney's driveway, they'd probably have parked here."

"Okay, that explains it," he said. "So yeah, anyone who was here would have no problem sneaking off to town. I'll let the chief know that he's going to want me to check the location history on pretty much everyone's phones. See who might have gone rogue at a suspicious time."

"Yeah," I said. "Of course, it might cast suspicion on someone if her phone shows her going downtown last night at a time when she claims to have been partying. But it won't clear anyone whose phone stayed here. It could just mean that she was smart enough to leave it behind if she went to town for some nefarious purpose."

"I have a hard time imagining any of them voluntarily leaving her phone behind, but you never know. And that would suggest premeditation, wouldn't it?"

"As would the fact that the killer showed up with a gun," I said.

"Yeah." Kevin looked bleak. "Take the gun, leave the phone behind—suspicious."

Then he grinned slightly and I knew what was coming.

"'Leave the gun. Take the cannoli,'" we recited in unison. Kevin was fond of quoting that line from *The Godfather*. Our shared laugh cleared away the down mood I was starting to feel.

"I'm glad the chief's the one who has to sort all this out." He turned back to his monitor and started fast-forwarding through surveillance video again.

I went to the storage room, selected four medium-sized boxes in good shape, and took them upstairs to Horace.

I helped Horace carry his boxes out to his cruiser. And while I was out by the road, I took out my roster of the two bridal parties. I'd made them all give me the makes, models, and license plates of their cars, mainly so I could pass the information along to Ekaterina and reduce the likelihood that any of them would get towed if they parked in places that weren't valid parking spots. I did a quick check and yes, several of Team Emily had parked their cars here.

When I returned to the kitchen, the chief was there, nibbling on a fresh cinnamon roll and talking to Rose Noire.

"Don't tell Nikki that her van caused problems," Rose Noire was saying. "She'd be mortified."

"Not her fault," I pointed out. "She parked where we told her to."

"Yes," the chief said. "But you can see why I'd be interested in knowing if any of your guests noticed anything last night."

"Of course," she said.

The back door slammed open and three bedraggled young women marched in. One of them was Emily.

"What the hell is going on here?" Emily demanded. She scowled at me and Horace, and then turned to the chief. "I don't appreciate being interrupted when I'm trying to get my beauty sleep."

Not the way I'd start a conversation with a police officer. And not just any police officer, but the chief of police. Who was also the county's elected sheriff. And conducting a murder investigation. But maybe Emily didn't realize any of that.

Or maybe she was one of those people who think a good offense is the best defense. And I could absolutely see her acting defensively if she knew she was guilty of something.

But was she guilty only of theft? Or also murder?

"This is Emily," I said. "Emily Winningham. And . . . two of her bridesmaids."

I probably wouldn't have been able to identify the two bridesmaids under ordinary circumstances. Now, dressed in sweats and jeans, with their hair askew and smeared mascara giving them raccoon eyes, I wasn't sure even their mothers could recognize them.

"Good morning, Ms. Winningham," the chief said. "I'm sorry that you have been inconvenienced, but I'm afraid I need to interview you and your friends."

"What do you mean, interview us?" Emily snapped. "What are—"

"Mr. Austin Luckett, your wedding photographer, has been murdered," the chief said. "And I need to talk to everyone who interacted with him yesterday."

Emily's mouth fell so far open I could have counted her fillings. One of the bridesmaids uttered a small squeak and half fell into a kitchen chair. The other looked over her shoulder at the back door as if thinking of making a run for it.

"If you ladies don't mind," the chief said to the bridesmaids, "I'll start with Ms. Winningham."

The chief held the door to the hall open for Emily. After a long pause—so long that I was beginning to wonder if she'd come up with some excuse for refusing to talk to him—she pulled herself up to her full height and strode out of the kitchen. The chief followed her.

The two bridesmaids looked uneasy.

"Sit down," Rose Noire said. "I'm fixing avocado toast."

The bridesmaids followed orders. I looked at Rose Noire with puzzlement. Avocado toast wasn't a regular feature of her cooking repertoire. Or if it was, I'd probably ignored it, since I intensely disliked avocado. And it wasn't as if these two were in good shape to enjoy what I considered a snooty gourmet delicacy.

Evidently Rose noticed my surprise.

"Avocados are high in potassium," she said. "Much like bananas. And toast has carbohydrates. Both good for helping someone recover from a hangover. And they need to rehydrate and replace their electrolytes—I've got some coconut water and Gatorades in the refrigerator. Put those on the table. And bring out the fruit salad and the yogurts. All full of nutrients that should help them feel better."

"Where were you the last time I had a hangover?" I asked, as I opened the fridge.

"Probably in middle school," she said. "You've always been a very sensible drinker."

I didn't try to refuse the compliment. I got the bridesmaids started on Gatorades and yogurts. It seemed to help. Or maybe just having someone fuss over them did.

"You think Emily is going to tell the police about Jenna?" one of them said to the other.

The other bridesmaid shrugged, her eyes on the plate of avocado toast Rose Noire had just set on the table.

"What about Jenna?" I asked.

The first bridesmaid tried to feign reluctance, but she didn't have the patience for it.

"She sneaked out of the party," she said, after a truly minimal hesitation. "For an hour."

"More than an hour," the second bridesmaid said, through a mouthful of toast. "Almost two."

"And she pretended she'd just gone to the bathroom," the first bridesmaid said. "Which was a lie. I saw her sneaking out the back door."

"Do you know where she went?"

They both shook their heads.

"I told her I knew she was lying about going to the bathroom," the first bridesmaid said. "Because I saw her sneak out the back door. And she said yeah, she went outside for a minute to make a private phone call, but then she came back inside and went to the bathroom. And when I told her I'd looked in the bathrooms, she said I couldn't possibly have, or I'd have found her."

"She might be telling the truth," the other bridesmaid said. "There are a lot of bathrooms. At least the house has that going for it."

Her tone suggested that she wasn't impressed with Rob and Delaney's house. I thought the renovations they'd been doing to their large, hundred-year-old farmhouse were excellent—a judicious mix of respect for tradition and appreciation for modern convenience. If the bridesmaid thought otherwise, I could only hope she'd kept her criticisms to herself in front of Delaney.

I'd worry about that later. I left the bridesmaids to Rose Noire's ministrations. Under the combined influence of her nonjudgmental sympathy and her well-researched hangover recovery breakfast, they were starting to perk up.

I went out to the living room and called Delaney.

Chapter 28

"The sleepers awake," Delaney said, by way of greeting. "I even sent a couple of them over for Rose Noire to feed, because I'm not sure I could resist the temptation to poison the wretches."

"They arrived," I said. "Do you still have one named Jenna over there?"

"Probably," she said. "I sent three over and I've got five left. What do you need her for?"

"I don't, but the chief does. Can you bring her over?"

"Bring? Not send?"

"We don't want her disappearing before the chief gets to talk to her." I gave her a brief rundown of what the two bridesmaids had revealed.

"Damn. I hope Jenna's not the killer. She's one of the nicer ones. I've actually heard her utter the words 'thank you.' And she didn't want to be here in the first place, you know."

"She told you that?" Interesting. "Did she explain why?"

"She and Blaine, Lexy's groom, used to be an item," Delaney said. "And she didn't know about the two weddings happening at the same time when she accepted Emily's invitation to be a bridesmaid."

"I'd have found an excuse to bow out if I were her," I said.

"You and me both. I think she tried, but Emily guilt-tripped her about what a hassle it would be if she withdrew, so she's sticking it out. Not having a very good time, though, poor thing. I get the idea she bowed out of last night's festivities pretty early on, so she's probably less hungover than the rest of them. I'll deliver her as soon as I can."

I hung up and headed back for the kitchen. But as I was passing the doorway to the dining room, I heard wailing inside. The door opened and the chief stepped out.

"Meg," he said. "You've got quite a few attorneys in your family. Are any of them here for the wedding?"

"Probably," I said. "I could ask Mother. And there's always Festus." My cousin Festus Hollingsworth specialized in fighting corrupt corporations, foiling environmental malefactors, and overturning unjust convictions, but he was always willing to step in and help out family members in a pinch. And although he traveled extensively for his cases, he loved Christmas, so I knew this close to the holiday he'd be home on his farm on the other side of the county, looking forward to the town and family celebrations. "I gather Emily will need an attorney?"

"I'm having her taken down to the station, where I'll be charging her with destruction of property," he said. "And since she denies going near the church and refuses to say anything else without a lawyer—"

"I'll call Festus and then Mother," I said. "We'll send someone over to the station as soon as we can. But before you take her away, we have someone else you might want to talk to. In case she also needs to go downtown with you."

He reached behind him and closed the dining-room door.

"One of the young ladies Rose Noire is presently feeding?" he asked.

"No," I said. "But they told me one of their number sneaked out of Rob and Delaney's game room for nearly two hours last night. They're kind of vague on the time, so I have no idea if her absence overlaps when the murder happened—"

"Where is she?"

"I'm having Delaney bring her over," I said. "On the pretext that Rose Noire's breakfast—correction, brunch—will help her hangover."

"Good," he said. "Her name?"

"Jenna." I pulled out my phone and opened up my list of wedding party members. "Jenna McCracken."

"I've already called Vern in to escort Ms. Winningham down to the station," he said. "I'd do it myself, but I had to have Osgood Shiffley tow my cruiser to his repair shop this morning and I'm driving Cal's car. And while it's nice of him to lend his wheels to his grandpa, I can't very well haul prisoners around in it."

"Since I assume it doesn't have that protective barrier between the front and rear seats," I said. "And even though Emily doesn't look like much of a threat—"

"Doesn't even have rear seats," he said. "It's that vintage Miata he's been restoring. Keep your fingers crossed that he's finally got the engine running reliably."

"Yikes," I said.

"And let me know when Ms. McCracken has arrived." He started toward the dining room, then turned around. "Any chance you could bring me a box of tissues? I should have found one before I started interviewing Ms. Winningham."

"Coming up," I said.

I went back to the kitchen and snagged a box of tissues from the pantry. And then I decided that under the circumstances, we could use a few more strategically placed boxes, so I grabbed two more. When I emerged with them, I saw Delaney coming through the back door, escorting three more of Emily's bridesmaids. The two of Lexy's who had just arrived, seeing they were outnumbered, scowled and took places as far as possible from Emily's pack.

"Morning," Delaney said. "Jenna, Kailee, and Andrea could use some of Rose Noire's hangover-curing breakfast."

She pointed to them as she named them. Jenna was the slender, pretty brunette I remembered as the nice one—the one who'd helped us clean up the front hall. She shed her coat to reveal jeans and a baggy black-and-gold sweatshirt from Virginia Commonwealth University. She didn't look nearly as miserable as the other bridesmaids. Was that because while the rest of them had spent the whole night carousing, she'd sneaked into town and killed Austin? I hoped not.

"I told them about what happened to Austin," Delaney said. "I hope that was okay."

"It's fine," I said. "And Chief Burke wants to interview each of you," I added, turning to the bridesmaids. "It's routine, you know," I hurried to explain, seeing the alarm on their faces. "When did you last see the deceased, and do you know anyone who might have it in for him and stuff like that. He wants to start with . . . let's see." I pulled out my phone and pretended to be studying a list. "Jenna. Would you like to get it over with?"

Six of the seven other bridesmaids present pointed at her. The seventh might have, except that she was holding a Gatorade in one hand and a slice of avocado toast in the other, but her eyes shot over to Jenna.

"That's me," Jenna said.

"Chief's in the dining room." I handed Rose Noire one of the tissue boxes, in case any of the bridesmaids grew weepy, and turned to the door. "I'll show you the way."

I led Jenna to the dining-room door and knocked. When the chief opened it, I handed him a box of tissues.

"Are you ready for your next witness?" I asked. "This is Jenna."

"Yes, thank you. Could you keep Ms. Winningham company while we're waiting for transportation?"

Translation: don't let Emily go anywhere.

"Of course," I said. "Come on, Emily. Let's sit here in the living room where you can have some privacy."

Emily followed me obediently and sat on one of the sofas, at the end closest to the fire. She seemed to be shivering.

I poked up the fire, then pulled out my phone and called Festus.

"Afternoon, Meg," he said. "I hear you had some excitement last night."

"We did," I said. "And we have a cousin who needs an attorney."

"Uh-oh," he said. "You mean one of them did it?"

"I'm sitting here with Cousin Emily," I said, and followed that up with the customary brief but specific explanation of where she fit into the family tree. "She is under suspicion of breaking into Trinity last night and stealing some of the decorations."

At this point Emily broke down in tears. I shoved the final box of tissues in her direction.

"Nothing to do with the murder?" he said.

"That I don't know," I said. "The chief is taking her down to the station in a few minutes. Any chance you could either meet her there or round up someone else who can? Mother can fill you in on whether any of the other family lawyers are in town for the weddings."

"Sure thing," he said. "I'll head down there now. Have your mother call me if there's anyone else who can pitch in."

"Will do."

I hesitated, wondering if I should call Mother now or wait until Emily wasn't there, so I could vent with a clear conscience. I glanced over at Emily.

"I didn't do anything," she said.

"The angels found their way over to Delaney and Rob's trash can all by themselves?"

"Oh, I did that," she said. "I know it was stupid, but I'd had a couple of drinks and I wasn't really thinking straight and I talked Kelsey into going with me. And if there had been any cars in the parking lot or lights in the church, I think we'd have given it up. But there wasn't anything."

"And you didn't see anything in the graveyard?"

"We didn't go anywhere near the graveyard!" She shuddered. "We parked on the other side of the parking lot and went down to the other side of the church. We tried all the windows and doors, and if they'd left any of them open, we wouldn't have had to break the window."

I thought of remarking that it was a little much, blaming Trinity's good security for her destruction of property. But I wanted her to keep talking. So I shot off a quick text to Mother, saying "We may have a family member in need of a defense attorney. Call Festus for details." Then I turned back to Emily.

"What time was this?" I asked.

"No idea." She pouted. "They're going to try to figure it out from my phone. They can do that, you know."

I nodded.

"Drives me crazy, not having my phone," she said. "I keep thinking of things I need to do with it. It's like being blind."

I understood how she felt, but I found I didn't feel much sympathy. "If you can't do the time, don't do the crime" popped into my head, but I didn't say it aloud.

"They'll be able to figure out that I didn't do it, right?" she asked. "That I had nothing to do with killing that man."

I nodded.

The doorbell rang. When I opened the door, Vern and Horace were both standing on the front porch.

Chapter 29

"Come in," I said, stepping back to give them room. "But isn't this a bit of overkill? I think Emily will probably go quietly."

"Might need to ferry a few more people down there before we're done," Vern said. "For fingerprinting if nothing else."

"I was already on my way to the station with my evidence," Horace said, his tone a little fretful. "A good thing I was able to fit it all into the trunk."

I nodded.

Emily had stood up when she saw them. Now she plucked half a dozen tissues from the box, then came out to the coatrack and claimed her wraps. Vern helped her into her coat and escorted her outside.

"You think she did it?" Horace asked, as soon as the door was closed.

"The break-in at Trinity, yes," I said. "The murder, no idea."

"I'm betting not the murder," he said. "We got tons of really clear, useful fingerprints at the break-in site. On the window, and some of the big glass shards that they probably had to pick out of the frame, and the ladder they used to get up to the decorations. And no useful fingerprints whatsoever on the other side of the church, where the murder happened. I'm thinking if whoever killed Luckett also did the break-in, they'd have been a lot more careful about fingerprints. Done what they could to avoid leaving any fingerprints anywhere at the church."

"Sounds logical," I said. "By the sound of it, breaking in and stealing the angels was a drunken stunt, so I'm not sure they were in any shape to be careful about anything. They're lucky they didn't get pulled over for a DUI on the way back."

"They?" he echoed. "Does that mean she had accomplices?"

"Probably one accomplice," I said. "A bridesmaid named Kelsey."

"That's helpful," Horace said. "We got a lot of really clear prints, and I'm almost positive there's more than one set. Can you point out this Kelsey?"

"I haven't learned their names," I said. "But I bet Rose Noire has. And can tell from their auras if we should suspect any of them."

"I'll settle for fingerprints," he said. "Since I doubt if an evil aura would be admissible in court. Any idea where this Kelsey would be?"

"She may be in the kitchen eating avocado toast," I said. "And if not, we can have Delaney bring her over."

"Good idea."

So I called Delaney. I started off with an apology for bothering her again.

"No need to apologize," she said. "The murder investigation is *so* much more interesting than the weddings."

Not a surprising reaction—Delaney and Rob hadn't wanted to disappoint their mothers by eloping, as Michael and I had, but they'd made it perfectly clear that within reason, the mothers could plan whatever they liked, as long as all Rob and Delaney had to do was show up. And she seemed not just willing but enthusiastic about helping round up the chief's interview subjects.

"I have no idea which one Kelsey is," she said, "but I'll herd the rest of them over as soon as possible. We don't want to keep Rose Noire catering for those wretched young women all day."

And within fifteen minutes, all seven of Emily's bridesmaids were crowded around our kitchen table, along with Lexy and three of hers. Kelsey was Emily's maid of honor, a freckled redhead who seemed more alert than most of the others, which made sense if she'd taken an hour or two break from partying to burgle the church. We sent her in to see the chief next.

Delaney stayed around to help, taking some of the cooking burden from Rose Noire, and the three of us did our best to keep the bridesmaids pacified while the chief called them in one by one to be interviewed. Rose Noire's hangover-cure breakfast did seem to perk them up a bit, and I doled out aspirin, Tylenol, or Excedrin as requested. But most of them didn't stick around long after they'd been interviewed.

"Do you have anything exciting planned for today?" I asked, when there were only three of them left.

"Emily didn't plan anything until this evening," one of her bridesmaids said. "She figured we'd need some recovery time."

"Lexy was going to treat us to a day of beauty," one of her team reported. "But I think she canceled it this morning."

"Not a big loss," Emily's bridesmaid retorted. "A day of beauty is one thing at a fancy spa. But at a beauty shop in a hick ... er, small town?"

I could tell Lexy's bridesmaid was groping for a suitably stinging retort, but eventually gave up and returned to her Gatorade.

I was relieved when the last of them returned from her interview and slipped away to her room. I stopped by the dining room to see if the chief needed anything.

"I don't suppose you could require all the young ladies to wear name tags," he said. "Sixteen of them, all skinny, all but two or three blond—did your cousins order up these bridesmaids from Central Casting?"

"It's not unheard of for brides to pick bridesmaids based on how they'll look in the photos," I said.

He nodded.

For that matter, I wondered if Lexy and Emily picked their circle of friends based on how they'd look on social media. I'd glanced at their social media a time or two, and saw nothing but pretty young people, fashionably dressed and in fashionable locales.

"You're probably hoping to get the use of your dining room back." He stood, picked up his notebook, and went out into the hall.

"Are you heading back to the station to interview Emily and Jenna?" I asked, as I helped him find his coat and hat. It surprised me that he'd spent so long interviewing the rest of the bridesmaids if those two were waiting downtown for him.

"Jenna, maybe," he said. "Emily's being arraigned for the break-in at Trinity, and will probably be out on bail in a few hours."

"That's good," I said. "Well, actually it's not great, but at least she's not going to be sitting in jail on her wedding day."

"And good that Robyn is determined to press charges," the chief said. "I was afraid she wouldn't be, but I suppose she felt the culprit needed to learn a lesson. Anyway, I'll need to talk to Emily again, but I think I'll wait until she's been through the system for the break-in. See if that makes her a little more cooperative."

"You could always take her down to the scene of the crime and interview her there," I suggested. "Evidently she's superstitious about graveyards—we could barely coax her to walk past the one at Trinity."

"Now there's a thought," he said, as he went out the front door.

I followed along.

"Is there anything we should be doing?" I asked. "Like letting you know if any of the bridesmaids show signs of packing up to leave?"

"Definitely give us a heads-up if that happens," he said.

Outside I was relieved to see that Bestitched's mobile dressmaking shop was now parked down by the barn. If only I'd thought to set them up down there in the first place, because this was definitely a case of shutting the proverbial barn door after all the horses were long gone. I hoped the new location wasn't inconvenient for Nikki and the ladies. If it was, we could move them back. After all, with any number of police coming and going from the house, the odds were that the security cameras weren't mission critical at the moment. And if—make that when—the snow started, it might be a good idea to have them closer to the house.

Then I noticed an unfamiliar car parked where the RV had been. A new-looking white Toyota Corolla. A man was leaning against it with his back to us, looking at Austin's van. He was muffled up against the cold, so all I could tell was that he was tallish and Caucasian.

"Rental car," the chief said in an undertone. "You expecting company?"

"Lots of it for the weddings, but that's still a day or two off," I said, keeping my tone low. And deciding to ask later how he knew it was a rental car, and why it mattered. "Could be one of the groomsmen. They're arriving earlier than the rank-and-file guests, and I haven't met them all yet. How about if I play hostess and see who he is?"

He nodded. I could tell he was watching closely as I strolled over to the new arrival. The man looked up and frowned when I approached.

"Can I help you?" I asked.

"No, I'm fine," he said. "Just waiting for him to come back."

He jerked his head to indicate the van.

"I'm afraid you're in for a long wait," I said.

"No problem," he said. "I can be patient."

I was tempted to say that I wasn't so patient, especially with strangers I found loitering suspiciously on private property, but I looked back at the chief. He stepped forward.

"Was there anything in particular you wanted to see Mr. Luckett about?" he asked.

"Yeah." The man laughed sardonically. "You could say that. He's holding me over a barrel, refusing to give me the rest of the pictures from my wedding."

The chief and I exchanged a glance. It suddenly occurred to me that this might be the disgruntled customer who'd been repeatedly calling Austin and Maddie. And also that since the chief was driving his grandson's sporty red Miata and wearing a heavy down jacket over his uniform, our new arrival would have no idea that he was talking to a cop.

"You must be Mr. Random Wilson," the chief said.

"Yeah. What about it?" Wilson sounded defensive.

"I'm Chief Burke from the Caerphilly Police Department," the chief began.

"That jerk," Wilson muttered. "Has Luckett filed a complaint about me? Can I file a countercomplaint?"

"Mr. Luckett is deceased," the chief said.

"Deceased?" Wilson looked puzzled. "How? He seemed fine yesterday."

"We're investigating it as a homicide," the chief said. "May I—"

"Oh, no," Wilson said. "I can see what you're up to. You can't blame it on me. Whatever happened to him, I had nothing to do with it."

"Then I won't need to take much of your time," the chief said. "But I'd like to talk to you. If you wouldn't mind—"

"Now we won't ever get our photos, will we?" Wilson said.

"I'm afraid I can't answer that," the chief replied. "If you wouldn't mind—"

"I told you, I had nothing to do with it," Wilson repeated. "But I bet I know who did. You know that crazy assistant of his?"

"I've talked to Ms. Brown," the chief said.

"I figured out Luckett was staying here, so I was kind of staking out the place last night," Wilson said. "Pretending to be one of the crazy tourists going all paparazzi on the sheep for a while, and then when they cleared out I just found a place where I could keep an eye on the house without being too obvious about it. And she drives up like a bat out of hell, gets out, and starts slashing the tires."

"And you didn't report this?" the chief asked.

"Didn't want to get mixed up in anything." Wilson shrugged.

"Interesting," the chief said. "Since Ms. Brown reported that you had made multiple threats to her and Mr. Luckett, and suggested we investigate whether you slashed the tires."

"Yeah." Wilson gave a humorless snort that was probably supposed to be a laugh. "I figured maybe she'd try to blame me. So I took this."

He pulled his phone out of his pants pocket, turned it on, and tapped on the screen a couple of times. Then he held it up with the screen turned our way. The chief and I both moved to get a closer view.

It was Maddie Brown all right. She had a blade of some sort—was it a box cutter? And she was slashing the van's tires with it.

Tears were running down her face, which was contorted with—was it anger? No, more like fear. Even panic.

We watched as she attacked the two rear tires. I gathered that she'd already done the front two by the time Wilson had started taking the video. She stood up and panted for a few moments. Then she took the box cutter and wiped the handle off on her scarf—ten, twenty, several dozen times, with tears streaming down her face all the while. Then she flung it in the direction of Seth Early's sheep pasture. She had a good arm—it cleared the fence.

I saw the chief's eyes flick in that direction, and suspected before long a deputy would be out among the sheep with a metal detector.

"What time was this?" he asked.

"I don't know," Wilson said. "Eleven thirty or midnight. You can probably figure it out from the video."

"If you would be so kind as to forward it to me."

The chief carefully recited his official police email and Wilson tapped on his phone. After a bit of a pause, the chief nodded, which I assume meant that the video had arrived.

"And as I said, it would be very helpful if you could come down to the station with me," the chief said. "I'd like a statement to go with this video, and you may be able to shed some light on last night's events."

I could see the man's face set in a stubborn expression.

"Remember," I said, "with Luckett dead, the chief's the person who's most apt to be able to get you those photos you're looking for. Besides, I gather you're not the only customer he's done that to."

"Precisely," the chief said. "I already have an officer down in Richmond going through Mr. Luckett's files to get a complete list of his customers, along with any emails or letters of complaint. I'd like to understand why so many people are angry at him, so it would help if you could take me through how the dispute between you and Mr. Luckett arose."

"But I bet you're gonna ask for my whereabouts at whatever time Luckett got wasted," Wilson said. "Because I know damn well I'm not the only one he's done this to, but I'm the only one here."

"That we know of," the chief said. "Until we know who those other unhappy customers are, we have no way of determining whether any of them are also here."

That seemed to reassure Wilson a little.

"I've heard that there are others," he said. "But I don't know who they are. Never met any of them."

Why did those words make me think, just for a moment, that he was lying? Covering up the existence of a vast conspiracy of disgruntled brides and grooms, plotting together to exact revenge on Austin for holding their wedding photos hostage? Perhaps Dad's fascination with mystery books—and their sometimes fantastical plots—was having an effect on me.

"If it would be convenient," the chief continued, "I'd appreciate it if you could come down to the station. Or I'd be happy to give you a ride down there and back."

"I'll go under my own steam," Wilson said. "That way I won't have to come all the way back here when we're finished."

"That's fine," the chief said.

Wilson got into his car and drove off.

Chapter 30

"I guess he must be pretty confident that his interview with you won't end up with him being arrested," I said. "But aren't you afraid he'll bolt? Drive straight through town and across the county line and back to wherever he comes from?"

The chief smiled.

"Richmond," he said. "And no."

He was already holding his phone. Now he made a call.

"Sammy," he said. "Were you heading out here to the Waterstons? . . . Good. Where are you? . . . Uh-huh. Turn around, pull over, and keep your eye out for a white Toyota Corolla heading into town. Rental vehicle. The driver is supposed to meet me at the station for an interview." He rattled off the license plate number, which was impressive, since he hadn't had his notebook out and must have memorized it. "When you spot him, follow him to the station and get him set up in an interview room. And if he seems to be heading anywhere other than the station, pull him over and bring him in . . . Thank you."

He tucked his phone back in his pocket.

"Question answered," I said. "You're not that worried about him bolting."

"If he tries, it will be interesting to ask him why." His smile reminded me of how Lurk and Skulk, our barn cats, looked when they had a hapless mouse cornered. "We know where he lives and works. In the unlikely event that he does try to bolt and succeeds in evading Sammy, we'll get out a statewide BOLO on him and charge him with fleeing the scene of a crime and interfering with a police investigation and anything else the county attorney can think of. And it's not as if I want to take him downtown with me in that tin can of Cal's."

He frowned slightly at the bright red convertible.

"He's vastly proud of it," he said. "But compared with my cruiser, that thing feels as flimsy as tinfoil, and I don't think he's got the heater working all that well. Ah. Here comes Osgood Shiffley to transport the van. Good timing—if he'd gotten here any earlier, it might have chased Mr. Wilson away and delayed my being able to talk to him."

Osgood hopped out, waved to us, and began the process of loading the van onto a flatbed truck. The chief and I stood for a few minutes, in case he needed help, but he'd brought along a young Shiffley cousin and the two of them were making short work of the job.

"So," I said. "You'll be heading downtown to interrogate—sorry, interview Wilson? Not to mention Jenna."

"I think first I'd like to have another talk with Ms. Brown. She's staying here, isn't she?"

"She is," I said. "No idea if she's here now, but I can show you which room she's in. And if she's not here, Rose Noire might know where she's gone."

I led the way into the house and upstairs to the bedroom where Maddie was staying. I knocked on the door.

"Yes?" Maddie's voice.

"Shall I leave you to it?" I asked quietly.

"Perhaps not just yet," he said. "You might be able to serve as a . . . calming influence." He nodded toward the door.

"May we come in?" I called out.

A pause.

"Yeah, okay."

I opened the door. Maddie was sitting on the bed. She looked up and flinched visibly when she saw us. Make that when she saw the chief. It looked as if she'd been crying. And packing.

I glanced back at the chief, to make sure he'd seen the nearly filled suitcase open on the bed. And to ask if he wanted me to leave. He just nodded slightly, so I turned back to Maddie.

"Going somewhere?" I asked.

"I want to go home." I could see that tears were welling up in her eyes, and her mouth was trembling. "I just want to get away from here. And start looking for a new job."

Tears began running down her face. The chief took half a step back, and I deduced that maybe helping him deal with this was why he wanted me to stay. I stepped into the room, grabbed the box of tissues that was on the dresser, and sat down beside her on the bed.

"But don't you already have a job?" I plucked out a tissue and handed it to her. "Who's going to photograph the weddings if you go back to Richmond now?"

"You actually want me to do that?" She sounded incredulous.

"It's what you've been wanting to do, isn't it?" I asked. "Start your own wedding photography business. Well, congratulations. You're here, and you've got us over a barrel. Do you really think we're going to have much luck finding another photographer on this short notice?"

"Oh." She looked dazed. "I never thought of that."

I glanced at the chief, who was frowning slightly, probably

because this didn't seem to be going in the direction he wanted it to.

"Of course, before you can focus on that, I think the chief has a few questions he wants to ask you."

"Of course." She looked up, more expectant than anxious.

The chief nodded. He stepped in, reached over to pull out the tiny room's one chair, and sat down facing us.

"I'd like you to look at something," he said.

Maddie nodded. Her face had taken on an expression of eager helpfulness, as if talking to him was a minor hurdle between her and the start of her new profession.

The chief held up his phone and started the video of her slashing the van's tires. A few seconds into it, she burst into tears, whirled around, and buried her face in the pillow.

Maybe it was cold of me, but I let her cry. I just made sure she could reach the box of tissues.

"Ms. Brown," the chief said, "there seems to be a discrepancy between the statement you gave me last night and what's shown on this video. I'd like you to come down to the station with me to discuss this."

"I didn't do it," she wailed. She sat up and faced him. "I mean, yes, I slashed the tires, but I had nothing to do with killing him. I was supposed to meet Austin at the church to play gopher, but it took a while to get away from those horrible parties, and then when I took off from here I realized the van was running on fumes, so I went by the gas station, and all that made me really late for meeting him, and when I got to the church there were all these police cars and an ambulance and I overheard someone say that they weren't going to move the body yet, and I panicked. I just knew it was Austin, and I was afraid you'd blame me, so I came back here and I thought maybe if you thought someone had slashed the van tires you'd think I couldn't have gotten to town to do it so it couldn't be me. Because it wasn't! I swear it wasn't!"

She threw herself down on the bed again and buried her face in the pillow. When this was over, if she wasn't in jail, I was going to suggest that Michael recruit her to demonstrate her vocal technique to some of his acting students. I couldn't remember the last time I'd heard anyone manage so many words with so few breaths.

"Ms. Brown." The chief's voice was gentle but firm. "As I said, you need to come down to the station with me. You're going to have to make a new statement—a truthful one this time. And I'll be charging you with destruction of property and making a false statement to the police."

She continued sobbing, and I wasn't sure she'd heard him.

"Meg, can you arrange to have Festus or whatever other attorney your mother has found meet us down there?" he asked.

"Absolutely," I said. "Maddie, we'll get you a really good lawyer, but you need to come clean so we can bail you out in time to photograph the weddings. Can you do that for us?"

That seemed to improve her mood a little. She sat up and began wiping her eyes with a corner of the top sheet. I pulled it away from her and handed her the box of tissues. Just in time, since she used the tissues to blow her nose.

"Let me have your cell phone." The chief held out his hand. "We'll need to have our forensic phone expert check the location data to verify your revised statement."

Of course, Kevin would also be checking her emails and texts and whatever other evidence he could find. I was reassured by how willingly she handed over her phone—a not-very-new iPhone with a badly cracked screen. Her willingness probably meant that she wasn't worried about any guilty secrets it might hold.

"Could you ask Kevin to meet us downstairs to take custody of this?" the chief said, holding up Maddie's phone.

"Sure thing," I said.

So while the chief escorted Maddie downstairs, I called Kevin.

"Kind of busy," he said. Which was so typical of his method of answering the phone that I'd long ago given up even suggesting that he consider niceties like saying hello.

"Then I should tell the chief you don't have time for him to hand over the latest suspect's phone for forensic examination?"

"Where is he?"

"Waiting for you in the front hall."

"Be right up," he said. "Do you know what Great's doing here?"

"No idea," I said. "I thought he was out at the zoo feeding indigestible beetles to frogs and toads."

"Heard about that." He chuckled. "Right now he's out by the llama pen with a bunch of rugrats."

"I'll check it out."

I stayed long enough to lock up Maddie's room before heading downstairs. Kevin beat me there, and I caught only a quick glimpse of him vanishing into the kitchen with the phone. I paused long enough to shut and lock the door behind the chief and Maddie.

Then I went out to the kitchen where I could peer out the window to see what Grandfather was up to. He seemed to be giving a crowd of a dozen kids a lesson on llamas. Which was probably harmless, but I stayed where I could keep an eye on him while calling Mother.

"Morning, dear," she said. "Festus says he should be able to get Emily out on bail by this afternoon."

"That's good," I said. "Does he have time to take on Maddie Brown's case? Because the chief's about to take her downtown for booking."

Just then the doorbell rang, so I headed for the front hall.

"Oh, dear," Mother said. "I suppose it's a good thing your cousin Stephanie has agreed to come."

"That's the photographer?" I asked. "The one who's technically on maternity leave?"

"Yes," she said. "She's bringing her husband and the twins—can you possibly put them all up? Because even if they let Maddie out on bail, I'm not sure she'd be really focused on the weddings, and will they even give her bail on a murder charge?"

"The chief isn't charging her with murder," I said. "Not yet, anyway. She slashed the tires on Austin's van and lied to the chief about it. And yes, we can find rooms for Stephanie and her family."

I peered out the front door peephole and saw the chief and Maddie.

"Hang on a sec," I said to Mother, as I opened the door.

"Sorry," the chief said. "I don't have my cruiser, and I didn't realize all my officers had taken off. Vern's headed out here to transport Ms. Brown. In the meantime, may we—"

"Of course." I waved them in. The chief escorted Maddie into the living room. I headed back to the kitchen.

"I'm back," I said into the phone.

"Do we think she did it?"

I waited a few seconds until I'd closed the kitchen door behind me.

"The video looked pretty solid to me," I said.

"I meant the murder, dear."

My first impulse was to say, "Of course not." I liked Maddie, and I felt a lot of sympathy for her. Austin had treated her abominably.

But after seeing her slashing furiously at the van's tires . . . I could imagine her killing him. If she'd gotten mad enough. She'd alternated between anxiety and anger the whole time she'd been here. I'd assumed it was the kind of helpless anger that she turned inward, hurting only herself. But what if I was wrong? What if something Austin had done or said had been the proverbial last straw that made her lash out?

Of course, for that to happen, she'd have to have been carrying around the gun. I had a hard time seeing her as a gun owner. Unless she was one of those people who panicked at the very thought of leaving the big city and had armed herself to face the perils she thought she'd encounter in a county where sheep and cattle outnumbered humans.

"We'll have to let Festus figure that out," I said finally.

"And he's so closemouthed," Mother said with a sigh. "Well, I'll see you soon."

"Do we have something scheduled that I would have missed if not for the timely reminder you're about to give me?" I asked.

"No, dear," she said. "But the hats have arrived."

Chapter 31

Hats? This didn't ring a bell.

"What's this about hats?" I asked.

"The hats for Lexy's bridesmaids," she said. "Although don't use that word in front of her."

"That word 'hat'? Since when is that an unseemly term?"

"She prefers to call them 'fascinators.' Which is a type of hat—brimless, usually small, often very ornately decorated."

"You mean like those silly things you always see British women wearing at royal weddings?" I asked.

"Exactly. And Lexy is very . . . particular about what she considers the proper terminology. So unless you want to provoke her into another half-hour rant on the difference between a hat and a fascinator . . ."

"Thanks for the warning," I said. "See you soon."

I glanced out the window again to see what Grandfather was doing. He and his audience were all squatting down now, peering closely at the llamas' feet, so I deduced that he was explaining the difference between the hooves you saw on horses, cows, and sheep, and the llamas' unique two-toed feet. I could tell from his gestures that he was explaining how their foot structure made them more sure-footed on mountain trails while causing less damage to the environment than horses or mules.

I hoped he was being careful not to do anything that would annoy the llamas while his head was in such a perfect position for them to demonstrate the speed and power of their kick. But I knew better than to warn him—warnings only made him dig in his heels. If his last encounter with an irritated llama hadn't taught him anything, no use my nagging him. He was lucky his video crew were too loyal to share the footage of him covered in green llama spit, his forehead bleeding from the llama kick that had propelled him into a mound of llama dung.

Besides, I saw Nikki headed my way from the RV. She was carrying a large box. Mrs. Nguyen was following her, carrying a similar box, and Mrs. Giap, laden with what looked like a garment bag, brought up the rear.

I went to open up the door for them.

"Thanks," Nikki said. "And please tell me it's okay for us to have the bridesmaids try on the hats in here, because I predict they'll all want to do it at once, and there just isn't enough room in the RV."

"Use the living room," I said. "It should be big enough."

If Maddie and the chief were still there, I could suggest they move into the dining room. A pity the library was still a disaster area, or I could have sent them there and not had them underfoot for what I feared would be the lengthy process of trying on the hats.

The hats that we weren't supposed to be referring to as "hats."

"Aren't we supposed to be calling them 'fascinators'?" I asked, as I watched Nikki and the ladies settle in.

"Whoops!" Nikki exclaimed. "Good catch. No idea why she's so picky about that, but yeah."

"I can't wait to see them," I said. It wasn't exactly a lie. Morbid curiosity, maybe.

"Same here," Nikki said. "We didn't make them," she added, seeing my puzzled look. "She got them from some fancy millinery shop in New York City. Which was supposed to have used exactly the same colors as the dresses, but it's been making me a bit nervous, waiting till the last minute like this to put them together with the dresses."

The door to the dining room was closed, so evidently the chief had retreated there. I'd find out later if Maddie was still with him or if she was on her way downtown.

Mrs. Giap had carefully draped the garment bag she'd been carrying over one of our chairs and was opening it and taking out its contents—a slinky, one-shouldered minidress made of black lamé and trimmed with pale lavender marabou feathers. Normally I'd have at least tried to *ooh* and *ahh* over one of Bestitched's creations, but Nikki already knew what I thought about Lexy's design for her bridesmaid dresses—because it was absolutely Lexy's design. And it looked remarkably like a bad remake of "Solo in the Spotlight," one of the iconic outfits my childhood Barbie doll had worn. But "Solo in the Spotlight" had been elegant, its slinky floor-length black lamé skirt finished with a flounce of tulle and a red rose. These dresses . . .

"Not something we'll be featuring on our website anytime soon," Nikki said. "But we do what we can to keep the customer happy."

She shrugged and opened up the box she'd carried in. She lifted out a wad of tissue the size of those exercise balls trainers were always trying to get us to sit on when I took classes at the gym. She began unwinding the tissue—several miles of it, apparently—to reveal . . .

"Oh, my God," Nikki muttered.

"It looks like a slug," I said. "A black velvet slug wearing lavender marabou feathers."

Nikki and the ladies were silent, their glances darting back and forth between the hat—sorry, fascinator—and the dress.

"They did a great job of matching the colors," Nikki said finally.

Mrs. Nguyen nodded. Mrs. Giap brought the dress over and held it up beside the hat.

"Yes," I said. "A perfect match in every way."

"Oh, God," Nikki said. "What if they hate them? What if they refuse to wear them?"

"Then sic Lexy on them," I said. "Unless Lexy hates them, in which case it's between her and the milliner."

"And the milliner isn't here to take the heat," Nikki said. "If she's not happy, she'll take it out on us."

"Then tell her to call the milliner," I said. "You can probably look up the number before she gets here."

"No need to look it up," Nikki said. "It's right here on the packing list. And I already told Lexy to gather her bridesmaids to try on the hats. Bother."

"I think Mother was planning to come over and help." I pulled out my phone and dialed her. "Let me encourage her to hurry."

"It doesn't have to be a disaster if they hate them," Nikki said. "We could make a very nice substitute. We've got some of the lavender marabou left over. A little puff of that, with maybe a purple rhinestone as an accent."

"What's wrong, dear?" Mother said, instead of hello.

"Why do you think something's wrong?" I said. "But you're right. Lexy's fascinators have arrived and they're beyond hideous, and we're bracing ourselves to deal with her reaction. How soon will you get here? Because we could use your moral support."

"I'm already on my way," she said. "And you never know—if they're hideous, maybe she'll like them."

"Here's hoping," I said.

"And really—are they any more hideous than the dresses?"

"Definitely," I said.

"Oh, dear," she said. "Now I'm almost eager to see them. I'll be there in five minutes."

We ended the call.

Nikki and Mrs. Giap had put the fascinator on Mrs. Nguyen's head, and were fussing with it. Trying to adjust it into a flattering angle. If anyone could manage that, they could, but I wasn't optimistic.

But, curiously, I wasn't dreading the moment when Lexy and her minions saw the fascinators. I was rather looking forward to it. Was this the same impulse that makes most of us rubberneck when passing an accident?

No, I decided. It was the joy—yes, definitely joy—of having a problem to cope with that had nothing to do with the murder. Even though I knew the sight of Austin lying dead on that tombstone would fade over time, along with the fear and shock I felt at that moment, last night would never turn into a happy memory. The Incident of the Velvet Fascinators would. The next hour or two might be tense, stressful, and downright unpleasant. But when we looked at it in the rearview mirror of our family's shared memories, we'd be laughing.

We just had to get through the next hour or two without laughing out loud. Or uttering the unforgivable phrase "I told you so."

Just then Grandfather, surrounded by his class, came strolling in from the kitchen.

"There you are," he said. "Where's Rose Noire?"

I suspected she was still out in her herb shed, rehabilitating the damaged Barbie angels—not something I wanted him to interrupt.

"She's off performing a vital wedding-related task," I said. "Want me to give her a message when she gets back?"

He frowned.

"My zoo interns here have worked up an appetite. Any chance you could throw together a meal for us?"

"No," I said. "We're having a small crisis here. But you're welcome to help yourself—anything in the refrigerator is fair game." Since Michael and I knew that we and our guests would be keeping crazy schedules—and since we didn't want Rose Noire to get sucked into spending long hours at the stove every day, like an unpaid short-order cook—we'd made sure to lay in a good supply of foods that could be eaten cold or nuked in the microwave. "There's sandwich fixings—ham, turkey, roast beef, multiple kinds of bread and cheese—and several pre-made salads. Also a lot of chili and chicken soup and mac-and-cheese, and I'm sure Josh and Jamie can show anyone who doesn't already know how to work the microwave."

Jamie and Josh both gave that idea a thumbs-up, and led the rest of the small cousins back to the kitchen. Grandfather stayed. He perched on the arm of one of the sofas and cocked his head curiously as he studied the fascinators. Nikki had unwrapped several more, and all three of them were fussing with the hats, trying to find a flattering way to wear them.

"What are those things on their heads?" Grandfather asked.

"Hats," I said. Lexy wasn't here to correct me, and I wasn't in the mood for explaining to Grandfather what a fascinator was.

"Reminds me of what the orcas are doing in the Pacific Northwest," Grandfather said. "I've heard rumors that they've taken to wearing dead salmon on their heads again."

"Why?" I asked. "And what do you mean 'again'?"

"They were doing it for a while in the eighties," he said. "Someone spotted a young orca wearing a dead salmon like a hat, and before long it spread to several nearby orca pods. That's what you call a group of orcas, you know. And then the whole thing died out as mysteriously as it started, and until recently we haven't seen it for a couple of decades. And we have no idea why. They're very playful, orcas."

"Aren't orcas the ones who have started attacking fishermen's boats?" I asked.

"Yes," he said. "And luxury yachts. And throwing porpoises around like Frisbees. But they don't really mean any harm by it. It's usually immature male orcas playing a game."

"Tell that to the people whose boats they sink."

"And one scientist has come up with a very good theory about why they've started attacking boats," he went on. "He thinks they like the feel of the jet of water coming from a boat's propeller when it's on. So they come up to a stationary boat and bump it a few times as a subtle hint that they'd like the propeller turned on. And when nothing happens, they escalate, and sometimes it gets out of hand and they sink the boat."

"Sounds like wearing dead salmon hats would be an improvement over that," I said. "But don't mention that to any of the bridesmaids."

"Don't worry," he said. "I have no plans to talk to any of them."

"Then you might want to join your interns in the kitchen," I said. "Because we're expecting a whole pod of bridesmaids any second."

"Thanks for the warning." He heaved himself off the couch arm and strode away.

I wondered if I should have a word with Mother. Because now that Grandfather had put the image into my head, I could see that the shape of the fascinators wasn't all that different from what you'd see if you plopped dead fish down on the bridesmaids' heads.

And when I tried to drive that thought out of my head, the image that replaced it wasn't much of an improvement. I found myself imagining a group of juvenile delinquent orcas with contraband cigarettes in their mouths, catcalling at nearby female orcas.

And maybe swimming off armed with spray paint and Silly String to vandalize some poor fisherman's yacht before they sunk it.

If this was my brain on too little sleep, maybe it was time for a nap.

I snapped to attention when Lexy strolled in, accompanied by two of her bridesmaids.

Chapter 32

"I hear my fascinators have arrived!" Lexy exclaimed.

Maybe it was Grandfather and his orcas, but for some reason the way Lexy strode into the living room, with one bridesmaid flanking her and another trailing behind, tickled my visual memory. Had I seen that maneuver before . . . in one of Grandfather's wildlife documentaries?

No. The velociraptors in *Jurassic Park*. I recalled a scene where they heard a noise and all three turned in unison, with an eager, predatory expression.

I reminded myself not to confuse *Jurassic Park*'s special effects with reality—after all, according to Grandfather, they'd depicted velociraptors as being more than three times the size they were in real life. And I focused on being ready to rescue Nikki and the ladies if Lexy was disappointed in her fascinators.

And to our relief, Lexy didn't seem particularly disappointed in them.

"They don't quite look like the picture I gave the milliner," she remarked.

"Difference in materials," Nikki said smoothly. "The fascinators in your pictures were tulle and lace. Velvet and marabou have a more substantial feel."

"More suitable for winter, don't you think?" I added. "Tulle feels more like a light, spring material."

"Exactly," Lexy said. "More suitable for winter."

Nikki shot me a grateful look, and Mother, who had just arrived and was taking off her wraps in the front hall, beamed at me.

Mrs. Giap disappeared for a few minutes, returning accompanied by Josh and Jamie, who were each carrying a large floor-length mirror. They set them down under Nikki's instructions and then returned to what I deduced, from the sounds of merriment, was a festive if impromptu feast in the kitchen.

By now, all six of Lexy's bridesmaids plus the maid of honor had joined us in the living room, and were trying on their fascinators as fast as the ladies could unwrap them. None of them appeared to be squealing with delight, but neither were they showing the signs of rebellion I'd be displaying if one of my so-called friends seemed intent on making me appear in public wearing something that so closely resembled a dead salmon. Mother and Nikki were brilliant—the moment a bridesmaid, looking at herself in one of the mirrors, began showing signs of dismay, one of them would swoop over, make minute adjustments to the velvet lump, and then make small exclamations of faux delight. I couldn't quite manage that, but I did what I could to help by beaming cheerfully the whole time and responding with an energetic thumbs-up whenever called upon to give my verdict on the results.

To my relief, Mother seemed to be enjoying herself.

"So much more pleasant," she murmured to me at one point. "If I have to reassure Betty and Letty one more time that Caerphilly is perfectly capable of handling a few inches of snow . . ."

Lexy seemed content with the wretched hats. Then again,

there were only seven dead salmon fascinators. I didn't remember what she'd be wearing on her head, but I'd bet money that it was something a little more flattering.

I found myself speculating that perhaps "The Emperor's New Clothes" had been partly inspired by a similar experience. I seemed to remember that Hans Christian Andersen had never married, but that didn't mean he hadn't been dragooned into helping out with the nuptials of some friend or family member.

My brother, Rob, came through the front door while the trying-on process was underway. He took one look into the living room and quickly scuttled past us to the kitchen.

"Isn't anyone going to take any candids?" Lexy asked, when all seven of her friends had been crowned with fascinators. "I know Austin's out of the picture but where's that assistant of his?"

"Down at the police station, helping the police with their inquiries," I said.

Not being big readers of mystery books—in fact, probably not being big readers of anything other than bridal magazines—Lexy and her troop were probably unaware that, at least in books and movies, those were the words British police used when they thought they'd nabbed their culprit.

Mother simply smiled, nodded, and added, "And we have an additional photographer on the way, just in case. But we'll do our best with our phones. And of course, we can model the fascinators again for the photographer. Re-create the moment."

Nikki, who had been suppressing laughter, suddenly rushed out of the room, calling back that she'd left something in the RV.

I decided I was probably going to give way to laughter if I stayed much longer.

"Got to check on my kids," I said, and headed for the kitchen.

And just walking into the kitchen improved my mood enormously. The table was crowded with kids—Josh, Jamie, their friend Adam Burke, and eight or nine younger cousins. Grandfather was at the head of the table, telling tales about his adventures while rescuing wildlife. Rose Noire was at the stove, cooking doughnuts in a huge vat of hot oil. Rob was sitting at the foot of the table, eating an enormous ham sandwich and keeping an eye on what Rose Noire was up to.

"Meg, do you want some doughnuts?" Rose Noire called over her shoulder.

"Of course," I said. "If you have plenty."

"Let's let Mom have the next one," Josh said. "And after that she can take her turn in the list."

I glanced over to see that Jamie had a list of all those present—including Grandfather and Rob—with a series of check marks beside their names—presumably to indicate who had just received a doughnut and who had dibs on the next batch. Judging from the number of check marks, some of them must surely be nearing capacity by now.

I grabbed a folding chair and set it up in the nearest convenient space, which happened to be right by Rob.

"How do you suppose they keep them on their heads?" Rob was saying to Jamie.

"Hairpins," I said. "Lots and lots of hairpins."

"Very funny."

"No, seriously," I said. "Or they might also have little tiny combs sewn on the inside that catch the hair."

"What are you talking about?" Rob asked. "Orcas don't have hair."

Damn.

"Sorry," I said. "I didn't realize you were talking about orcas. I thought you were asking how Lexy's bridesmaids were keeping those silly little hats on their heads."

Rob looked at me for a few seconds with an odd expression on his face. Then he burst out laughing.

"Lexy will have a cow if she finds out you've been comparing her bridesmaids to killer whales."

"Yes," I said. "Which is why you are never, ever going to mention this conversation to anyone."

"What's it worth to you?"

"I'm serious," I said. "And see if you can get Grandfather to shut up about orcas. At least until Lexy and Emily and their mothers are all gone. Because they'll take it out on Mother, not me, and you don't want that happening."

Rob's face went sober.

"Are they . . . Is it just me, or are they being pretty nasty to Mother?"

"To Mother, and Rose Noire, and anyone else who comes into contact with them."

"Mom's right," Jamie said. "They're already being pretty mean to Grandma. We don't want to do anything else to upset them."

Just then Rose Noire came over with a plate that held two piping hot doughnuts in a bed of powdered sugar.

"Let them cool a bit first," she said.

"Thanks." And then, as she was turning back toward the stove, I thought of something. "How are the angels coming?"

"Very well," she said. "Delaney went into town to see if she could find some more glitter. As soon as she comes back with that, we should be able to finish up."

About the time I finished my second doughnut, Kevin stuck his head out of the basement door.

"Come have some doughnuts!" Jamie called out.

Kevin shook his head.

"It's Rose Noire's doughnuts," Josh added, although Kevin almost certainly knew that, since he could see our cousin at the stove.

"Too busy," he said.

"Want us to bring you some?" I asked.

His face brightened.

"Yeah. Thanks," he said, before disappearing into the basement again.

"He's doing a lot of work to help my granddad solve the murder," Adam said solemnly.

"He needs energy," Jamie said. "Let's let him have the next batch of doughnuts."

"Some of the next batch," Josh countered.

"Most of the next batch?" Adam suggested.

"Here." Rose Noire handed me a plate with four freshly cooked doughnuts, so hot their heavy dusting of powdered sugar was melting into a glaze. "Tell Kevin there's more where these came from."

"Roger." I took the plate and descended into the basement.

Kevin was seated at the long counter that held a dozen or so computers, along with monitors, keyboards, and a host of peripherals whose name and purpose I didn't know. He was wearing headphones and probably hadn't heard me come in, so I set the plate in a spot where he could see it. And tried not to drool at the sight.

"Thanks." He pulled off the headphones and reached for a doughnut. "And go ahead and take one while they're hot. Carrying charge."

"I won't say no."

We munched on doughnuts in contented silence for a minute or two. I heard the occasional shriek of laughter from above. At least I hoped it was laughter, from the kids in the kitchen, not sounds of the bridesmaids finally rebelling against their dead salmon hats.

"Between suspects' phones and all this video, the chief's keeping you pretty busy," I said. "How's it going?"

"Don't know if the chief will be happy or sad about it," he said. "But I'm pretty sure I've cleared one suspect."

"Happy, I suspect, if it gets him even a little closer to solving the case. Which suspect, if I'm allowed to ask?"

"A bridesmaid named Jenna," he said. "Who was a hot suspect, for a little while."

"According to whom?"

"All of the other bridesmaids."

"'Used to laugh and call her names,'" I sang, to the tune of "Rudolph the Red-Nosed Reindeer." "Sorry—I guess I've been listening to too much Christmas music."

"Understandable," he said. "And actually all of the other bridesmaids kind of were. I get the feeling maybe she isn't really a part of their tight little group. Like maybe Emily needed a sixth bridesmaid and decided she'd do."

"Or maybe Emily picked her deliberately to annoy Lexy," I said. "Remember, Lexy's groom used to date Jenna."

"Would Emily really do that to her cousin?" he asked.

"In a heartbeat," I said.

"Then maybe it's kind of ironic that Lexy probably owes her alibi to Jenna," he said. "Watch this."

He pointed to a monitor and started a video. Our backyard, after dark—I recognized the familiar shape of the llama pen. As I watched, Lexy crept into the picture—and yes, crept was definitely the word. Her body language absolutely shrieked "Look at me! I am doing something illicit!" We watched as she crossed the yard and disappeared into the opening in the woods where the trail led to Delaney and Rob's house.

Kevin touched a couple of keys and a new picture emerged: Lexy, still moving with ostentatious stealth, emerging from the woods and sneaking toward Rob and Delaney's house. Kevin switched to another camera view, this one showing Lexy crouched in the azalea bushes that nestled against the foundation of the house. She was peering into one of the basement windows.

"It wasn't Austin spying on the hens in Rob and Delaney's basement," I said. "It was Lexy."

"Yeah," he said. "And I'm pretty sure I've figured out what—or rather who—she was spying on."

Chapter 33

I got the feeling Kevin was enjoying this show-and-tell—and maybe also finding it useful. A dress rehearsal for demonstrating his findings to the chief. His fingers danced over the keyboard as he showed me more snippets of video. Jenna, emerging from the back door, struggling into a coat, with her phone held to her ear, then hurrying across the yard until she was beside the duck pond. Lexy, still crouching in the shrubbery, but now with her back toward the window, and her eyes focused on where Jenna was pacing. Lexy, taking alarm and running away from the basement window. Emily and her remaining bridesmaids erupting from the back door and, finding no Peeping Tom at the window, surging away from the house and into the woods. A shot of them arriving at our house and barging in through the back door.

"So this was happening about the time of the murder?" I asked.

"I'll cut to the chase," he said. "Jenna stayed out there, pacing up and down by the pond, for close to two hours. And Lexy hid behind the garage the whole time, watching her like a hawk. After a while she snuck up closer—I bet she was trying to hear what Jenna was saying. When Jenna finally hung up and hurried back into the house, Lexy came back here. But this whole thing started a little before ten, and by the time Lexy got back here it was well past eleven. Almost midnight. No way either of them could have done it."

"That's good," I said. "And this doesn't just help Jenna. Lexy's off the hook, too."

He nodded. And I wondered if, like me, he cared more about Jenna being proven innocent than he did about Lexy. Which some people might find a little odd, since Lexy was a cousin and someone I'd known for years, and I'd only just met Jenna. Then again, I felt a little sorry for Jenna, who, on top of being relatively nice and apparently the odd girl out in Emily's bridal party, was having to watch her ex's wedding at close range.

And what if Jenna wasn't really that close to Emily? What if Emily had included her in her wedding party for the sole purpose of annoying Lexy? I could easily imagine a scenario in which Jenna was flattered to be invited to be a bridesmaid—thinking it was a sign that she was accepted by the local in-crowd. How would she have felt when she realized that Emily only wanted to use her?

"Still kind of weird how secretive Jenna's being about her phone call," Kevin said. "I hadn't yet gone through very much of the video when the chief interviewed her, so all we knew then was what the other bridesmaids told us—that she snuck out of the party and was gone for nearly two hours. And she would only say that she wanted privacy to make a phone call and she'd been on the call the whole time. Wouldn't say who the call was to, or what it was about. Just that it was a private conversation and had nothing to do with Austin. Turns out she was telling the truth."

"About being on the phone," I said. "We only have her word for it that the call had nothing to do with Austin."

"You think maybe she hired an assassin to bump off Austin?" he said. "And watched the whole thing over FaceTime?"

"Probably not," I said. "Still weird that she's stonewalling the chief about a stupid phone call. A phone call that actually helps prove her innocence."

"Yeah. He asked her to let me look at her phone and she refused, and the county attorney has been working on getting permission to access her phone records, but so far she didn't think there was enough probable cause for a judge to sign off on it. And now that she's alibied, there never will be, I guess."

"That's a pity," I said. "Because now I'm really curious. What could she possibly be calling anyone about that—"

And then an idea hit me, and I paused in mid-sentence to consider it.

"What's wrong?" Kevin asked finally.

"Jenna's not the only one who was making really long private phone calls last night," I said. "Blaine went to the basketball games with Michael and the boys, but he spent more time pacing up and down and talking on his cell phone than watching the game."

"Blaine?" Kevin echoed. "That's Lexy's groom?"

"And Jenna's ex."

"Yikes," Kevin said—although he sounded less alarmed than entertained. "The plot thickens. Maybe he's not so ex."

"Did the chief ask to look at Blaine's phone?"

"Blaine offered, and the chief didn't think it would be that useful, since when the murder took place the guy was in full sight of Michael and several thousand basketball fans."

"Only several hundred," I said. "The Chargers aren't having that great a season. But if he was willing to give up the phone then, maybe you or the chief could think up an excuse to look at it now?"

"We could probably come up with something," he said. "Like that we need to corroborate what someone else told us. But not sure the chief would go for that, given that they're both alibied and it's just us being nosy."

"Don't you think it's a really odd coincidence that their marathon phone call happened to overlap the murder?" I asked. "And you know how the chief feels about coincidences when he's working on a case."

"Yeah," he said. "Probably not a bad idea to clear it up completely. I'll talk to the chief. And now I think I'll get back to my video."

He reached for the headphones he'd been wearing when I arrived.

"Could you use another pair of eyes for a little while?" I said.

"Sure," he said. "You don't have wedding stuff you need to do?"

"I'm sure Mother will find me if I'm needed," I said.

So he set me up with a monitor and a set of headphones, and I settled in to scan video for a while. I knew most of the chief's deputies hated doing this, but I found it strangely restful—at least when it came to video like this, where I was mostly staring at a static view of scenery and watching for the occasional bit of action. In this case the scenery was the view from a security camera at the high school. Since the school was on the outskirts of town, the area didn't get the same frantic level of traffic as the roads closer to the central tourist attractions. And this camera happened to overlook the road that led out of town and, eventually, to our house, with only a few driveways and unimproved lanes intersecting it. A good way to keep tabs on who had been coming and going from our house. I slowed the replay down to normal speed whenever a vehicle passed, but very few did. Apart from the ones I was expecting to see—Emily's car. Random Wilson's rental car. Maddie in Austin's van. None of the times contradicted what I knew of their statements, but they also didn't clear anyone.

At one point Kevin disappeared upstairs, taking a laptop with him. I wondered, briefly, where he was going, and then I went back to focusing on the video footage. I almost didn't notice when he eventually returned.

But when I spotted the chief's cruiser passing by in the video I was scanning, followed by my own Toyota, I looked at the time stamp on the video and realized that it was past when the murder had occurred. Maybe it was time to give my eyes a break.

So I gave Kevin the notes I'd taken—the times when each car had passed, and as much information as I'd gathered on it—and headed back upstairs.

The kitchen was empty. And quiet. And squeaky clean—I hoped Rose Noire had enlisted the doughnut eaters to help in the cleanup.

The sun had set while I was in the basement watching video. I glanced out the back window and saw lights in the herb shed.

The whole house was quiet. No riotously exuberant kids. No querulous bridesmaids. Someone had even turned off the sound system that would normally be playing soothing instrumental carols through tiny speakers hidden in the ubiquitous evergreen garlands.

On a hunch I went to the back door and listened. I could hear the faint strains of music coming from the herb shed. Loreena McKennitt's "The Mummer's Dance," which I knew was a favorite of Rose Noire's. Good. She was probably safely ensconced with her plants, her music, and even a few of her friends.

I closed the door and decided to see if the house was really as empty as it sounded. No one in the living room. I was trying to decide whether to check the library when I noticed that the dining-room door was open. Chief Burke was sitting at the table, writing something. And it occurred to me that I hadn't yet remembered to ask him about cleaning up the party sites.

So I knocked on the dining-room doorframe. He looked up and smiled.

"Just kick me out if you're about to interview yet another witness," I said. "Although I thought by now you'd be downtown interviewing Random and Jenna."

"No," he said. "No more interviews tonight, thank goodness. At least none planned. Vern's talking with Mr. Wilson. And we let Ms. McCracken go, once Kevin showed me what she and Ms. Turner were up to while the murder was taking place."

"Nice to know they're both alibied," I said.

"Yes." He frowned. "But Ms. Turner swore she never left your house last night, and all seven of her bridesmaids backed her up. I do not appreciate being lied to. I will be reinterviewing some of those young ladies tomorrow."

"Please let me know if you're going to charge them with making false reports and interfering with a police investigation," I said. "So I can arrange to have Festus or one of the other family lawyers available to bail them out before the wedding."

"Noted," he said.

"I wanted to ask if it's okay to bring in the Dirty Dogs to clean up after the hen parties, here and at Delaney and Rob's," I said. "I know you were going to have Horace take a look at them."

"I think he's finished," he said. "May I let you know after I've checked with him? Might not be till tomorrow."

"Sure," I said.

His phone dinged, probably signaling the arrival of a text. He glanced down at it, then smiled and quickly picked it up.

A message from his wife, Minerva? Or one of the grandsons?

His face fell.

"Osgood," he said. "I was hoping he was texting to say that my cruiser was ready. He was only confirming that he has delivered Mr. Luckett's van to the station and it's safely locked up, awaiting Horace's ministrations."

"I know you'll be glad when you get your cruiser back," I said. "Because having one less official vehicle than usual seems to be quite inconvenient."

"That it is," he said. "And I do need to get down to the station to handle things there—today was supposed to be poor Vern's day off. But I have to stay here for a little while longer. About twenty minutes ago, while I was on the phone, Father O'Donnell left me a message that he has something important to tell me, and he heard I was out here at your house, so he was going to come out here to see me. And he's not answering his phone, which probably means he's driving, and could be here any minute now."

"Something related to the case?" I asked.

"He didn't say, but I assume so. Do you mind if—"

Just then his stomach growled. He looked at his watch and sighed.

"Follow me," I said. "Your stomach just reminded mine how long it's been since breakfast, and the only thing I've had since then was a couple of doughnuts. We've got plenty of planned-overs in the kitchen."

"I won't say no," he said.

Chapter 34

I led the way to the kitchen and pulled out some of the salads and sandwich fixings.

"Help yourself," I said.

The chief made himself a huge ham-and-swiss sandwich on rye with a side of potato salad. I nuked a few Buffalo wings and fixed myself a plate of ham, Caesar salad, and slices of buttered French bread.

"Do you think Maddie did it?" I asked, while we were loading our plates. "Not that it's any of my business, so let me ask that another way—how worried should we be about finding another photographer?"

"Too soon to tell if she did it," he said. "So if I were you I'd do my best to find someone who can step in if I end up arresting her for murder on top of the damage to Mr. Luckett's van. I can see giving her bail on the current charges, but not on murder."

He took a big bite of his sandwich and chewed thoughtfully.

"Her defense attorney's going to have a lot of material to work with, though," I said.

He swallowed and sighed.

"All too true," he said. "With several suspicious persons wandering around near the crime scene during the relevant time period, it's going to be hard to figure out which one is actually guilty and even harder to make the charge stick. Apart from Ms. Brown, we also have our light-fingered bride and her sidekick, the groom who managed to wander around town for three or four hours without showing up on any cameras Kevin has access to, and Mr. Random Wilson, the disgruntled client."

"Random Q. Wilson," I added. "Wonder what the Q stands for."

He shrugged and took another bite.

"Yeah," I said. "Five hot suspects is about four too many. The video clears Wilson of the tire-slashing, but it doesn't rule him out for the murder. He could have committed that and then headed this way, hoping to search Austin's stuff for his photos. Just as Maddie could have killed him and then raced back to try to set up an alibi. Taking a friend along to help you commit a felony would be pretty stupid, and I don't think Emily is clever enough to think of leaving tons of evidence of breaking in and stealing the angels and none at all of the murder, but maybe I'm underestimating her. And who knows what Harry got up to after he bailed out of the basketball game."

He only nodded.

"Did any of the bridesmaids have anything useful to say?" I asked.

"Possibly," he said. "One of them said she hadn't done anything to him, but she completely understood why someone had, because he was a horrible man who took nasty pictures of women and then tried to use those pictures against them."

"Yikes," I said. "So he's a blackmailer? Or is she implying that he exerted pressure on women to trade sexual favors in return for suppressing embarrassing pictures?"

"She wouldn't say," he said. "We might be able to use her statements as probable cause to get the phone records for all of the young ladies, on the theory that any of them of whom he had embarrassing photos could have a motive to kill him. But we'd be in a stronger position if we could find some embarrassing pictures to strengthen our request. Aida's still down in Richmond, combing through Mr. Luckett's files, and Kevin's been going through all of the gear he brought here, but so far we haven't found any. For that matter, we don't have any pictures taken here in Caerphilly, apart from what Ms. Brown has on her camera, which is mostly candid shots at last night's parties. And she seems to have had the good sense to stop taking pictures when the parties started getting a little wild."

"So if we don't find that missing data card, the brides may not have any pictures of anything that happened yesterday. I don't want to be in the same room with them when they find out. In fact, I'd rather not be in the same time zone."

"According to Kevin, they'll have pictures—just not from Mr. Luckett. In addition to their wedding websites, both of them—and most of their bridesmaids—have been posting regularly on social media."

He pulled out his phone, tapped on it, then held up the screen for me to see. It was Lexy's Facebook page, which featured a posed picture of her and her bridesmaids, all waving liquor bottles. Below that was a shot of one bridesmaid puking into a toilet.

"Good grief," I said. "Don't these people realize that these days employers scour applicants' social media for stuff like this? And look at all the pictures of the wedding gifts—it's one thing to show them to the guests, but to the whole world on social media? Why not just come right out and say, 'Hey, burglars, you want a lot of expensive silver and electronics? Come and get it.'"

"You're preaching to the choir," he said.

Just then my phone rang. Michael.

"The boys and I are out at the zoo again," he said.

"And Grandfather?" I asked.

"Yes. Him, too." He chuckled. "I gathered from something Jamie said that you might be happier if your grandfather wasn't underfoot, saying things that might alarm the brides. So I rounded everybody up and brought them back here. We're busy feeding more water beetles to more pond frogs. And your grandfather has invited everyone to stay around tonight for Sleeping with Wombats, the sequel."

"Probably a good idea," I said, "as long as you don't get snowbound out there."

"No danger of that," he said. "Your grandfather already has his staff tuning up the snowmobiles. It's all we can do to keep him from trying to test them out in the penguins' habitat. Oh, and we're having a Christmas pageant rehearsal out here in the auditorium."

"Also wise," I said. "I bet the chief will be relieved not to have several dozen curious children trying to sneak into his crime scene."

Across the table from me, the chief nodded vigorously.

"Plus, some of the parents might feel a little nervous about bringing their darlings to Trinity, at least while the killer's still at large," Michael suggested.

"I doubt if the killer's still at large," I said. "The chief has four or five of the leading suspects down at the station. I suspect he'll be having a long night, but with luck the killer will be among them."

"Keep me posted," he said.

"Will do," I replied, and we signed off.

"I do wish Father O'Donnell would get here." The chief glanced up at our kitchen clock. "Technically, I only have two suspects waiting for me down at the station—Ms. Winningham should be out on bail by now, and I let Mr. Koenig go back to your parents' house after some initial questioning. But I'm eager to see what Ms. Brown and Mr. Wilson have to say."

Just then the doorbell rang.

"That's probably Father O'Donnell," I said.

I hurried out to the front hall, still nibbling on a Buffalo wing.

"Good evening." Father O'Donnell looked contrite. "And I'm so sorry I'm interrupting your dinner."

"You're not." I waved him in. "The chief and I have been too busy to eat, so we've been cleaning up some leftovers. He's back in the kitchen."

I led the way there, slowing down when I realized how badly he was limping, with a big blue boot on his right foot.

"Did you actually break your foot chasing the vandals?" I asked.

He nodded, and collapsed into a kitchen chair as soon as he could. I could tell he was eyeing the food with interest, so I set out a plate and some flatware for him and gestured toward the food. I knew that this time of year was a busy one for clergy, and if he was anything like Robyn, he'd probably been running around like crazy and skipping meals.

"I couldn't," he said.

"Don't be silly," I said. "You'll be helping keep this from going to waste."

"And we'll both feel like greedy pigs if you just sit there watching us," the chief said.

So I started him out with a large slice of ham, which I knew he liked, and he abandoned his scruples and dug in.

"You said you had some information for me," the chief said, when we'd all settled back to clearing our plates. "Something related to the murder?"

"Yes," Father O'Donnell said, through a mouthful of ham. "I heard that Harry Koenig is a suspect in your murder case."

"One of many, this early," the chief said, as he buttered another biscuit. "He claims to have been wandering around town for hours, thinking. And as a result, he has no alibi for the time of the murder. Kevin's been searching the video from all the cameras he's able to access around town, and so far he hasn't found anything that will alibi Mr. Koenig for the critical period."

"Well, I don't know where or how long he was wandering around," Father O'Donnell said. "And I also don't know why he's shy of mentioning this, but he spent quite a long time quietly praying at St. Byblig's."

"When was this?" The chief put down his biscuit and took up his notebook.

"He arrived at around nine-fifteen," Father O'Donnell said. "And I'm pretty darn sure of the time because I'd just taken my nine o'clock dose of the pain meds. The last hour leading up to each dose, I'm pretty much checking the time every few minutes. He went into the sanctuary and sat down in the last row of pews. I went out and asked him if he needed help or wanted to talk, and he thanked me and said he just needed some time to think and pray. So I decided to give him some space. I couldn't exactly lock up with him there, and I didn't want to kick him out—he looked so . . . unsettled. I was actually worried that he might be having suicidal thoughts. The holiday time is so hard on many people."

The chief nodded, and made some notes.

"And frankly, lately I've been trying to spend time there at the church in the evening hours. To keep an eye out for those vandals. With school out for the holidays and the kids having too much time on their hands—"

"My officers are all under orders to keep an eye out," the chief said. "And drive by all the local churches and temples a lot more often. Especially since . . . er . . ."

"Since you know very well who did it, but can't charge them if their parents are going to lie about it," I said.

"Precisely." The chief nodded. "We don't normally do major forensics on a mere vandalism case, but I've given Horace orders that if—sadly, I think it's more like when—the vandals strike again, he's to go all out. I'd love to see how those wretched parents try to explain it away when we've got DNA on their spoiled darlings."

"Setting a terrible example for those unfortunate boys." Father O'Donnell's normally cheerful face looked stern. "Anyway, I've been spending time down there, hoping to catch them in the act if they come back—or better yet, head them off before the trouble starts. So I settled down where I could keep an eye on my visitor without making him feel crowded or hovered over. Since I didn't know him, I had no idea what he might be dealing with, but clearly he was troubled."

The chief nodded. I wondered if Father O'Donnell had called upon Kevin to set up a camera that let him keep an eye on the church from his office, or if he had something old-fashioned like a peephole.

"He spent quite a long time, either kneeling in prayer or sitting with his head and hands resting on the back of the pew in front of him. The longer he stayed the more convinced I was that I shouldn't leave him alone. Then after a while he sat up and I began to think he was about to leave, so I came in—trying to make it look as if I was just stepping back in to take care of something. And I was relieved to see that he looked much better. Calmer and, well, resolved. So I said something like 'You look less troubled, but are you sure there's nothing I can do to help you?' and he said that when he came in he'd been feeling something like despair, but spending time here helped, and he'd come to a very difficult decision. And then he saw my face and said, 'Oh, don't worry, Father. Not that kind of a decision. I've decided I have to take back control of my life and do what my conscience tells me to do.' And so I gave him a blessing, and told him I'd pray for him, and that he could come back anytime, either to talk or to pray. And he left. With what I'd call a spring in his step."

"And what time was it when he left?"

"A little after midnight."

I marveled, for a moment, at his patience. Hovering around for three hours in case a young man he didn't even know needed his help.

"And you're sure he stayed there the whole time?"

"I made sure to peek at him regularly," Father O'Donnell said. "Every ten minutes or so. And there's no way he could have sneaked out while I wasn't watching. You remember we pulled up that nasty old carpet this spring and had those beautiful hundred-year-old oak floors refinished."

"They're lovely," I said.

"But unbelievably noisy." Father O'Donnell frowned. "The last time the bishop came to visit, he said it was like trying to say mass in the middle of a tap-dancing performance. I'd have heard the young man if he tried to sneak out."

"And you're sure it was Mr. Koenig?" the chief asked. "I thought you said you didn't know him."

"I didn't," Father O'Donnell said. "Not then. I just knew that he looked slightly familiar. Last night I assumed he was one of the college students who'd come over occasionally for mass. But then this afternoon I sat down to read this week's issue of the *Clarion,* and I saw the feature about the weddings and I recognized him at once. It was definitely him. The only thing different from his photo was that he was wearing round wire-rimmed glasses."

"His fiancée is quite militant about him always wearing his contacts," I said. "Which is a pity."

"You have something against contacts?" The chief sounded curious.

"No, but he doesn't seem to be adjusting well to them," I said. "He's constantly batting his eyes and dabbing at them. If they made me that uncomfortable, I'd just stick to glasses."

"Anyway," Father O'Donnell said, "I thought you might like to know where the young man was."

"You've been very helpful," the chief said.

"And I should be going." Father O'Donnell stood up.

"As should I," the chief said. "I have a few suspects to interview down at the station."

Neither of them turned down my offer of a few Christmas cookies for the road, and we said our goodbyes.

While I was in the kitchen, putting away the food, Rose Noire came in. She was wearing her cloak and carrying the basket that would have made her look like Red Riding Hood if the cloak had been the right color. Pale Lavender Riding Hood just didn't have the same ring to it.

"Oh, good," she said. "I didn't want to bother you if you were busy—but I wanted you to know that we've finished the angels."

Chapter 35

Rose Noire opened her basket and began carefully setting the angels down on the kitchen table. They were as good as new. In fact better. The angels' original gowns had been decorated with just random globs of glitter. The glitter on these angels was in delicate patterns—spirals, snowflakes, moons, and stars, all accented with silver rhinestones.

And there were six of them.

"Wonderful," I said. "Did Horace give you back the doll he took as evidence?"

"No," she said. "We bought another one. Not hard to find them in the thrift shops. You know, this really might be a lovely way to raise funds for local good causes. We could collect unwanted dolls throughout the year and buy the glitter and rhinestones in bulk."

"I bet they'd go like hotcakes at the next year's Christmas mart," I said. "Let's ask Robyn."

"Could you possibly get these back to her?" Rose Noire said. "I've got company."

"Of course."

She thanked me and began putting on her cloak.

Just then Kevin emerged from the basement carrying two large cardboard boxes.

"Rose Noire said to give you these," he said, setting one box down on the kitchen table. "So you can take them down to the Inn."

"You were able to do it, then?" Rose Noire asked.

Kevin nodded.

I peered in. The first box contained three plastic eagles. I recognized them as something that Flugleman's Feed Store and Garden Center sold—the theory was that having even fake-looking plastic owls or eagles in your garden would help keep birds from eating your crops. These eagles had been completely covered in gold glitter and had green rhinestones for eyes.

"A replacement for the eagles they had to move," Kevin said. "I think Ekaterina rather liked the eagles, before they started causing problems."

"Perhaps," I said. "But I think by the time they left she was quite happy to see the back of them."

"A peace offering, then," Rose Noire said. "As an apology for all the trouble the eagles caused."

"And she should like these ones," Kevin added. "No chance of them puking."

"What's in the other box?" I asked. "More eagles?"

"No need for more," Kevin said. "There were only three to start with. This one's for the angels."

He set down the second box, which turned out to be empty. We carefully packed the angels in it.

"And let's take the boxes out to Meg's car," Rose Noire said.

So Kevin borrowed my keys, and they disappeared with the boxes.

I rummaged around until I found a small canister in which Rose Noire had stored a few leftover doughnuts. They weren't hot, but they were still fabulous. I grabbed one and sat down at the kitchen table to call Robyn.

"I have your angels," I said.

"Why does that sound like a ransom demand?" she said. "Do you mean that you've found the ones that were stolen, or that you've sneaked into the church to bag the remaining six?"

"I found the ones that were stolen, and Rose Noire and her friends have repaired them."

"Should I ask why they needed repair?"

"You're better off not knowing," I said. "But I'll fill you in later. And anyway, they're as good as new now—in fact, better. How about if I bring them to the church by tomorrow?"

"Could you make it early?" she said. "We're having the Advent crafts and carols event tomorrow at nine—you know the one where we bring in the seniors from the assisted-living facility. I'd really like to have the sanctuary back in shape for that."

"How about if I drop them off tonight?" I asked. "Because I'm not sure I want to commit to getting up early enough to get there for the event, and you're going to need at least an hour or two to reinstall the angels. And maybe it would be a good idea to deliver them before the snow starts—assuming it ever does."

"I saw a few flakes just now when I was driving home," she said. "So tonight will be perfect. Remember to bring along your key. I managed to escape the Finance Committee meeting a few minutes ago, and for all I know they'll still be there, arguing over next year's budget. But if they've finally called a truce, there won't be anyone on site to let you in. Just leave the angels behind the altar. I'll go call a few early birds to see if they can come in tomorrow to do the redecorating."

"If you ask me, we should be making Emily help with the redecorating," I said.

"I'd insist on that if she wasn't so busy with the wedding preparations. And speaking of Emily—is it Betty or Letty that's her mother?"

"Um . . . Letty, I think."

"Whichever one's her mother brought her by this afternoon to make a formal apology and deliver a check to cover the damage to the church."

"An adequately large check, I hope."

"More than adequate," Robyn said. "And she said to let her know if it wasn't enough, and consider any surplus a donation to the church."

"Just one thing," I said. "Who was the check from—Emily or her mother?"

"Emily," Robyn said. "And she seemed quite genuinely contrite. I have to say, I was pleasantly surprised."

"Good," I said. "Maybe there's hope for Emily. I do hope if there's jail time involved it can wait till she's back from her honeymoon."

"The chief will be recommending that she do community service," Robyn said. "A lot of it. I've already started making a list of useful things she can do around here. I gather she'll probably end up staying with you when she does it—I hope that isn't going to be too annoying for you."

"With luck you'll keep her so busy that I'll hardly notice she's here," I said. "And I hope she'll bring her new husband—him I don't mind having around."

We said our goodbyes and ended the call. I pulled out my notebook and checked on the wedding schedule, to see what the brides and their parties were up to this evening, and whether any of it was likely to involve me. Or cause any hassles that I should help Mother cope with.

Emily was having a rehearsal dinner down at the Inn—to which Mother and I, obviously, weren't invited. And why was she having the rehearsal dinner before tomorrow's rehearsal? Lexy was also having a dinner, but hers was described as "A Celebration of the Joining of the Turner and Marshall Families." I wasn't sure how that differed from a rehearsal dinner, but I didn't think Mother was expected to show up at that either, and I knew I hadn't been invited.

I checked the time. Nine thirty. Where had the day gone? I gave way, just for a moment, to feeling put upon. Couldn't someone else deliver the eagles and the angels?

But then I reminded myself that neither errand was likely to involve any of the wedding party. And that once I'd made my deliveries, I could come home, crawl into bed, and maybe read another chapter or two in my book club's latest selection.

Better yet, maybe I could see if the Caerphilly Library had the audiobook. It would be closed this late, of course, but if they had the electronic version, I could check that out online. I liked the idea of closing my eyes and letting some silver-tongued narrator read me to sleep. In fact, if the library didn't have it, I could splurge and buy the audiobook.

So I wrapped up warmly and headed for my car.

There were fewer tourists photographing the decorations at Seth Early's and the Washingtons'. Was that because of the late hour, the arctic temperatures, or the looming threat of snow? Or maybe word had gotten around that tonight's concert in the town square was by the justly famous New Life Baptist Choir, and everyone had gone to that.

Either way, I appreciated the dearth of traffic.

I wasn't so sure I appreciated the snow, which began falling while I was driving into town. Not falling heavily yet, thank goodness, and I should be able to get home before road conditions got bad.

When I arrived at the Caerphilly Inn, I found Hector and another hotel employee in the parking lot, doing some kind of maintenance to the Inn's small all-purpose tractor. Which was already fitted with its snowplow blade.

"Aren't you afraid you'll jinx us?" I asked as I passed them on my way to the door. "And scare off the snow?"

"Would scaring off the snow be such a bad thing?" Hector answered. "Me, I do not enjoy it so much."

"Normally I'm fine with having snow," I said. "But it would really complicate all the wedding arrangements. So I'm hoping for a false alarm—but don't tell my sons that."

"Snow is for the young," Hector said. "They will have the sledding and the skiing and the snowball fights. But for us, it only means extra work. Ah, well."

At the door, Jaime bowed me in and insisted on carrying the box containing the eagles. At my suggestion he set it in the alcove, by the fireplace.

"It's something for Ekaterina," I said.

"She is in the meeting area," Jaime said. "Checking to see that the dinners are going smoothly. Shall I fetch her?"

"No, thanks," I said. "I know the way. I'll go and find her."

I took a few minutes to appreciate the Christmas tree, now restored to its original glory. Then I left the lobby proper for the Gathering Area. Along its side walls and in front of the glass front wall that echoed the one in the lobby were a few tables and chairs, along with several groups of upholstered chairs arranged in conversational groupings. The space was in its evening mode, with most of the light appearing to come from floor lamps and table lamps placed by the tables and conversation areas.

And it was empty except for two people sitting in easy chairs at the far end, sipping cups of tea. I waved at them and went over to say hello.

"You weren't invited to either of the fancy dinners?" Terri asked.

"I think they're mostly for the people in the actual wedding parties," I said. "Which I'm not, thank goodness."

I could hear a hum of noise coming from the bigger of the meeting rooms. Emily's dinner, if memory served. Lexy's would be in the ballroom.

"Terri's been having a great time, watching all the fancy outfits the ladies are wearing," Frank said.

"Oh, yes," Terri said. "Just fabulous. But I don't think I'm going to be able to stay awake to see them all leave. We've had a lovely day, but a tiring one. I could fall asleep sitting up."

"We'll call it a night when we've finished our tea," Frank said.

"I hope I'm not bothering you," Terri said. "But do you know if . . . if the police will be arresting someone for the murder soon?"

"This whole thing has her a bit nervous." Frank reached over and patted her hand.

"It's making me a bit nervous, too," I said. "But not so much about the killer still being at large—I think it will turn out to be someone with a grudge against Austin, without any sinister designs on the rest of us. I'm mostly worried about the effect this will have on the weddings. We're already down a photographer and scrambling to find a replacement. If the killer turns out to be someone from one of the wedding parties . . ."

"Oh, dear," Terri said. "Do you think that's likely?"

"Not likely, no," I said. "But possible."

"It really would make everyone feel so much better if the police would make an arrest," Frank said.

"Absolutely," I said. "But keep in mind—it hasn't even been twenty-four hours since Austin was killed."

"True," he said. "And I suppose solving a murder is harder for a small-town police department."

"Well, I bet it's easier if the people involved are local," Terri said. "But in this case, where the victim's from out of town, and perhaps the killer is, too, it must be difficult."

"Very," Frank said. "Do you think they'll call in the state police?"

"Or the FBI!" Terri seemed to find this idea exciting. I wondered if she was a fan of any of the various TV shows focused on the FBI. There were certainly enough of them—*Criminal Minds, Mindhunter*—even *Twin Peaks* and *The X-Files*.

"I'm sure he will if he needs any help," I said. "But Chief Burke is a pretty experienced investigator. He was a homicide detective in Baltimore for over a decade."

"Oh, my," Terri said. They both seemed impressed.

"So while I'm sure he enjoys the quieter life he has as the police chief of a small town—and one that's normally pretty peaceful—he's definitely up to taking on a murder investigation."

"Good to know," Frank said.

"And I happen to know he's got the most likely suspects down at the station even as we speak," I said. "Nothing's certain yet, but with luck we'll hear news of an arrest soon."

That seemed to reassure them both. They broke into smiles of relief.

"Do let us know if you hear anything," Terri said.

Frank nodded vigorously.

Just then the door from the lobby opened. I turned to see if it was Ekaterina, but it was the desk clerk. She bustled over to us.

"Meg, I have something for you." She handed me an envelope. I recognized the Inn's thick, elegant off-white stationery.

I opened the envelope to reveal . . .

"A data card?" I asked. "Not mine, actually."

"No," she said. "We found it in the parking lot. Ekaterina assumed that poor photographer must have dropped it there. She thought perhaps you could give it back to his assistant."

"Actually, that's probably ours," Terri said. "We've misplaced the one from our camera—so distressing since it has all those lovely pictures we took of the Christmas decorations. I can't tell you how glad we are that you found it."

She smiled and held out her hand, palm up.

"I don't think it's yours," I said. "Unless you normally write someone else's name on your data cards." I picked the card up by the edges and held it so she could see that it had "A. Luckett" printed on it in tiny black letters.

"I found ours, dear," Frank said. "I'm sorry—I should have told you. It was on the car floor, under your seat."

"Oh!" Terri put both hands to her mouth. "I'm so embarrassed. I wasn't trying to steal your card! I just assumed . . ."

"Not a problem." I turned back to the desk clerk. "Tell Ekaterina thanks, and I'll make sure this gets into the right hands."

She nodded and hurried off.

"I'm sure his assistant will be relieved to get it back," Frank said.

"I'm sure she will," I said. "Unless, of course, she turns out to be Austin's killer, in which case I don't think Chief Burke will be letting her have it anytime soon. She's one of the suspects he's interviewing."

"Oh, my," Teri murmured.

Just then I spotted Ekaterina approaching us from the corridor that led to the ballroom.

Chapter 36

I waved to her and she strode over to join us.

"If you're here for the dinners—" she began.

"No, I just came to drop off something for you," I said. "A peace offering from Rose Noire and Kevin. It's in the lobby, by the fireplace."

"Is it supposed to be a surprise?" she said. "That I should not open until Christmas has actually arrived?"

"Of course not," I said. "It's three artificial golden eagles. For decorative purposes only. Guaranteed not to cause any of the damage the real ones did."

"That was kind of them." Then she frowned slightly. "Are eagles a part of the American Christmas tradition? I was not previously aware of this."

"I think they will become part of the Caerphilly Christmas tradition, if Rob has his way," I said. "But let's make sure it's fake eagles, not the messy live kind."

"Yes." She shuddered slightly. "It is good that you are not here for the dinners, because they have both already begun, and both brides brought almost twice as many guests as they told us there would be, so the kitchen has been scrambling, and I doubt if we could fit another chair in either room."

"And I wasn't invited, and would have begged off if I had been," I said. "I just dropped by to give you the eagles. I'm on my way to drop some repaired decorations at Trinity, and then I'm going home to make an early night of it."

"I wish I could." She sighed in the dramatic manner of someone who wants the world to know that she has been put upon. "Both brides want to have a viewing of their presents after dinner. So I am on call to unlock the rooms when they're ready, and then lock them up again when they're finished."

"You couldn't delegate that to one of your security personnel?"

"I could," she said. "But I don't want to. I am not sure any of them understand how much vigilance this requires."

"Or how much chaos the brides will cause if anything goes wrong."

"You understand," she said, with a quick nod. "And now I must go check on something in the kitchen. Sleep well."

She nodded to all of us before striding off.

"The gifts are in good hands," Terri said. "I'm sure everything will go smoothly."

"Here's hoping," I said.

And then I wished them good night and went back out to my car.

But before starting it, I called the chief.

"I have what I think is Austin's missing data card," I said. "Someone at the Inn found it in the parking lot and turned it in to Ekaterina."

"How did you deduce that it's his?"

"It's got his name printed right on it," I said. "No clever deductions needed."

"Nice," he said.

"And while I can't guarantee that whoever found it hasn't left fingerprints and DNA all over it, I have been careful to hold it by the edges. Look, Rose Noire has repaired the angels Emily stole, and Trinity's Decorations Committee is going to restore them to their proper place."

"I'm sure that will be a relief to Robyn."

"But the committee is coming at oh-dark-thirty tomorrow, so I'm dropping off the angels tonight. How about if I continue on to the station and hand over the data card?"

"That would be excellent," he said. "See you soon."

I started my car and headed for Trinity. The snow was definitely underway. So far it was a light scattering of flakes, but they were the kind of tiny, dry flakes that, according to the local weather experts, presaged serious accumulation. Or as Judge Jane Shiffley—whose left knee was considered more reliable at predicting precipitation than the Weather Bureau—was fond of saying, "Big snow, little snow; little snow, big snow."

I wanted to hurry, to finish my errands before the snow began to pile up. But I knew rushing in bad weather was an invitation to have a fender bender, so I kept my pace slow and steady.

All was quiet at the church. No cars in the parking lot. No lights in the building. I was relieved, since I remembered that Robyn had said she'd escaped from a Finance Committee meeting. This time of year their meetings tended to run long and could even be slightly contentious, And for some reason—possibly because Mother had told them I had a good head for numbers—they kept trying to recruit me to join their ranks. If the church was deserted, that probably meant that they'd had a relatively efficient and harmonious meeting. Or maybe they'd all given up and gone home in a snit, but at least they weren't still around to spot me and suck me into their debate.

I parked near the side door and used my flashlight to keep from tripping on the brick walk, which was already half covered with snow. I let myself in and locked the door behind me. I could have turned on the lights, but familiar as I was with Trinity, the beam of the flashlight was quite bright enough for me to see my way. And the darkness felt peaceful and fit my mood. Tonight was a little oasis of calm before the real craziness of the weddings began. Hordes of guests arriving and filling what few spare rooms we had left, with tents and camping trailers in the backyard for the overflow. Feeding crowds of fifty to a hundred people at every meal. Wedding rehearsals. Then the ceremonies themselves, and the receptions.

Tonight's quiet was a gift.

I inhaled the scent of the evergreen garlands that festooned every hallway. In the sanctuary it mingled with the heady aroma of the incense.

As I was tucking the box of angels behind the altar, something suddenly struck me. Incense. Emily was allergic to so many things. Or claimed to be. What if incense was one of them? It was for a lot of people—to the point that Robyn always noted in event announcements whether or not incense would be a feature. What if walking into the church and inhaling the residual incense smell set Emily off on her way to the altar?

She hadn't reacted when we'd come here to scout out the photo angles, so it should be all right . . . shouldn't it?

Or had she been so focused on the Barbie angels that she'd forgotten that she was supposed to be allergic? Maybe that was an unkind thought. Then again, Mother and I had discussed my theory that maybe Emily didn't have physical allergies so much as an intense revulsion for certain smells. And that she didn't seem to suffer any ill effects from those smells if there was something to distract her from noticing them. Even if that theory was true, it wouldn't change how we treated her. Of course we'd try to avoid inflicting unwanted smells on her, whether she was allergic to them or just deeply repulsed. But try as we might, we couldn't protect her from encountering unwanted smells all the time.

And clearing Trinity of all incense smells might not be possible. Surely if the Barbie angels were enough to distract her from an unloved smell, the excitement of the wedding would have the same effect, wouldn't it?

My notebook was in my tote, but I'd left that in the car, so as I headed back to the side door I made a mental note to ask Robyn if we could put an embargo on incense between now and Emily's wedding. And to do a little probing to see if there was a smell Emily actually liked and found restorative. If there was, we could figure out a way to flood the sanctuary with it on Saturday.

Just coming up with that idea improved my already mellow mood. And we could worry about how to do it tomorrow.

I opened the side door, stepped out—

And saw Frank standing just outside. He was pointing a gun at me.

Chapter 37

"Put your hands up where I can see them," he said.

I obeyed orders. I liked the way the beam of my flashlight shone up onto the trees overhanging the graveyard. The chief had his deputies patrolling in the neighborhood of all the town churches. If someone spotted the beam—

"And turn that flashlight off," he barked. "Before someone sees it."

"Just drop it," Terri said, from somewhere nearby.

I did as I was told. My flashlight fell to the brick walk with a loud clink and rolled onto the mulched flower bed. I heard steps behind me, as Terri walked over, picked it up, and turned it off.

"Let's take her back inside," Terri said. "In case anyone comes by."

"Why are you doing this?" I asked.

"I'm sorry," Frank said. "But you have something we want. That data card the desk clerk gave you."

"You can't just ask me for it?" I figured it was worth trying to play dumb.

"Don't be stupid," Terri said. "Inside."

I went inside, and they followed me in.

"That's better," Frank said. "It's beastly outside."

"The data card," Terri repeated.

"I don't have it." I wondered if I should try telling them I'd already turned it over to the chief.

"Do you think we're stupid?" Terri snapped. "We saw the desk clerk give it to you, and then you went straight out to your car. And don't try to tell us you've already taken it to the police station, because we followed you here from the hotel. Hand it over."

"I'd love to," I said. "But it's still in my car."

They exchanged a look.

"She could be telling the truth," Frank said.

"Keep the gun on her," Terri said. "I'll search her."

Terri's search was embarrassingly thorough. If I had been trying to conceal the data card, nothing short of swallowing it would have worked.

"I can't find it," she said. "I'll go out and look for it."

She reached into my pocket and pulled out my keys.

"I'll come with you," Frank said.

"Don't be silly," Terri said. "I don't need your help to search her car."

"But what if she comes at me while you're outside?" he asked. "Better safe than sorry."

"Yes," I said. "What if I did that and he had to shoot me—when you've already killed one person to get that data card. You don't want to up the ante."

"Why would we care?" Terri said. "In for a penny, in for a pound."

"Ah, but killing more than one person in such a short stretch of time would be a special circumstance," I said. "Increases the penalty. Title eighteen point two. Chapter five, I think."

I had no idea if this was true since, unlike Vern Shiffley, I hadn't memorized the criminal section of the Virginia Code. Although I did know it was Title 18.2, since Vern had often remarked how odd it was that there was no Title 18.1. If they knew anything about the Virginia Code, they might be at least slightly impressed.

"Just bring her along if you're so nervous," Terri said.

So we went back outside—Terri leading the way, with my car keys jingling in her hand, followed by me, with my hands raised, and Frank, holding the gun close against his belly, as if hoping to keep any onlooker from noticing it.

Suddenly I realized something.

"You're after the gifts," I said. "All those expensive wedding gifts. You were always kind of hovering near them. And then Austin recognized you from some other wedding where you'd pulled the same thing."

"I told you she was dangerous," Terri said.

"The jerk was trying to blackmail us." Frank's tone suggested that he thought this justified killing him. "He was going to report us to the local police."

"Just shut up for a minute, can't you?" Terri turned to snarl at him. "Just until we get the damned pictures and— Oh!"

A spot had appeared on her forehead. Not the red of blood—although in this light, blood would have looked more black than red. This spot was a luminous lime green.

More spots appeared on her face and body. And a few on Frank, who was so startled that he whirled around and fired the gun. I heard the tinkle of glass as the bullet struck a window.

"Down, Meg!" someone shouted.

The gate to the graveyard was hanging open, so I sprinted through it and dropped to the snowy ground behind one of the slab tombstones. Then I peered over it to see what was happening. Spots of color continued to appear on Terri and Frank. And then not just spots but also streaks, along with tangles of Silly String.

Terri and Frank sprinted for the parking lot. Pursued by three ... four ... no, five figures, clad all in black, like ninjas. Some of them carried paintball guns. Others were waving spray cans of paint and Silly String.

One of the ninjas hurried over to where I was hiding.

"Are you okay?" he asked, in a voice that wobbled uncertainly between baritone and soprano. I was pretty sure I recognized him as an eighth grader from the Shiffley clan.

"Fine, thanks to you guys," I said.

"Maybe you could guard this." He set down Frank's handgun on the nearest flat stone slab. "We called nine-one-one when we saw them pull it on you, but we're going to keep chasing them until one of the deputies shows up."

"Be careful," I said. "For all we know they could have another gun."

Just then a cruiser pulled into the parking lot, its siren silent but lights flashing.

"Here comes the cavalry," I said.

"Cool beans," the adolescent ninja said. I stood up and we watched as Vern hopped out of the cruiser, drew his service weapon, and ordered Terri and Frank to halt and put their hands up. The other four ninjas stopped, but instead of running away, as I more than half expected, they remained nearby, spray cans and paintball guns at the ready, until two more cruisers had arrived and Sammy and Horace had reinforced Vern.

And once Terri and Frank had been handcuffed and loaded into the cruisers—one in Sammy's and one in Horace's—the ninjas remained, talking to Vern.

"I should go turn myself in," the nearby ninja said. "Maybe you could put in a good word for us when the chief gets here?"

"Absolutely," I said.

FRIDAY, DECEMBER 19

Chapter 38

"Good morning, dear," Mother called, as I walked into the lobby of the Caerphilly Inn, stamping my feet on the mats to shake off the last bits of snow.

Technically it hadn't been morning for a good ten minutes, and under other circumstances Mother might have issued a mild reproach about the late hours I was keeping. Especially since she and other family members had almost certainly been down here for several hours coping with whatever wedding preparations were on today's agenda. But evidently she was making allowances for how late it had been when I'd finally arrived home from the police station. And maybe also acknowledging that I'd overcome my well-known preference for staying home and cocooning whenever it snowed. It was a light, fluffy snow, and since Caerphilly's two snow-plows had been working all night, the roads were in good shape. Michael and the boys were keeping all the needed paths shoveled at our house. And of course, here at the Inn, no amount of snow was allowed to affect the comfort and enjoyment of the guests. Still, left to my own devices, I'd have stayed in bed another hour or so, and then settled in by the fire with the dogs and this month's book club selection. But we had two weddings to keep on track, so I'd dragged myself out of bed and braved the snow.

"How's it going?" I asked. "And what needs doing?"

"It's going rather oddly," she said. "Let's sit down for a minute. I have news."

She took a seat on one of the sofas and patted the seat beside her.

"Bad news, I assume." I took the seat she indicated and braced myself.

"That depends on your point of view," she said. "The weddings are off."

"Off?" To my surprise, I was torn between stress and relief. "What happened? Did Robyn finally decide to ban them from Trinity? Are they rescheduling or looking for a new venue for Saturday?"

"No need to reschedule or find a new venue," she said. "Neither couple is getting married. Ever. Lexy's young man has eloped with one of Emily's bridesmaids. They got married this morning down at the courthouse."

"Blaine and Jenna?" I asked.

She nodded.

"Wow." It takes a lot to make me speechless, but for several minutes, "wow" was all I could come up with.

"And Emily and Harry?" I said finally.

"They've broken up, too," Mother said. "Though I don't quite know all the details. Emily said something about him running off to join a convent, but I think she must be confused."

"How are the brides taking it?" I asked. "And their mothers?"

"Both Letty and Betty were back at our house, the last I heard." She sniffed slightly. "Betty is having a migraine. Letty is having hysterics. Or maybe it's the other way around. I've left a few of your aunts there to cope with them. I haven't seen the brides yet this morning, but I assume eventually there will be drama. In the meantime, we have a lot to do down here."

"Like what?"

"We've had a busy morning notifying everyone who was coming to the wedding," she said. "So at least that's off our minds. And I have been having some discussions with Ekaterina. Obviously the cancellation of the weddings does not cancel the families' financial obligations to the Inn. The cost of the room rental, for example."

"Obviously," I said. "It's not as if the hotel could book any other weddings in the space on such short notice. And then there's all the food from the rehearsal dinners and the receptions."

"Ekaterina is being very accommodating about the food," she said. "She will not be charging us for anything that can simply be returned to the Inn's supplies or made use of in the next few days. And as for the rest—well, we've agreed to throw a lovely holiday party this afternoon for all the friends and relatives who have traveled to town for the weddings. Your father and I are chipping in a bit, so the two families aren't stuck with the whole cost. Five o'clock in the Dolley Madison ballroom."

"I'll be there with bells on," I said.

"Spread the word," she said. "And at the moment, we are dealing with the gifts, which all have to be returned as soon as possible, of course."

"Is that what the etiquette books say?" I asked. "I thought you had a year to deal with the gifts."

"That's for writing thank-you notes, dear," Mother said. "And the best sources say three months is much more acceptable. The etiquette books absolutely say that you need to return all engagement, shower, and wedding presents, but none of them give a timeline for it, so we're trying to get it over with as soon as possible, while we have many hands to make light work. Even your grandfather is pitching in, although I'm not sure what he's doing is all that helpful. The job is to pack the presents, not critique the impact they have on the environment. Anyway, I've brought over all the packing materials I could find, and we're boxing up everything."

"Feel free to raid our stash of boxes if you need them," I said.

"We already did, dear," she said. "Rose Noire told us where to find them. And luckily the brides—or perhaps their mothers—seem to have kept a reasonably good inventory of who sent what, so we should be able to ship most of it directly from here. Dorcas from the Caerphilly Pack 'n' Ship will be coming by to pick up everything as soon as we have it ready. And anything for which we don't have shipping information will be going home with the brides."

"Or perhaps their mothers," I suggested. "Because I bet Aunt Letty and Aunt Betty would be a lot better at figuring out where to send the remnants."

"True." She sighed. "Although as I said, I haven't seen them and I suspect both brides are alternately sulking and having temper tantrums. But not, thank goodness, in the Lafayette Room, where the packing is going on. I should go back and make sure it's going well."

"I'll come and help, if you like," I said. "I just need to take care of a few things first."

"You'd be welcome to help," she said. "Both with the packing and the note writing. But you don't have to, if you don't feel up to it. You have had a trying time the last few days. So take all the time you need."

With that she stood and strode purposefully across the lobby, toward the door that led to the meeting-room area.

Just then I spotted Caroline and the man I'd taken to calling

Donor Guy leaving the Inn's restaurant. They were both all smiles. I watched as they walked across the lobby to the front door, where Jaime hastened to produce the man's suitcase—a wheeled, leather one that looked both expensive and well worn.

They stood chatting for a few minutes. Then started to shake hands, which turned into an enthusiastic hug. Donor Guy tipped Jaime and the bellhop and strolled out, no doubt to hop into the car that another bellhop had already brought around. From the expression on Jaime's face, I deduced that Donor Guy wasn't a stingy tipper.

Caroline waved at him for a minute or so. Then she turned back, spotted me, and headed over—still smiling.

"All's well with Donor Guy?" I asked.

"Very well indeed." She patted one of her pockets. "I have here a check for his donation. A very large donation. More than twice what I hoped for."

"Congratulations!" I said.

"And it's a good thing I didn't take your grandfather to task about trying to snake my donor."

"So he didn't try?" I was relieved. I'd been optimistic that Grandfather wouldn't do something like that to her—but not quite positive.

"Not only that—apparently he spent a good part of the Sleep with the Wombats event singing my praises. Pointing out zoo animals I'd rehabilitated and mentioning bits of good advice I'd given. And encouraging the boys to do the same."

I wasn't sure if it was Grandfather doing the encouraging or Michael, but either way, good to hear.

"And you know what my donor told me just now?" she continued.

I shook my head.

"He said that if a top-notch scientist like your grandfather approved of the sanctuary, he figured he could be confident that his money was well spent. And he said he was also highly impressed with how I'd managed to get kids and laypeople fired up about the sanctuary's mission. Remind me to do something nice for Michael and the boys. And Monty. You think I should apologize for doubting him?"

"Just thank him," I suggested. "That will give him enough of a swelled head."

"True. Is he around someplace?"

"Probably," I said. "I think he's helping out with the packing of the gifts."

"Helping out?" She snorted in derision. "Scoffing at the whole thing, probably."

"He's fond of observing what he calls bizarre primate behavior," I said.

"Oh, yes." She nodded. "Your mother was quite provoked with him yesterday afternoon when Lexy's bridesmaids were doing each other's hair and nails."

"Don't tell me," I said. "I bet he was comparing it to how monkeys constantly groom each other and pick off lice and ticks."

"Yes," she said. "But your mother chased him off before he could get to the bit about the monkeys eating the lice and ticks."

"Thank heaven for small favors," I said.

"Well, I think I'll go see if they could use my help," she said. "I'll see you later."

"At the party," I said. And then, seeing her puzzled look, I added, "the one we're having to use up all the food that won't be eaten at the canceled receptions. Five p.m. in the ballroom."

"Ah," she said. "Good use of resources."

And she strode off toward the meeting-room area.

I was about to follow her when I noticed the chief coming into the lobby. I waved, and he came over to greet me.

"Please tell me you're not here on business," I said. "We don't need any more crimes this close to Christmas."

"Not to worry," he said, with a smile. "Just wrapping up a few loose ends from the crimes we've already had. Horace is on his way to examine the room our wedding bandits have been occupying, and then we'll pack up all their stuff so Ekaterina will have it for more guests. Oh, and she's going to give me some information from her files about them."

"She has information Kevin hasn't been able to find?" I asked.

"With Ekaterina, you never know," he said. "Anyway, I can't imagine that any of it will interfere with the wedding preparations, but just let me know if we're underfoot."

"You won't be interfering with any wedding preparations," I said. "Because apparently there won't be any weddings."

"No weddings?" He looked stunned. "They're both off? What in the world happened?"

"Jenna and Blaine—the ones who had the two-hour phone call the night of the murder—got married at the courthouse this morning. And Harry and Emily are off, too, though I haven't yet heard exactly why."

"Goodness," he said. "That's . . . quite a change."

"And Mother's arranging a party to eat up all the food that's already paid for and would otherwise go to waste," I said. "You're hereby invited. Five o'clock in the ballroom. Bring Minerva and the grandsons."

"I'll be there," he said. "If the Moffetts' attorney finally shows up at five, they can all just cool their heels until the party's over."

"The Moffetts?"

"That's their real name," he said. "The two people you knew as Terri Meredith and Frank Graves. Frances and Henry Moffett. They've refused to talk until their lawyer arrives—a high-powered criminal defense attorney from Northern Virginia. But I'm pretty sure it's going to turn out that they're responsible for a string of thefts all up and down the East Coast."

"Thefts of wedding presents?"

"Along with fancy anniversary and birthday parties, and a few conferences with inadequate security in the exhibit halls. They've been exercising their right to remain silent, but we've been comparing the list of weddings over the past few years at which Mr. Luckett has been the photographer with what information we can find out about big wedding thefts. About eight months ago, he was photographing a wedding at a fancy Richmond hotel, and someone cleaned out the presents. We strongly suspect it was the Moffetts. They probably thought enough time had passed—and Caerphilly was far enough away—that no one who'd seen them there would show up here."

"They implied that he was trying to blackmail them," I said. "And seemed to think that made it okay to do him in."

"He may have been a blackmailer." He looked thoughtful. "Or maybe he wanted to get even for all the trouble they caused him. The Moffetts—well, whoever pulled off that Richmond theft, but obviously my money's on them—dropped something at the crime scene that pointed the finger at Luckett. Some bit of camera gear that was traceable to him. The Richmond police sweated him pretty hard before he was able to prove that he was miles away with an alibi the night that theft occurred, and I suspect he was still holding a grudge about it. And unfortunately, instead of reporting his suspicions of them to the police, he stupidly tried to confront them. Maybe even tried to blackmail them. We may never know."

I nodded. It felt as if I should be saying something valedictory about Austin. Something like what a pity it was that someone so talented had been cut down in his prime. But I had no idea if he was a particularly talented photographer or just a fashionable one. And if you want people to feel bad when you go, you should refrain from mistreating your staff and making every woman feel uncomfortable the minute you walk into a room with them. About the only thing I could think of to say was that even Austin didn't deserve to be murdered. A good thing no one was apt to ask me for a comment, or I'd have to work on coming up with something a little more positive.

"What about your other arrestees?" I asked. "Emily and Maddie."

"The county attorney cut deals with them," he said. "They both agreed to plead guilty to lesser charges—I think they settled on disturbing the peace or some such thing. They'll be going before Judge Jane this afternoon, and I expect she'll sentence them to a small fine and quite a lot of hours of community service."

"So we'll be seeing them back in town from time to time," I said.

"You don't sound entirely thrilled by the prospect," he said. "I gather you expect your cousin will want to stay with you when she does her community service."

"They probably both will," I said. "We'll cope. Maddie's okay. And for all I know, Emily might be pretty tolerable when she's not in full-bore bride mode. I guess we'll have the chance to find out. And what about those middle schoolers who saved me?"

"Community service," he said. "Alongside their parents, who have pleaded guilty to making false reports to law enforcement and interfering with a police investigation. I've got every church in town making a list of things we could include in that community service. If you've got any suggestions, let me know."

"I will," I said. "I hope you won't be too hard on them. After all, they probably did save my life."

"We're letting the kids off pretty easy," he said. "Since they did step in to save you, even though they knew it would mean getting caught for the vandalism. The parents, on the other hand . . ." He set his jaw and shook his head slightly.

"If the parents haven't figured out by now why it was a bad idea to cover up the vandalism, they're probably past fixing," I said. "But let's brainstorm on how to help the kids take away the right lesson from this."

"Yes," he said. "Let's talk about that. And here's Horace. I'll go help him with his equipment."

"Make sure he knows about the party," I said.

The chief gave me a thumbs-up and hurried over to Horace's side. The two of them, now each pulling one of the two large, wheeled suitcases in which Horace stowed his growing supply of crime-scene tools, headed for the elevator.

Chapter 39

The lobby door opened again. I wasn't sure I was all that happy to see Random Wilson show up. What could he possibly want here at the Inn? He found a seat at the far corner of the lobby and seemed to be trying very hard to make himself inconspicuous. Unfortunately, that was the kind of thing where the harder you try, the more you fail.

Was it paranoid of me to hang around to see what he was up to? Or maybe just sensible?

"Hey, Meg!"

I turned to find Nikki Tran had just strolled into the lobby.

"You look none the worse for wear," she said. "But can you believe it? Both weddings canceled!"

"If you have any trouble getting paid by anyone, let me know," I said. "And I'll sic Mother on the deadbeats."

"Nah." She shook her head. "We're fine. We don't let anyone walk away with a finished dress until we have the money in the bank. And who knows? We might make a little extra on this one. I've let all the bridesmaids know we're available if they'd like some alterations to turn their dresses into something they might actually want to wear in public."

"Do you think that's even possible?" I asked.

"I'm not sure even the ladies could turn those horrors into something you or I would wear," she said. "But we might be able to come up with something that some of these chicks would go for."

"Did Mother tell you about the party?" I asked. "Five o'clock."

"She did. And Ekaterina said it's okay to park the RV here so we can carouse as much as we like and just stagger outside at bedtime. And then in the morning, we head back to Yorktown."

"You're not staying for Rose Noire's Winter Solstice celebration?"

"I'm taking the ladies home so they can start having some holiday cheer with their families," she said. "And then coming back for the Solstice. Anyway—got to run right now. The ladies heard about a fabric clearance outlet a little way down the road. We're going to drop by there before the party starts. Catch you later!"

She gave me a quick hug and ran back out.

On her way out, she passed Maddie Brown coming into the lobby. Maddie looked around and, when she spotted Wilson, strode over to where he was sitting.

I moved a little closer, as unobtrusively as I could. Call me nosy, and I won't argue.

"Here." Maddie handed him a flash drive. "That's all of the photos I could find. If I come across any more that he put someplace weird, I'll let you know, but I think this is probably it."

"Thanks." He stuck the drive in his pocket.

"And if you find any that you need cropped or enlarged or whatever, let me know."

"And what will that cost me?" His tone sounded a little harsh.

"Nothing," she said. "You already paid Austin more than

enough that he should have been taking care of it. I don't do that kind of thing."

He looked surprised for a second. Then he held out his hand.

"Thanks," he said as they shook hands. "And I'm sorry if I was kind of . . . um . . ."

"Obnoxious?" she suggested. "It's okay. Austin was worse. You've got to fight fire with fire."

He chuckled at that. Then he headed for the front door, struggling into his coat as he went.

Maddie turned and noticed me. I tried to look as if I hadn't been eavesdropping, but from the way she smiled I suspected she saw through me. She looked at me for a moment, then joined me.

"Good job," I said. "Giving him his photos."

"Keep it under your hat," she said. "Technically those photos weren't mine to give."

"Photos? What photos?"

She smiled. Then she dug into her purse and handed me another flash drive.

"Any chance you could share these with anyone who wants them? It's just the ones I've taken. I don't have anything that Austin took."

"The police have those," I said. "And I guess they'll eventually give them back to . . . whoever should get them."

"Austin's parents." She closed her eyes for a moment. "They own the studio now. They've already asked me to help them shut down the business. I want to get there before they do, so I can make backups of all his digital files and his client lists. And then maybe I can hunt down all those people he mistreated by holding up some or all of their photos until they paid him whatever ridiculous phony extra charges he was asking. But keep that under your hat, too. I've never met his parents. For all I know, they might be just as grasping as he was."

"Understood," I said. "And then what?"

"Well, I'm going to make them an offer for the business," she said. "Somehow I doubt they'll take it, but you never know. And if they turn me down or if they want to charge way more than it's worth, I think I'll go back home and see if I can start a business there, where Austin hasn't poisoned the whole wedding vendor community."

"Where's home?" I asked.

"Newport News," she said.

"Let me know if you end up there," I said. "I grew up just down the road, in Yorktown, and we still have a few hundred relatives in the Tidewater area. I can ask Mother to sic them on the case. Make sure you get off to a good start."

"That would be great," she said.

"For that matter, if you end up buying Austin's business or staying in Richmond on your own, Mother knows plenty of people there, too. Let us know where you end up, and we'll do what we can to help you."

"Thanks." She stood for a moment, blinking back tears. Then she gave me a quick hug before turning and almost running for the door.

Ekaterina strolled over to me.

"You heard the news, I assume," she said.

"I did indeed," I said. "Sorry. I know even if the families cough up everything they're contractually obligated to pay, the Inn and the staff will lose on this."

"It cannot be helped," she said. "The staff will lose tips, but then they will have more time off around the holiday. Some of them will be happy for that."

It occurred to me that some of them would be hurting without the overtime pay the wedding events would have brought, but that wasn't exactly her fault.

"They will not suffer," she said, as if reading my mind. "It is not any of their faults that the weddings were canceled, and they have all worked long hours under difficult circumstances to prepare for these phantom weddings. Fortunately, I have it within my budget to increase their holiday bonuses so they will not lose."

"You're a good boss," I said.

"I have never found treating my staff well to be incompatible with running the hotel effectively." She shrugged.

"You have the power to render them happy or unhappy; to make their service light or burdensome; a pleasure or a toil," I said. "Paraphrasing a line from Michael's production of *A Christmas Carol*," I added, seeing her puzzled look.

"We should all learn from Scrooge," she said. "And do our best to be good employers without having to be frightened out of our wits by ghosts."

"Amen," I said.

And I wondered, just for a moment, what would have happened if Austin had treated Maddie better. Not that it was her fault that the Moffetts killed him. But what if he'd been a good employer—one she enjoyed spending time with. I imagined, for a moment, the two of them companionably roaming the streets of Caerphilly together with their cameras before strolling over to Trinity. Maybe the Moffetts wouldn't have tried anything on two of them.

Or maybe she'd be dead, too. We'd never know.

"Oh, dear," Ekaterina murmured. "Look who is arriving."

I followed her line of sight. Aunt Letty was standing just inside the door, allowing Jaime to help her take her coat off. And out on the sidewalk, Aunt Betty was just handing her car keys to a bellman.

"Should we distract them?" Ekaterina asked.

"Good idea." I hurried toward the entrance. But Betty stepped inside before I could reach Letty's side. The two looked at each other—

Then they both burst into tears and hugged.

"Isn't it terrible," Letty said.

"Maybe it's for the best," Betty replied.

They both nodded to Ekaterina and me and plopped down on the nearest sofa.

"I think it is for the best," Betty said. "I think perhaps Lexy knew he wasn't really the one."

"Exactly!" Letty exclaimed. "I've been thinking it's the same with Emily. Maybe that's why they were both being so . . . difficult about everything connected with the wedding."

"Maybe," Betty said.

"Oh, who am I kidding," Letty said. "They've both been behaving like the spoiled brats they are."

"Yes," Betty said. "Spoiled and entitled. If I could turn back the clock . . ."

"And raise them differently." Letty was nodding vigorously. "Maybe we wouldn't have . . . drifted so far apart."

They looked at each other for a second, then hugged again.

"If Lexy ever finds anyone else crazy enough to marry her, she can organize her own wedding," Betty declared.

"Well, I'm not sure I'd go quite that far," Letty said. "But I certainly won't run myself ragged and watch Emily walk all over people. It's been eye-opening, this whole wedding thing."

They were both shedding tears, though I decided they were mostly happy tears. I dug into my tote, found a travel pack of tissues, and handed it to them.

"Thank you, dear," Betty said. "For everything you've done. I know that if the weddings had come off, it would be thanks to you and your mother and your whole family."

"What are your plans?" I said. "For the immediate future, that is."

They looked at each other.

"There are a lot of fun things to do here in Caerphilly this season," Letty said.

"Things we haven't had a moment to think about, what with

all the wedding nonsense," Betty said. "Meg, do you think your parents would mind if we stayed a few more days, as originally planned?"

"I'm sure they'd be fine with it," I said.

"Let's stick around and enjoy some time together," Letty said.

"You're on," Betty said. "How about starting with tea at the Frilled Pheasant?"

"Perfect!" Letty said. "Meg, we'll see you later."

And they headed for the front door, arm in arm. I watched as Jaime dispatched a bellman to retrieve one of their cars from valet parking and scurried to fetch their wraps.

"You don't want to tell them about the party at five?" Ekaterina said.

"Well, if they get back in time, of course they're welcome," I said. "But somehow I think we'll have a merrier time without them."

"You could be right," Ekaterina said, nodding. "And I confess, I am relieved that they did not come here to talk to me. Having your mother serve as an intermediary has been much more productive."

"Mom!"

I turned to see Josh and Jamie racing across the lobby toward me.

"Guess what!" Josh said. "Grandpa's going to get us beetles for our science fair project!"

"The indigestible beetles?" I asked.

"*Regimbartia attenuata*," Jamie said, with only a slight hesitation. "I'm doing those."

"And I'm doing bombardier beetles," Josh said.

"What about Adam?" I asked, since I knew their friend had also been casting about for a project.

"Horace is going to help him with a project on luminol," Josh said. "You know, the stuff that glows bright green when you spray it on invisible bloodstains."

"He's going to see how much blood it takes to show up," Jamie said. "And what other stuff also makes the luminol glow."

"Fantastic," I said. "I look forward to seeing your projects."

And I meant it—partly because these days the boys really did work rather independently on their science fair projects, even going down to the stationery store themselves to buy the inevitable trifold presentation boards that science projects always seemed to require. And partly because they'd have other adults they could call on for expertise—Adam could turn to Horace for help, and the boys would have Grandfather. Well, and Manoj, who would probably be the one who took care of any hands-on science fair work.

"Can you tell Adam's granddad about the party?" Jamie asked.

"I already did," I said. "And he's planning to come."

"Great!" Josh exclaimed. "See you later."

And the two of them raced back toward the door to the meeting-room area.

"Oh, my!" Ekaterina murmured.

I turned to see what had alarmed her. Jaime snapped to attention. He called over one of the bellhops and sent him on an errand. Then he looked around in what seemed like an almost furtive manner.

Curious, I strolled over.

"What's up?" I asked

He started at my words.

"Oh, it's you." He wiped his forehead, which was slightly sweaty. "Can you let me know if you spot either of the brides coming?"

"Sure thing," I said. "But why?"

He pointed out the hotel door. Blaine and Jenna were standing outside on the Inn's front walk.

Chapter 40

"What do you suppose they're doing here?" I murmured. Blaine's car was parked right in front of the entrance, with its trunk open. But Jaime had scurried off.

Just then Blaine and Jenna spotted me. They waved.

And they were both smiling broadly. I went outside to see them.

"I hear congratulations are in order," I said.

"Yes," Blaine said. "We did it. Went down to the courthouse this morning and got hitched." He held out his left hand, now adorned with a plain gold wedding band. Jenna's was, too, as I could see when he grabbed it and pulled it forward.

"Your brother was very helpful," Jenna said. "He picked up my luggage from your house and Blaine's from your parents' house, and brought it all over here."

"We didn't want to run into . . . anyone." Blaine nodded, his face solemn.

"Smart move," I said. "Where are you headed now? Although

you don't have to tell me if you're worried that I might spill the beans to Lexy or her mother."

"We're going to stay at this cool bed-and-breakfast in the Blue Ridge Mountains," Blaine said.

"It's right on a lake and miles from everything," Jenna said. "And there's hiking and fishing and birdwatching."

"We lucked out," Blaine said. "It's my favorite vacation spot. Normally it's booked months in advance, but we called, just to see if maybe they had an opening, and they had just gotten a cancellation a few minutes before."

"Isn't that wonderful!" Jenna exclaimed.

"It is," I said. "And if any vengeful members of my family ask me where you've gone, I'll suggest they try the Jersey Shore."

Blaine guffawed at that, and Jenna giggled.

Then Jaime and the bellhop emerged with their luggage and began stowing it in the trunk of Blaine's car.

"Thanks, man," Blaine said. He handed each of them a folded bill. Jaime merely bowed, but I saw the bellhop's eyes widen when he unfolded his.

"Well, till we meet again," Blaine said. "Or if we don't, have a great life!"

"You, too," I said.

They walked back to Blaine's car, holding hands.

Just then a police cruiser pulled up right behind Blaine's car. I spotted Vern at the wheel and waved to him. Then Harry Koenig hopped out of the passenger seat. He hurried over and shook hands first with Blaine, then with Jenna. They exchanged a few words, but so softly that I didn't catch them. Then Blaine and Jenna hopped into the car. Harry joined Jaime and me on the front walk, and we all waved as the newlyweds drove off.

"All's well that ends well," Jaime said as he went back inside.

"They look happy," Harry said.

"So do you," I said. "I hear you've postponed your wedding."

"Not postponed," he said. "Called it off entirely."

I wasn't sure whether congratulations or commiseration was called for, so I just nodded.

"What are your plans?" I asked.

"I'm going back to Holy Cross. The Trappist monastery in Berryville," he added, seeing my puzzled look.

"Back to it? You used to be a monk?"

"No," he said. "I've done retreats there as often as they'd let me over the last couple of years, and I'm pretty sure I have a vocation, but they won't take you as a candidate until you turn twenty-five. So I figured I'd spend the time I had to wait developing my culinary skills. They make fruitcakes, you know—best fruitcakes in the world! And creamed honey and chocolate truffles. That's pretty much how the abbey supports itself, so I figured if I could turn into a decent baker, they'd be happy to have me."

I was so surprised that it took me a moment to digest the news.

"Good luck with it," I said. "If it's what you want to do, I'm glad you're going for it."

"Almost got sidetracked," he said. "I'm still not quite sure how that happened, but I feel like I'm on the right path now."

I rather hoped he hadn't explained it quite that way to Emily.

"Oh—could you do me a favor?" he asked.

"Name it," I said.

He ran back to Vern's cruiser and opened the rear door. Vern got out, and the two of them each reached into the back seat, gathered up an armload of boxes, and headed my way. Vern nodded and carried his load inside. Harry stopped beside me and set his stack down.

"Deputy Shiffley was kind enough to take me up to Berryville for an interview with the abbot," he said. "And now he's going to take me back there to stay. I wanted to bring back some of the bakery treats as a thank-you for everything you and Michael have done. And maybe you could share them with . . . well, with anyone I've hurt or upset here."

"Thank you," I said. "And I'll gladly share the bounty with anyone I can find."

"Not Emily, though," he said. "She hates fruitcake. And under the circumstances, I doubt if she'd enjoy the creamed honey or the truffles."

"Probably not," I said.

"But her mom might," he said. "I'll leave it to you to figure that out. Oh, and here."

He handed me the volume of *David Copperfield*.

"You can keep that if you like," I said.

"We're not allowed a lot of personal possessions," he said.

"As a loan," I said. "And we can collect it from you when we come out to buy more fruitcakes and truffles."

"It's a deal," he said, with a quick grin. "Thanks."

He set down his boxes at my feet, scurried back to Vern's car, and got into the passenger seat.

Vern emerged from the hotel accompanied by Jaime, who picked up the stack of boxes at my feet and carried them inside.

"Don't you want to take a few?" I asked Vern.

"He already gave me at least this many, to thank me for running him back and forth between here and Berryville," Vern said. "I was happy to do it without any payment, but I have to admit, this kind of gets me out of a jam. I was originally going to take the last two days off so I could get all my Christmas shopping done. The murder derailed that. Now I can relax. Everyone on my gift list is getting either fruitcake, creamed honey, or truffles."

"Good deal," I said. "Have a safe trip."

"Don't worry," he said. "I think I can resist the temptation to sign on as a fruitcake baker. See you later."

He ambled down to his cruiser. He had to wait there for a few minutes, until Beau Shiffley, driving his snowplow, had done a circuit of the parking lot.

I stayed put to wave at Beau, and then to wave some more at Vern and Harry as they took off.

Then I scurried back inside.

"Isn't it grand?" Jaime said, as he ushered me inside. "So many people are so cheerful! So full of the holiday spirit!"

"Don't look now," I said. "But here comes someone who probably isn't all that cheerful."

Lexy was handing her keys to the bellman outside.

"Maybe I should go help out with the packing," I said.

"Courage!" Jaime exclaimed.

And then Lexy was upon us.

"Afternoon," I said.

"I notice you didn't say 'good afternoon,'" she replied. "Smart call. Mom told me I was supposed to come down here and help pack up all the wedding presents. How ridiculous is that? I mean, here I am with my whole life ruined, and she's worried that some great-aunt will fuss because I don't send back some stupid Crock-Pot fast enough."

"Don't worry about it," I said. "Mother has organized a whole bunch of people to do all the packing. They'll let you know if they have any questions about who sent something. Why don't you just relax. Do something that will make you feel better."

"Like what?" she asked. "Pulling all of Jenna's hair out? Giving Blaine a good, swift kick where it hurts the most?"

"Talk to the hotel desk," I said. "They can book you a massage. And the bar can make your favorite cocktail while you wait for the masseuse to show up."

"I like my ideas better."

I was about to suggest that she go home—either home to the room she was staying in at our house, or all the way home to Richmond. But suddenly I realized that Emily had just walked into the lobby. And was headed our way.

Lexy saw the expression on my face and turned to watch as Emily approached. They both had glum expressions on their faces. But they didn't immediately start shrieking at each other. Or, worse, physically attacking each other.

"It's all your fault, you know," Emily said.

"My fault?" Lexy looked surprised. And, curiously, a lot less combative than usual.

"Remember when we were kids and you told me I was fat and ugly and stupid?"

"I seem to recall telling you that pretty regularly back then," Lexy said. "And you'd usually snap back something about it being too bad, since everyone always said we look so much alike we could almost be twins. Which usually shut me up because it was true."

They both laughed at that, a little ruefully.

"Well, one time when we were in seventh grade, you told me that I was so ugly that of course you'd be the first one to get married," Emily said. "I don't know why that stuck in my mind, but it did. I kept hearing you say it, like an echo. I kind of got this stupid superstition that if you got married first, maybe I never would."

"That's—" Lexy stopped herself and started over, her tone almost gentle. "That's kind of silly, don't you think? I mean, that you'd care that much about something I said."

She sounded uncharacteristically sane and sensible.

"I said it was stupid," Emily said. "And a superstition. I didn't really believe it."

"But you don't walk under ladders, either," Lexy said.

Or go near graveyards.

"Neither do you," Emily countered. "So anyway, when your mom told my mom that you thought Blaine was going to pop the question, it kind of weirded me out."

"And you went out and got engaged to Brother Harry just to spite me?"

"Not to spite you." Emily sighed. "I got depressed and desperate, and I thought about all the guys I'd ever dated, and most of them turned out to be such jerks. Just party animals, and not reliable or anything. And then there was Harry. He was . . . he was nice."

Instead of repeating one of her usual uncomplimentary comments about Harry, Lexy just nodded.

"And he was kind of struggling at the restaurant. Not because of his cooking—he's a genius cook. But you get a lot of big personalities in a kitchen, and he wasn't one of them, so they'd kind of run over him, and I tried to help him out. We started, I don't know, bonding."

"So when he proposed, you accepted." Lexy nodded as if this was a perfectly reasonable thing.

"He didn't ever actually propose," Emily said. "I thought it was because he was just too shy and had no self-confidence."

"So you proposed to him?"

"More like I sort of made it our understanding that he had proposed, or as good as, and we should get on with planning the wedding. He seemed okay with it."

"I had to tell Blaine to propose to me," Lexy said. "I think maybe he thought he had to. Working for my dad and all. Plus his parents never liked Jenna and they liked me."

"He didn't have to," Emily said.

"But maybe he thought he did."

They seemed to have forgotten I was there. And I was starting to feel a little uncomfortable, being the forgotten eavesdropper on this very personal conversation. Would they notice if I quietly slipped away?

"I'm never going to another football game," Lexy said suddenly. "Basketball's fine, and hockey's not bad, but football bores me to tears. Plus, I'm sick to death of freezing outdoors just to see a bunch of hulks smash into each other. Blaine can have his stupid Cowboys."

"And I don't ever have to read *The Sun Also Rises*," Emily said. "I don't care if it's only two hundred and twenty-eight pages. That's two hundred and twenty-eight pages more of Hemingway than I ever want to read. Or is *The Sun Also Rises* Faulkner?"

"Hemingway, I think," Lexy said. "Or maybe F. Scott Fitzgerald. One of those high-school reading-list people."

"Either way, no." Emily lifted her chin and assumed the expression of someone who was valiantly taking an unpopular moral stand. "Harry can just go to hell with his reading lists."

My sympathy was with Harry. But it occurred to me that maybe he wasn't the only one who'd had a lucky escape.

Emily suddenly seemed to notice that I was nearby.

"Oh, Meg," she said. "I'm probably going to be taking off pretty soon, so I wanted to thank you for having us."

"Me, too," Lexy said. Something about their tone made me imagine I could see their mothers urging them to make their manners, as our aunts would call it.

"You're very welcome," I said. "And please don't feel you have to rush off."

"Thanks," Emily said. "But I think maybe getting away from here might be the best thing."

"Yeah," Lexy said. "Where are you going?" she added, turning back to Emily.

"Home, probably." Emily shrugged. Then her face brightened. "You know, there's one thing that's kind of okay. Harry insisted that he get to plan the honeymoon. And he made reservations at this bed-and-breakfast off in the middle of nowhere. Like in the Blue Ridge Mountains, where there's nothing to do but sit around appreciating nature. According to its website, the place doesn't even have reliable Wi-Fi."

"The only kind of nature I care about is the kind that comes with bright sun, white sand, and an endless supply of piña coladas."

"Same here," Emily said.

"Then why did you let him pick that for your honeymoon?" Lexy sounded incredulous.

"Well, he was being really good about letting me make all the decisions about the wedding," Emily said. "I thought maybe it wouldn't be too bad. But the closer I got to actually going there the more I was dreading it."

She shuddered, and Lexy nodded in sympathy.

"It was actually kind of satisfying," Emily went on. "Calling them this morning to cancel it."

"And losing your deposit, I bet."

"No, I lucked out on that. They had someone call asking if they had any vacancies, so they were willing to refund us."

Emily's description made me wonder if her cancellation was what made Jenna and Blaine's honeymoon in a Blue Ridge bed-and-breakfast possible. I made a mental note to find out.

"Lucky you," Lexy said. "We were going to the Virgin Islands. We had an Airbnb right on the beach, with a hot tub and a sauna."

"Why not go anyway?" I said. "You could use a getaway."

"All by myself?" Lexy asked.

Then she and Emily looked at each other. They just stared for so long that I started to worry.

"It's a three-bedroom house," Lexy said finally. "Plenty of room. All you have to do is buy a plane ticket."

"You're on," Emily said.

"Let's go make some plans," Lexy said.

"I was thinking maybe this would be a good time to get blotto," Emily said.

"We can do both," Lexy said. "This place actually has a decent bar."

With that, they linked arms and marched together into the restaurant.

"Would you look at that?" Michael appeared at my side. "The wolf shall dwell with the lamb, and the leopard shall lie down with the young goat."

"In this case I think it's the wolf hanging out with the leopard," I said.

"Whatever," he said. "I think this is the beginning of a beautiful friendship."

"Maybe," I said. "I'm not putting money on it lasting. But even if it doesn't, maybe they can help each other heal from this whole experience. And speaking of healing—I gather you and Robyn managed to settle whatever disagreement Josh and Jamie were having over their directing project?"

"We did." He rolled his eyes. "We managed to convince Josh that nobody wanted fart jokes in a Christmas pageant."

"Well, nobody who's not a preadolescent boy," I suggested.

"Precisely. And then we talked Jamie into loosening up and letting us add a little family-friendly comic relief. So all's well that ends well."

"That's good," I said. "Although I confess I won't be completely reassured until I actually see for myself that you straightened them out."

"You're in luck, then," he said. "I'm here to watch the latest rehearsal—Ekaterina's letting us have a dress rehearsal here in the lobby so the staff will have a chance to see the show. Looks as if they're about to get started."

I glanced around and realized that while I'd been worrying about the possibility of conflict between Emily and Lexy, the lobby had been filling up with costumed Nativity cast members, the dozen or so adults and teens who'd volunteered to ride herd on them, and a growing crowd of curious guests and uniformed hotel staff members.

Josh and Jamie chivvied the cast members into place—they'd chosen the space in front of the glass wall to be their stage. When they were all settled down—sheep and shepherds to the left, wise men and camels to the right, and the inhabitants of the stable in the center—the boys took their places in front of their cast.

"Places!" Josh bellowed. "And everyone should be quiet now!"

"Except for the singing," Jamie added. "You can join in on the singing."

So, led by the twins, everyone in the lobby joined in on a rousing few verses of "While Shepherds Watched Their Flocks by Night" and the pageant began.

Josh and Jamie had done a fabulous job—and I was sure I could see Michael's influence in the gentle notes of humor that livened up the familiar story. The addition of an overzealous Border collie, who refused to let the sheep and shepherds abide in peace and kept trying to herd them all into the smallest possible space around the feet of the angel. The one wayward black sheep who kept interrupting the angel's tidings of great joy with sarcastic baas. The moonwalking camels. The transformation of Gaspar into a charming klutz who kept dropping his frankincense and making the other two wise men sneeze. The addition of three wise women who delivered diapers and a covered-dish meal before sternly shushing the noisy shepherds.

The whole thing ended with a rousing rendition of "Angels We Have Heard on High," followed by half a dozen curtain calls for the cast and directors.

In fact, the only thing that brought the applause to an end was the arrival of several serving carts loaded with hot chocolate, hot cider, and freshly baked cookies from the Inn's kitchen.

"That was splendid," Ekaterina said to Michael, as she watched staff, guests, and cast members descend on the refreshments. "I'm glad you suggested it. But I hope it doesn't keep you from enjoying the snow."

"As soon as we're finished here, I'm going to see if the boys want to do a little sledding while it's still light. If we think the gift-packing project can spare them," he added to me.

"I suspect it can," I said.

"And I'm glad to see that you've managed to repair the damage to your Christmas tree," Michael said to Ekaterina. "You can't tell anything ever happened to it."

"We have Meg's mother to thank for that." Ekaterina turned toward the alcove that held the tree. "And I think it's better than before."

"Mother probably added in a few more decorations," I said. "Things she didn't have time to do before. That's usually what she does when she has to repair any of her decorating schemes."

"She did," Ekaterina said with a smile. "Although I think the best new additions are the eagles Rose Noire and Kevin provided." She pointed to where the three glittering birds were hanging in a triangle at the front of the tree. "While I wish the real live eagles well, I think these are a significant improvement when it comes to forming a part of our Christmas decorations. And look what they can do."

She strode toward the alcove that held the tree, pulling out her phone as she went. Michael and I followed her. She did something with her phone. The eagles' beaks began opening and closing, and music emanated from them.

"On the twelfth day of Christmas, my true love gave to me." A chorus of voices emanated from the eagles—I recognized Rob's as one of them. But it only took a few bars for the crowd of guests, staff, and pageant cast members to join in, drowning the recording out as they sang, with great enthusiasm:

Ten lords a-leaping,
Nine ladies dancing,
Eight maids a-milking,
Seven swans a-swimming,
Six geese a-laying,
FIIIIVE GOLD-EN WIIINGS!

Acknowledgments

Thanks once again to everyone at St. Martin's/Minotaur, including (but not limited to) Claire Cheek, Hector DeJean, Stephen Erickson, Nicola Ferguson, Meryl Gross, Paul Hochman, Kayla Janas, Andrew Martin, Sarah Melnyk, and especially my editor, the fabulous Ellery Queen Award honoree, Pete Wolverton. And thanks also to the art department for another beautiful cover.

More thanks to my agent, Ellen Geiger, and all the folks at the Frances Goldin Literary Agency, for taking care of the business side of things so I can concentrate on writing.

Thanks to Irina Heidt and Ellen Crosby, who helped with the bits of Russian that appear in this book. Here's hoping I didn't misspell any of it! And thanks to Robin Templeton, who spent many years as a wedding photographer before starting her new career as a crime writer, and who provided much useful guidance on her former profession. But she wanted me to make it clear that she never did any of the awful things Austin does in this book.

Many thanks to all the friends who brainstorm and critique with me, give me good ideas, or help keep me sane while I'm writing: Stuart, Aidan, and Liam Andrews; Deborah Blake; Chris Cowan; Kathy Deligianis; Margery Flax; Suzanne Frisbee; John Gilstrap; Barb Goffman; Joni Langevoort; David Niemi; Alan Orloff; Dan Stashower; Art Taylor; Robin Templeton; and Dina Willner. And thanks to all the TeaBuds for two decades of friendship.

Above all, thanks to the readers who make all of this possible.

About the Author

Joe Henson, NYC

Donna Andrews has won the Anthony, the Barry, and three Agatha Awards, a Romantic Times Reviewers' Choice Award for best first novel, and four Lefty and two Toby Bromberg Awards for funniest mystery. She is a member of the Mystery Writers of America, Sisters in Crime, and Novelists, Inc. *Five Golden Wings* is the thirty-eighth book in the Meg Langslow series. Andrews lives in Reston, Virginia.